THE LAZARUS GAME

THE LAZARUS GAME

STEPHEN J. VALENTINE

SWEETWATER
BOOKS
AN IMPRINT OF CEDAR FORT, INC.
SPRINGVILLE, UTAH

This is a work of fiction. The characters, names, incidents, places, and dialogue are products of the author's imagination, and are not to be construed as real. The opinions and views expressed herein belong solely to the author and do not necessarily represent the opinions or views of Cedar Fort, Inc. Permission for the use of sources, graphics, and photos is also solely the responsibility of the author.

ISBN 13: 978-1-4621-1554-9

Published by Sweetwater Books, an imprint of Cedar Fort, Inc.
2373 W. 700 S., Springville, UT 84663
Distributed by Cedar Fort, Inc., www.cedarfort.com

LIBRARY OF CONGRESS CATALOGING-IN-PUBLICATION DATA

Valentine, Stephen, 1972- author.
The Lazarus Game / Stephen Valentine.
    pages cm
Summary: When fifteen-year-old genius Carter Chance agrees to help create the "most advanced video games ever imagined"--something he hopes will impress the hottest girl in town --Carter gets himself involved in a dangerous adventure.
ISBN 978-1-4621-1554-9 (perfect bound : alk. paper)
[1. Video games--Fiction. 2. Virtual reality--Fiction. 3. Brothers--Fiction. 4. Genius--Fiction.] I. Title.
PZ7.1.V34Laz 2015
[Fic]--dc23
                    2014032420

Cover design by Kristen Reeves
Cover design © 2015 by Lyle Mortimer
Edited and typeset by Melissa J. Caldwell

Printed in the United States of America

10 9 8 7 6 5 4 3 2

For Linda.
In my writing, as in all other aspects of life,
you made all the difference.

CHAPTER ONE

You think my life is perfect.

Okay, it's true I'm a genius. I will graduate high school this year at age fifteen. I scored a perfect SAT score. I can skip college if I want to—I already have my pick of jobs at Google, Apple, and GameStop. The President awarded me—Carter Chance—"Most Likely to Succeed" out of every teenager in the United States. Girls want to date me, teachers adore me, enemies fear me. Life is good.

That doesn't mean my life is perfect, though. Far from it.

I have the normal teenager problems: my brother is an idiot; the girl of my dreams ignores me; an ancient cult just invaded my town; the Russian mafia wants to kill me. Like I said, normal problems.

But the day the Lazarus Game Shop opened—the day this all started—I didn't know anything about secret societies or labyrinthine conspiracies or immortal geniuses. All I knew was that the five gangsters prowling the back of the school parking lot had come to kill me.

You may think I'm overreacting. I saw no switchblades, no guns, not even pots or pans. I didn't need to. I knew their intentions better than they did. How? I had run predictive regression analytics using a self-learning neural network to forecast . . . okay, relax. Sit back down. Take a deep breath. Keep reading. I promise not to bore you with complicated subjects like mathematics while telling my story. Point is this: my genius brain predicted these men would try to kill me.

And here they were, at Merewether High School, precisely on schedule.

I decided to get right to the point. I stepped smartly off the curb and approached my would-be killers. No sense waiting around to get a bullet to the head.

The bad dudes were Russian mafia. They wore the usual assortment of black sweaters, leather jackets, diamond-stud earrings. It was *so* last decade. The future is all about cybercrime: identify theft, bank account scraping—the sort of thing a self-respecting criminal can do in his bathrobe and fuzzy pink slippers. Yet here in my backward hometown, criminals still did it the old-fashioned way.

The five surly men watched warily as I approached. They gathered into a neat little gangster pack near a black Cadillac Escalade, putting their backs to the automobile. They huddled together as though I had startled them. Hands went for pockets, and I saw the dull glint of knives and the barrels of handguns poking out from leather jackets. I smiled as I walked, pleased that my impressive five feet six inches instilled such fear and trembling.

"You're here to kill me," I said, "but this is a bit public, don't you think? School just ended. All sorts of kids and parents and teachers around. Too many witnesses."

"We no here to kill you," said one of the Russians. He

must have missed the day they taught English at Mafia School. "We kidnap your sorry buns."

I nodded. Mishandled euphemism, but I got the general point.

"Well, that makes me feel better," I said. "My buns certainly thank you. Same problem, though. Witnesses everywhere. Cameras on the roof. Could be a drone airplane overhead."

"We take the chances," the man said as he glanced at the sky.

"Out here?" I asked. "Terrible statistical odds for success. Why not wait until I'm home? Much more private. You'd only have my brother to deal with, and I don't mind if you take him out. You'd be doing the world a humanitarian service."

"We do it now," said the leader. "No wait. No talk. Shut face and get in car."

"Hey, maybe boy's right," said one of the others. "Look at kids coming out door."

I raised my hand. The Russian nearest me jumped and pulled out his gun. I smiled and asked: "Can I make a suggestion? Some advice?"

The leader frowned, eyes narrowed. "What advice?"

"You need to use a definite article in your sentences. You're dropping the *the*. It should be 'look at *the* kids coming out of *the* door.' If you speak like an idiot, the other criminals won't respect you. You'll be the laughingstock of the Pacific Northwest."

"Shut up, the boy," the leader said. "Get in car . . . the."

I winced. I had created a grammatical monster.

"Get in car!" the man repeated, waving his gun at me.

"Just my buns?"

"What you mean . . . ? No, not just buns! You and *the* buns. *You and buns!* Now! We make you pay! You should not got Dmitri arrested!"

I shrugged. "He should have stayed out of my town. For sure he shouldn't have shot my girlfriend's dad."

"It is your fault! You caught Dmitri! You got him arrested!"

"Of course I caught him! An infant could have caught him!"

That was actually a bit insulting. To infants, that is. A freaking fetus was smart enough to catch him. It really had not been that hard to track down the man who shot Sidney's father. In fact, catching Dmitri had been the least exciting part of my evening.

—

Last night should have been entirely simple. I had it all planned out. Like all my plans, it was foolproof. Given the idiots I hang with, that is highly important. It would go like this:

1. Track the gangster to his lair
2. Avoid personal maiming or death at hands of said gangster
3. As much as was convenient, avoid maiming or death for my friends—within reason and as long as it doesn't comprise point #4
4. Impress Sidney Locke with my daring deeds, thus convincing her to . . .
5. Go out on a date with me!

Foolproof, no? You would think so. But then you don't know my friends.

I had fashioned a little crime fighting investigative unit out of my group of friends. Think Sherlock Holmes with some nobody helpers. I was Sherlock, of course, and they were the nobodies. They're like the guys in movie credits who don't even warrant a name. Given that I am a magnanimous fellow, however, I'll name them for you.

First, there is my entirely unfortunate brother, Clinton. He's a senior. This is a bit embarrassing to admit, but it took him *all four years* to complete high school. He is seventeen and about six inches taller than I. I got all the brains and he got the proverbial brawn. He can punch his fist through brick walls. He can also bust his head through brick walls. I encourage him to use his head instead of his fists. He needs it less.

There is my so-called best friend, Darek Branderson, that bucket of spit. Darek would as soon stab me in the back as look at me. But then he hates everyone, and in relative terms hates me less. Darek should have been drowned at birth along with a bag of unwanted kittens, except he did have one redeeming quality. The jerk is an absolute mechanical genius. He could build anything out of anything.

Then there's Kyle Chamberlain, or Chambers, as we call him, who has absolutely no value to me, my gang, or society as whole, except for a fluke of genetic fortune that makes him absolutely irresistible to women. I mean it. It doesn't matter the age, marital status, body fat index—they all love him. Why include him in the gang? Are you kidding me? You have any idea how much easier life is when every female in town will do your bidding? Chambers is my secret weapon.

Finally, there was my girlfriend, Sidney Locke. She

wasn't technically part of our team. For that matter, she wasn't technically my girlfriend either. I'd rather not talk about Sidney right now.

Sidney is only the hottest girl in town. In the state. In the Western Hemisphere. Sidney is so hot she caused global warming. I mean it. The lousy polar ice caps are melting because of her. Our town is in the fifteenth year of drought because she lives here—rain evaporates before hitting the ground.

She's smart, too, for a non-genius normal person. She has musical talent—plays the piano or violin or tuba or something like that. I'm not the world's expert on ancient forms of music. She has athletic ability, if you consider soccer a real sport. She's witty and funny and doesn't immediately bore me when she opens her mouth. Did I mention she's the hottest creature on God's good green earth?

But I don't want to talk about Sidney right now.

I mean, we've known each other ever since we were little snot-nose toddlers. Her dad's a cop, my dad's a cop, so we were obviously destined to be together, like Darcy and Elizabeth or Bella and Edward. Of course *I* see it. Sidney still hasn't realized the perfect, predestined nature of our union, but then she's not a genius like me. Eventually she'll get smart enough to see we are soul mates.

Look, I refuse to talk about Sidney. In fact, I've decided to ignore her completely until she grows up and can love me for more than just my IQ. She makes me crazy. I'm going to stop thinking about her.

So, in an attempt to prove how *over her* I am, I assembled my gang and decided to risk my life (and theirs, though that hardly matters) to capture the criminal who had shot and wounded her father. I was only doing this for civic duty. If she happened to be impressed and felt compelled to throw herself at my feet out of overpowering gratitude, so be it.

I led my faithful band to a dark alley nestled between matching four-story apartment buildings. From the alley we could observe the rear of several stores across a narrow service road: Gus's Gun and Pawn Shop, the abandoned Capitol Theater, and Greets and Eats Diner. A mirroring alleyway between the theater and diner stared back at us. Dingy apartments squatted on top of the pawn shop. Yellow light flickered behind tattered drapes in the upstairs apartment window. Our criminal was at home.

I averted my gaze from the gaunt Capitol Theater that huddled on the street like a sad old woman: forlorn, scorned, and forgotten. I spent many Saturday afternoons at the theater. My dad had regaled me with stories of watching the original *Star Wars* in the place, the awestruck wonder he felt when that infamous Star Destroyer crawled across the screen. I watched strictly dollar movies, only the finest of Hollywood entertainment. I saw every chainsaw-, hacksaw-, and axe-murderer movie available. That was all gone now. The place sat as empty as my brother's head. I felt a pinging stab of sadness.

As I well know, nothing lasts forever. Sighing, I turned to the task at hand.

Four cars lined the narrow service road. A lone streetlamp cast oily light across the spine of the building. Nothing stirred from the pawn shop or diner. Shadows wrapped us in darkness inside the alley. I had a perfect stakeout. I had tracked the criminal to this apartment. Soon, he would be my prisoner.

I assembled my team and gave instructions for the

infiltration. As usual, they listened patiently and respectfully to my plan.

"That's the stupidest thing I've ever heard," Darek interrupted. "What kind of moron came up with this plan? I'm telling you, we should climb up the walls using these special wall-grabber gloves I just created. These may look like rubber dishwashing gloves, but if you look carefully you'll see—"

"I say we bash down the front door and take him head on," said Clinton, my dear brother. "I'm sick of standing around talking. Let's just go up there and knock some heads."

"We just got here," I corrected my brother. "We barely started discussing it!"

"Too much talk! Let's beat up this loser before I'm too bored to move."

I sighed. I turned to my other trusted comrade.

"Chambers, what do you think?"

He gazed at me as though surprised to find me in the same dark alley.

"Hmm?"

"What do you think?" I repeated.

"About what?"

"The gangster! Didn't you hear my plan to take him?"

"Gangster? There's a gangster up there? I thought you said we were going to see your grandmother! Wait. Is your grandmother a gangster?"

"No, she's not . . . look, we're here to arrest the Russian criminal who shot Sidney's dad!"

"Arrest him . . . well, I don't know. Sounds like a lot of work. I can't mess up my hair. I have a date later tonight."

Before I go any further with this story, and lest you get any wrong ideas, I feel I should say a word about my friends.

Imbeciles.

My friends, how I love them. If I had trained monkeys—or, really, any monkeys at all—I'd use them instead of these losers.

"Carter, let me demonstrate the beauty of my plan," Darek said. He promptly pulled on the latex gloves and started a Spider-Man-like climb up the wall.

My brother—never to be outdone—initiated his own demonstration. Clinton rammed his head against the brick wall so hard dust fell in a shower around me.

"See!" he exulted. "If I can shatter brick, just imagine what I can do with that door!"

"We won't get blood on our clothes, will we?" Chambers asked. "I don't have time to change."

I grabbed Darek's foot and dragged him back down to the ground. Clinton staggered against the wall, dazed and bloodied after his head-butting. Chambers was staring into a small compact mirror while rubbing his teeth. I pulled the team together and repeated my plan.

"No wall climbing, door busting, or anything else," I said. "We do it my way. I'm the boss here."

Darek rolled his eyes. "This is stupid. I'm not risking my neck for your little romance."

"It has nothing to do with Sidney! This is about justice! It's about law and order! Bringing the criminals before the court! It's about . . . okay, forget it. How about a hundred bucks each?"

Darek nodded. Clinton smiled. Chambers looked up from his mirror and shrugged.

We poised to move on the apartment. I had taken only a single step from the alley when Clinton grabbed my arm. He pulled me back into the darkness.

"There's someone over there!" he whispered, breathy and annoying. "In the other alley!"

"I see them too," Darek murmured. "They watching us? Dmitri's gang? You think we're blown? You want to climb up the wall now?"

"No, I don't want to climb up the—just hold on, okay? Let me get a look at them."

I pulled my backpack from off my shoulders and stuck my hand inside, rummaging around until I found night vision goggles. Every self-respecting criminal investigator should carry a pair. My father is a cop and paramilitary wacko. Some of his crap comes in useful, though. I pulled the goggles over my head and peered across the road.

My vision became a milky green sheen. At first I could only discern the outline of a man perched near the edge of the alley. My eyes adjusted until I could see him clearly. Then I had no idea what I was looking at.

"Well?" Clinton whispered. "Is it the Russians or what?"

"One guy," I answered my brother. "One very weird guy."

"What's he doing? What do you see?" Darek asked, pushing up against me.

I shrugged. I honestly didn't know *what* I saw.

"A hobo warrior?" I returned. "A homeless hit man? You tell me."

I handed the goggles to Darek. I knew what he was seeing. The guy in the alley held a shotgun in his left hand, a pump-action bad boy straight out of Schwarzenegger-land. He had some kind of an assault rifle strapped to his back (I'm not the world's expert on guns, you understand). In his right hand he held a massive double-headed axe. Not a lumberjack kind of an axe. I'm talking about a battle axe. In addition to blades, it had a long pointy-looking thing sticking out of the top, like a bayonet on a rifle or whatever (I'm also not the world's expert on axes). The axe thingy seemed capable of cleaving chicken, dicing onions, and severing arms and necks. He whirled it through the air as though warming up to chop off a spare arm or practicing for a cheerleader audition (I do consider myself the world's expert on cheerleaders).

"Dude, you see that axe thingy he's carrying?" Darek breathed. "That's the coolest thing ever!"

"Axe thingy?" Clinton asked. "Why's he got an axe thingy?"

That seemed to wake Chambers up. "Axe thingy? Who's got an axe thingy? I don't have time for axe thingies if I'm going to make my date! We're not going to fight, are we?"

Hobo Warrior wore a long battered trench coat from the first *Matrix* movie, very ten years ago. Even in the weird green night vision, I could see his clothes looked haggard and worn. Topping it all off, he wore an old black fedora. Who wears fedoras nowadays?

"He's either a gangster or a loser," I said. "Not that I'd say that to his face."

"What's he doing here?" Clinton asked. "You think he's here for Dmitri?"

I shrugged, but I was worried. If his object was Dmitri, my infiltration was blown. I couldn't let that happen. I had Sidney Locke to think about. Oh, and the safety of the citizens in town.

"I'm going to scare Hobo Warrior off," I said. I rummaged through my backpack for the PlayStation AI.

"What are you going to do?" Darek asked, eyeing me suspiciously.

"You'll see," I said as I pulled out the device. I turned it on, preparing to launch one of my custom apps. "What I'm going to do is . . ."

Light flickered in the road, flaring across shadowed buildings. Headlights beamed into the service road as a delivery truck rumbled its way toward us. I retreated deeper into the alley, yanking my friends back. The mercenary dork vanished into deeper shadows. The truck growled up the road until I heard brakes whining and tires coming to a stop. The engine coughed once and killed.

Doors opened and slammed shut. Low voices. Something metal rattled, and I heard the rolling clicking sound of a large metal door pushed upward. More voices. A light came on from somewhere across the road, from one of the buildings. I inched back to the edge of the alley and peered out.

The truck had been backed up to the theater dock. The dock door gaped open, a yawning throat leading into the theater. A group of men emerged from inside the building, moving quickly to the back of the delivery truck. Within a few minutes the truck was opened and boxes removed, a steady line of men moving cargo from the truck to the theater.

"What's going on?" Clinton asked, stuck beside Darek. "What do you see?"

"There's something going on with the theater," I said. "They're taking boxes inside."

"Is that all this is?" Darek asked. He jammed his way beside me so he could look out. "It's just for the new video game store."

"Game store?" I asked. "What game store?"

Darek looked at me as though I were an idiot. "Dude, the new game store! Haven't you heard? That's what's inside the theater now. A brand-spanking-new video game store! Everyone's been talking about it."

"Well, I haven't heard about it," I muttered, feeling about as techno-savvy as an Amish person.

Darek went on: "Everyone's saying it's the coolest thing ever. It's been open a few days. They're supposed to have totally unique video games. Stuff you can't get anywhere else. Must be pretty fun, too, 'cause Jordan McInerny went there opening day and no one's seen him since. You know him. He's probably locked up in his basement playing nonstop, stinky and bacteria-infested and surviving off uncooked ramen noodles. Jeez, Carter, you have to know about the store! Facebook's lit up about it."

I felt my temper rising. How could I, the creator of the PlayStation Artificial Intelligence game console—the only such device in the world—not know about a new game store? I grumbled: "Only idiots are on Facebook. I don't care that your cat had kittens or your mother just got a belly button ring."

Darek punched me in the arm. "How'd you know Mom got another belly button ring?"

"I swear I was totally making that up and . . . hey, look at that!"

Two men pulled a rectangular crate from the truck, long and narrow, maybe six feet from end to end. They dropped the crate on top of a wheeled cart. Two other crates rested on gurney-like carts beside the truck. Workers came out of the store and pushed the carts into the store.

"Weird boxes, huh?" Darek asked. "Seem heavy too, from how those guys are moving them. Wonder what's in those crates."

I watched at least a dozen of the six-foot-long crates get

unloaded before gazing back up at the apartment window. Had the gangster heard the commotion in the road? Was he getting nervous, about to run? I had to get up there!

Darek fidgeted. "We could be here all night. It could take hours to unload that stupid truck."

"All night?" Chambers echoed from behind me. "Did I mention I have a social commitment?"

I turned to offer helpful insults to my friends, when I heard a crashing, splintering sound behind me. Twisting, I spied one of the crates lying sideways in the road. The lid had shattered, shards of wood all over the place. A heavyset man on the tailgate looked down in horror. Two men rushed from the store, scrambling to the crate. They tipped it upright. As they did something flopped out of the top.

I flinched as though struck in the face. Darek cursed and stumbled backward. I watched one of the men take hold of the object and shove it back in the box.

"Is that what I thought it was?" Darek whimpered. "Did I just see what I thought I saw?"

I nodded.

An arm. A pale albino-like human arm had flopped out of the open crate.

Only one thing makes skin that deathly white.

Death.

"That's what's in the crates!" Darek gasped. "They're moving human bodies inside those crates! Dead human bodies! They're not even crates, are they? They're probably coffins!"

I heard Clinton start laughing. I told you he was an idiot.

"Coffins? Dead bodies? What is this, vampires? Hey, maybe one of them's Edward! You guys are freaking hysterical. Vampires are lame. You can't come up with something more original than that?"

Darek turned and shoved his forearm against my brother's throat.

"Moron! I didn't say anything about vampires! But those are bodies! I'm sure of it!"

Chambers looked sickly pale as he heard the news. Clinton shoved Darek away but stopped his ridiculous laughter. I gazed back at the theater.

Dead bodies? Awesome new video games? I gotta check this out!

Movement caught my attention. Hobo Warrior had inched his way to the edge of the alley. He peered around the corner, spying on the truck. The axe had been set aside. He held the shotgun and rifle, one in each hand, fingers on triggers. I didn't need to be a genius to know what would happen next.

Darek saw it too. He seemed downright giddy about the prospect.

"We're going to see some action!" he whispered. "Check it out! Dude's going to take them down!"

I told you, Darek isn't worth a bucket of warm spit. He may revel in the possibility of seeing a good old-fashioned shoot-out, but not me. Once bullets started flying, my Russian would be flying too.

I lifted the PlayStation AI and punched in my passcode. The device flickered back on, displaying four rows of my custom apps. I didn't have time for anything fancy. I punched the app in the left corner.

At once four cars started honking. Headlights flashed on and off, horns blaring, dome lights flickering. Car alarms from the four cars pierced the night. The men on the loading dock froze in surprise. Hobo Warrior retreated back into the alley.

Drapes moved in the upstairs apartment. A man came to the window, peering down at the street. I cursed as I realized the flaw in my plan. I may as well have let the Hobo Warrior start shooting.

The car alarms did something to mobilize the men at the truck, however, for within seconds I saw guns in their hands. One minute they carried boxes, the next they had automatic rifles, handguns, and shotguns. A half dozen more men spilled from the back of the theater, all heavily armed. Behind them, long coat flapping in the breeze, came a towering, raven-haired, black-garbed mammoth of a man.

The huge man stared directly across the street, right past the honking cars, right past the truck and the crates of dead people and the gun-toting workers. He stared at the alley where I stood hidden. He stared at me as though knowing exactly where to find me. He stared with eyes glimmering fiercely in the dim light.

He stood tall and dark. He loomed upward at least six and a half feet. He wore a strange archaic coat, something out of the nineteenth century, a coat an English nobleman would have worn: high collared, heavy, long. Beneath the coat he wore a modern pin-striped business suit, silver tie, and dark shirt. A diamond necklace sparkled from his chest. Even at my distance I could see a dazzling sideways figure-eight symbol hanging from the man's neck, the "8" made entirely from nickel-size diamonds. The man was massive and dark and fluid. He moved lithely yet powerfully to the street, his steps purposeful and quick. His eyes bore right into me. The breeze caught his coat, billowing it around him.

I'll admit it, the guy looked cool. For some reason I also think he wanted to kill me. He kept moving down the dock and into the road, coming right at me. I turned and shoved my friends forward.

"Go! We've got to go, go, go! Come on!"

I started running, pushing my friends ahead of me.

We ran down the length of the alley. I scraped my elbows against the narrow brick alley walls as I ran, nearly tripping into my friends, frantic to get out.

We burst out of the far end of the alley. I kept running, cajoling my friends forward with threats and promises and cursing. We ran to the end of the block before I dared look back.

I saw nothing. No pursuit. No big black-cloaked man. No Hobo Warrior. Nothing.

We kept going, turning the corner and running head-first into Dmitri the Russian gangster.

I shouted at Clinton. My brother leaped at the Russian, tackling him to the ground. The gangster tried to sit up. Clinton head-butted the criminal, knocking him bloodied and dazed to the asphalt. Darek dove to Clinton's side. He whisked two yellow dishwasher gloves from his pockets. Darek slapped the rubber gloves over the man's wrists. The same adhesion that allowed Darek to scamper up walls held the Russian's wrists firmly to the sidewalk.

Chambers stepped into the road and waved at the next passing car. A middle-aged woman pulled her Toyota Sienna to the curb and lowered the window. Chambers arranged for her to take us to the police station. She didn't stop blushing the whole time he talked to her.

I turned to my prize of war. I forgot all about tall dark men and Hobo Warriors with double-bladed axe thingies and dead white arms flopping out of caskets. As I gazed triumphantly down at the criminal, I thought of only one thing.

Sidney Locke. She'd have no choice but to go out with me now.

I stood over the gangster and said: "I, Carter Chance, leader of the Merewether Criminal Investigative Team, place you under citizen's arrest."

CHAPTER

I had captured Dmitri, the Russian mafia boss. I should have been a hero. Everyone at school should have been talking about me. But the next day no one was talking about me. Everyone was talking about the Lazarus Game Shop. So when I stepped out of the school and into the hands of the Russian gangsters, I was already in a foul mood.

The fact that the goons pointed guns at me didn't make me exactly giddy, either. But I wasn't worried for my safety. I was a genius, and they were losers. I could easily outsmart them.

Because I'm a genius, I activated my PlayStation AI device while chatting with the gangsters, sending a satellite signal that started the engine of a white Chevy Suburban parked about twenty cars away. Keeping the PlayStation AI in my pocket, I managed to reverse the SUV out of its stall and send it hurtling thirty miles per hour toward me.

The entire exercise was easy. I calculated how many feet to reverse the vehicle, how much torque to apply to the wheels, how much acceleration to needed to get the object in motion. I figured when to turn the steering wheel at what degree of force based on speed, distance, mass, and friction. I entered all the variables into my game console while keeping my hand inside my pocket. Being a genius, I knew this was a piece of cake. What I hadn't planned was a baby stroller in the path of the speeding Suburban.

The lead Russian mobster aimed the handgun at me.

"No talk. Now you the die."

I was too busy guiding the Suburban to correct his butchering of the English language. I spied the stroller down the row of cars. I saw a woman bending over an open trunk. The stroller sat in the road beside her. The Suburban would smash the stroller in about three seconds.

I jammed my finger against the controls and slammed the Suburban into a rusty pickup truck. The Suburban pushed the truck over the cement curb. Both vehicles came to a screeching, smoking halt on the adjacent sidewalk. Metal crunching against metal at thirty miles per hour sent a shock wave across the parking lot. The Russians jumped, I swore, and the mother grabbed the baby from the stroller.

The baby was okay. Everything was okay. Everything would have been okay no matter if I'd run over that stupid stroller or not. The *mother* turned out to be a sixteen-year-old sophomore taking a Family Relations class. The *baby* was one of those lousy fake plastic babies who cry all the time and wake kids in the middle of the night, all the while teaching teenagers to NEVER get married and instead be monks or nuns and take vows of celibacy and basically have a lonely, miserable, rotten life.

Okay, I took that rotten class last semester. Can you tell?

Anyway, the stupid fake baby didn't make so much as a whimper. I cursed as I observed the wreckage. Fake baby? Safe. Real teenager about to get shot in head by Russians? Very much unsafe.

The collision must have convinced the Russians to kill me now rather than later in a more private and respectful manner, for all five pulled out handguns. The leader raised his gun, finger on trigger. One little motion—one insignificant flick of finger against metal—and the world's last, best hope would be extinguished. I would be dead. Or perhaps disfigured and horribly mutilated. Or maybe with just a flesh wound that would attract the sympathy of Sidney. But probably dead.

The Russian raised his gun to shoot me. Although a genius, I saw no way out of my predicament. Then I heard the guttural rumbling of what turned out to be the sickest, baddest, coolest car ever.

Now I may not know much about babies—fake or real—religion, philosophy, or basic human relationships (all nonsense subjects anyway), but I do know a thing or two about automobiles, particularly freaking awesome ones. What I knew about the Lamborghini Z 2025 Prototype is that it could not yet be built. We lacked the basic technology. And yet here it came, roaring its way toward me.

A tinted cockpit perched atop a gleaming black body about the size of a tank. The car rode an inch off the ground despite tires the size of small horses. Although riding lower than the lowest of the hub-spinning lowriders, the car could almost immediately elevate as high as Humvee as if it sensed disruption in the road. According to the prototype design, the car could literally *levitate* off the ground, propelled by jet-style engines underneath the body. It could *fly* for short distances. Handy in rush hour.

The ground shook as though a rocket were gearing up to take off. A Mini Cooper or Smart Car this was not. The car was as sleek as a stealth bomber but as subtle as your polyester-wearing blue-haired grandmother at a fashion show. It could go zero-to-sixty faster than an expletive. Though huge on the road, it turned, not on a dime, but on a microchip. This was the most advanced vehicle ever designed. Like I said, it could not be built. It would cost untold millions of dollars.

This unbuildable car rolled to a stop about five feet from me. I stared. The Russians stared. People in passing cars nearly drove off the road as they stared. For once in my life I was speechless.

The door slid open, lifting upward like a giant black wing. A foot hit the ground. I watched anxiously, eager to know who could own such a car. Nothing could surprise me now. A green pointy-antennaed alien from Mars stepping out of the car would not have surprised me.

What did emerge from the car didn't just surprise me. It scared the crap out of me.

Billowing black preceded the man out of the car, an undulating flow of inky fabric that floated on the wind like a drifting parachute. Through the black cloth, a man stepped out, a massive gorilla of a man with black beard and eyes shimmering like polished obsidian. Beneath the coat, he wore a stylish dark business suit, diamond cuff links twinkling from milky-white sleeves. Diamonds sparkled from his fingers and from the strange sideways figure eight necklace on his chest. My friend from the video game store poured out of the car and set his pulsating eyes on me.

I felt suddenly very glad the Russian mob was there to protect me.

The man turned his steely gaze from me to the gangsters. He barked something in Russian at the men. The gangsters shrank back against their getaway car, the Cadillac Escalade. Guns wavered, feet shuffled. I saw fear in their eyes. The men glanced at each other, eyes darting, wide. I thought they would turn and run, and they probably would have, but the leader grew a backbone and stepped forward, gun raised again, finger on the trigger.

I grimaced and prepared to watch the owner of this really cool car be gunned down. I wondered about the legality of my borrowing the Lamborghini after the man's death. Could it really fly? What would Sidney think of me pulling up in front of her house in a car like this?

But the Russians didn't shoot him. What happened was much more terrifying.

The Russian gangster put his finger to trigger. I watched as his finger began to pull. Then, a split second later, so fast I detected only a blur, something flew from the big dude's hand, a streak of metal, a shimmer of reflected light. I heard a bark from the Russian. The man's arm careened backward as though on a puppet string. His arm crashed against the Escalade door behind him and stuck there, pinned against the side of the SUV.

The Russian stared at his arm in obvious surprise. He struggled to pull his arm forward but could not. His arm held fast to the car door. He tugged on it, but it was pinned firm. I could see a metal object sticking through his arm, embedded all the way through the limb and several inches into metal. Game Store Dude threw a metal missile right through the gangster's arm!

Recognition must have registered pain, for the man squealed like a trapped pig. The cry sent his gangsters into action. Four guns came up. I grimaced and ducked, waiting for the barrage of bullets.

Instead I saw Game Store Dude flick his wrist four times and heard four corresponding cries of pain. Metal guns fell. Men yelped and screamed.

One man held his arm, a metal spike stuck clean through the palm of his hand. Another fell to the road, grasping at his leg, blood pooling at his feet. Another held his forearm, and a fourth stood stunned and gaping. I saw no wound in the man, no metallic throwing star or missile stuck out of him. The guy seemed totally untouched. Yet he stood riveted in place, eyes on the ground.

I looked down, following his gaze. I saw what appeared to be two halves of a Beretta handgun lying in the road. The gun had been severed by a ninja star, split right up the barrel.

Game Store Dude said something and immediately the four men scrambled toward their car. The leader had managed to pull his arm free from the car door, a big gaping wound in his arm, a clump of flesh and fabric left still pinned to metal. Within a few seconds, the entire gang had stumbled, groaned, and bled their way into the Escalade. The vehicle roared to life and the gangsters sped away.

I swallowed hard and remained perfectly still. I held my breath, wondering what Game Store Dude would do to me. I cursed myself for not jumping inside the car with my Russian friends.

I said nothing, fortunately. I almost said, *Hey, I didn't even notice the dead bodies last night—it's really none of my business*, but luckily I didn't, because Game Store Dude spoke first.

"My name is Geoffrey Chaucer," the man said in a pleasant, friendly, conversational sort of way. He smiled, but it was the leer of a hyena. He extended his hand to me. I didn't shake it.

Geoffrey Chaucer. Did I know that name?

I searched my memory for matches, pretty much like doing a Google search, only better. Let's see . . . *Geoffrey Chaucer, lead singer in British alternative rock band, underwear model and*—uh, no, probably not; *Geoffrey Chaucer, Wall Street private equity investor, killed himself after stock market crash in 2001*—nope, not him; *Geoffrey Chaucer, circa 1343–1400, widely regarded as the "father of English literature," author of* The Canterbury Tales, *and*—okay, obviously not *that* guy. Maybe he was—

"You must be Carter Chance."

The big man spoke, startling me out of my analysis. I gulped. How did he know me? Crap, *why* did he know me?

"Nope," I returned, forcing my voice to sound calm and cool. I resisted the urge to start begging for mercy. Instead, I said: "Never heard of him."

"The teen named by the president of the United States as most likely to succeed?"

"Not me."

"The kid who got a perfect score on the SAT?"

"Uh . . . no, no you're mixing me with . . . well . . . no."

"The only teenager ever awarded a Presidential Medal of Freedom? The teenager recognized for designing predictive algorithms that may eliminate all crime from the world?"

"It wasn't actually a predictive algorithm as much as it was . . . no, that's, uh, someone else."

"Not the kid who designed and patented the PlayStation Artificial Intelligence device with apps so advanced you can—"

"No, no, not me, probably mixing me up with my brother."

"Okay, then I suppose you're also not the one all the girls in town find irresistible, including Sidney Locke?"

"Hey! That's me! Wait, did you hear Sidney say that? Did she really say that about me?"

"So you *are* Carter Chance?"

I sighed. Well, when you are as famous and brilliant and accomplished as I am, it's a bit difficult to stay anonymous. I shrugged and nodded.

"Okay, yeah, that's me. But I swear I saw nothing last night! I mean it! Whatever you're doing there at that store . . . hey, none of my business!"

Chaucer smiled. "Actually, I'm hoping that won't be true much longer. Listen, I'm a very busy man, and I don't want to waste your time. Let me cut to the chase here. I own a video game company. We create the most advanced video games in the world. We sell them through our own stores. As you know, we just opened one here in Merewether. You saw it last night. The Lazarus Game Shop."

Yes, I thought, *I saw it all right. Along with coffins and dead bodies.* I said nothing. He continued.

"Mr. Chance, I am creating the most advanced video games ever imagined, and I need your help. You see, I want to hire you to come work for me."

I blinked. My mouth opened. My mouth closed. I stared. I gawked. I made grunting sounds. I must have looked like the biggest idiot in the world. Chaucer waited patiently while I gurgled and grumbled. I didn't know what to say.

"If payment is the issue, let me just say that with this position comes almost unlimited riches, power over nations, control of governments around the world, and, of course, immortality. If you're interested in such things, that is."

I laughed. I downright chortled. The guy was pretty

darn funny. What a sales pitch! Had he grown up selling Amway?

But the man who called himself Geoffrey Chaucer did not laugh. He didn't even smile. Maybe he didn't appreciate his own humor. I waited for him to explain his ridiculous comment. Instead he pulled something out of his jacket pocket and handed it to me.

"Don't decide now. Come see the store and check out our games. Please take my business card. When you're ready, come take a private tour."

I glanced at the so-called "business card." It was a small electronic device, the size of a business card, only awash in light and motion. A video played on the card, a promotional advertisement for what must be Chaucer's business. I held what looked like a card-sized iPad in my hand, as thin as paper.

While I stood gaping at the video card, the man pressed a wad of paper into my hand. I felt the comforting, heavy, embossed texture of cold hard cash.

"Call this a presigning bonus," Chaucer said. "Not much, just a small token of my interest. Go take your girlfriend out to dinner tonight, have a good time. Then come see me."

The man said nothing else. No explanation of how he found me. No clue as to how he knew so much about me. No mention of the way he diced up my Russian friends and sent them off bloody and wounded. He simply climbed inside his totally awesome futuristic car, black coat curling and flapping behind him, and disappeared from view.

I held a thick stack of hundred dollar bills, at least fifty of them, maybe a hundred. The wad was so thick I could barely wrap my hands around it. I'd never seen so much money. Having that much money made me think of only one thing.

Sidney Locke.

Just think of how much attention I can buy with this much cold hard cash!

If you can't earn their love, I've always thought, you can at least buy it. I broke into a run as I headed for home, my thoughts entirely on Sidney, all disturbing thoughts of whimpering Russians and severed handguns and dead white arms in coffins already forgotten.

CHAPTER THREE

Because I am a genius, I memorized several long romantic poems to impress Sidney, real woozers from Keats and Yates and other such hacks. I had Shakespeare's Sonnet #130 in my Cupid's quiver. I had song lyrics, I had flattery, I had pretend-caring about animals, babies, and the environment. I had this entire arsenal of romantic shock and awe. When I met Sidney at the hospital that evening, I would unleash the fury.

She sat at her father's side, holding his hand. He lay on a hospital gurney, tubes and wires and various medical devices on and inside and around him. The touch of Sidney's hand would have raised me from the dead, yet her father remained lifeless as a turnip.

I knocked on the half-opened door. She turned.

I steeled myself, ran through my litany of romantic weapons, and prepared to woo and wow her. She smiled. My heart hammered. My throat constricted. My vision blurred. I felt like fainting. But I called on my reserves of strength and used my towering intellect to produce this profound statement.

"Hey."

"Hey," she said back.

I swallowed hard. I thought my heart would burst just hearing that word. That word was completely directed at me, not one of her other friends, not at a teacher, nor a family member, but at *me*. There was feeling in that word. Real honest emotion. The way she said it! Wow. I still had so much to learn about romance . . . but she could teach me!

Now that we had that icebreaker out of the way I felt comfortable really bearing my soul to her.

"So . . ." I began.

"So," she returned. I smiled at her reply. Now we were really communicating!

"How's your dad?" I asked.

"The same."

"Hmm."

"Yep."

She looked lovely, seated by her father's prostrate, gaunt, nearly dead body. She had skipped school the past couple of days to stay by her father and had a grungy, unbathed appearance that really swept me off my feet.

"How are you doing?" I asked, gathering the courage to string four words together.

"Okay."

"Okay, good. Real good. So . . . uh . . . how's calculus coming?"

"I'm in geometry."

"Oh, yeah, that's right. I'm so sorry. How's that going?"

"Fine."

"Listen, if you need any help with your homework or anything, I'm happy to do it for you. It was like third grade when I took geometry, but I'm sure it'll all come back to me. Just let me know if I can help."

"That's nice, but I should probably figure it out myself."

"Okay."

Our deep, significant conversation lapsed into awkward silence. I felt a pang of disappointment, to be honest. Usually Sidney is a lively conversationalist. What was her problem today? Cat got her tongue? I figured I should lighten the mood.

"So, Sidney, I arrested the man who shot your dad. Did you hear that? Everyone's talking about it at school."

This was actually not true, since everyone was talking about the game store. Which reminded me of the video business card in my pocket, but I forced that out of my mind.

"Yeah," she said without looking at me. "I heard about it."

I kind of expected a bigger reaction. But then I've never had a father on the verge of brain death, so maybe that was dampening her mood. I sighed. Well, it was worth a try. Not an easy person to impress, this Sidney Locke.

Perhaps she heard the exasperation in my sigh, maybe she was in touch with my true emotions, or maybe she just wanted to get rid of me, but she did respond. She glanced up at me and smiled.

"Thanks, Carter. You did that for me?"

I shrugged. "Well, there was justice to be served, of course, the law to be upheld, the right of citizens to live without fear of gangsters and . . ."

Sidney grinned. A real smile.

"Carter! Really?"

"Okay, fine. Yes. I totally risked my life to impress you."

Her grin widened. "Thanks. That's sweet of you."

With that she turned her attention back to her father as though he were about to start dancing or whisper the location of hidden treasure. I could see I had to escalate my attempt.

"Hey, you wanna get out of here for a while? Go grab something to eat?"

She frowned. "I don't know . . ."

"Come on, Sidney. It's not like he's going anywhere."

She shot me an icy look.

"I mean, it's not like he'll be waking up anytime soon."

"Carter!"

"Uh . . . what I'm trying to say is . . . you know, nothing lasts forever. The coma, I mean. He'll come out of it, right? But you still gotta eat."

She hesitated. I decided to go with the nuclear option.

Pity. She couldn't resist pity.

"Hey, I know what you're going through here. I mean, not the whole brain-dead comatose thing, no, not that. But not having a parent around? Feeling a bit alone? Yeah, I know that. My mom may as well be dead, you know?"

She looked at me a long while, her eyes searching me. I saw real tenderness there, compassion, warmth. I almost felt guilty. Fortunately, that wasn't an emotion I spent any time worrying about.

She finally nodded. "Yeah, I guess you probably do. I never thought about it that way. I'm sorry you don't have your mom at home anymore, Carter."

For the record, my mom is not dead. She and Dad divorced about a year ago. It's not a huge deal. It's kind of a family tradition. I have two older sisters, also divorced, and my grandparents divorced, and pretty much all my aunts and uncles. No biggie. I guess the Chance side of the family is a bit hard to live with or something. Or maybe it's just that relationships suck. Or maybe just that nothing really lasts forever, if you know what I mean.

Don't feel sorry for me or anything. I'm totally over it. Really.

I shrugged bravely. "Well, we all have to keep moving on in life, right? We have to live each day. We have to go on fighting. We got to survive. And we have to eat. So what do you say? Come get dinner with me?"

She still didn't move. I had one last trick.

"We can bring the whole gang. Clinton, Darek . . ."

"Kyle?" she asked.

I nodded. "Yeah, Chambers will be there."

She sighed and stretched. She stood up.

"Well, I guess a daughter's gotta eat, right?"

So that's how I got Sidney out on a date with me. Yes, okay, maybe it was more of a "group date," and maybe she really only wanted to come because of Chambers, but I'll take whatever I can get. You see, I told you it was handy to keep an irresistible man in the gang.

———

I took Sidney, Clinton, Darek, and Chambers to IHOP for dinner. I couldn't exactly blow my wad of cash all in one shot, could I? Besides, I did let them all get a soda and dessert with their entrée, so it's not like I'm a cheapskate.

It was a fun evening at the restaurant, even though my brother is an idiot and kept making various foul bodily noises and that fat-butt Darek ate half of my entrée. When you're out with your best friends, it's always a good time. Even when you can't stand them.

I'm pretty sure I could have really made a breakthrough with Sidney over dinner had the circumstances been different. I mean, if I could have engaged in a deep meaningful discussion about something of real value, like the unified theory in quantum physics, then we could have really connected. But no one wanted to talk physics or science or even about our death-defying stunt last night. All my friends wanted to talk about was the new video game store.

"We're the biggest losers in the whole town," Darek said after shoving half my apple pie down his gullet. I stabbed at his hand with my fork, but he pulled away before I could severely wound him.

"What? Why?" Clinton asked. I couldn't look at him. He sported a flaky ketchup mustache like a three-year-old. "Why are we big losers?"

"Dude, go look in a mirror," I said. But Darek shook his head.

"We're like the last ones in the whole town who haven't been inside the Lazarus Game Shop!"

"I know people who haven't been there," Chambers said between bites of his dainty salad.

"You and your mom don't count," Darek said. "I'm saying that every normal cool person in town has already been there! Except us!"

"My mom's a normal cool person!" Chambers said, putting down his fork and placing his hands on the table. I knew that look. Chambers may be a pretty boy, but he could kick Darek's butt any day of the week. "Don't be dissing my mom."

"It's not just your mom. It's *every* mom," Darek explained. "Moms hate the place."

This got Clinton's attention. "They do? Really? If moms hate the place, then we definitely got to go there. It must be awesome."

Darek nodded. He leaned in, voice low, conspiratorial.

"The PTA is forming this big rally tomorrow to protest the store. They'll be burning games and everything. It's a big deal. Total violation of the Second Amendment."

"First," I corrected.

Clinton ignored me. "Game burning? Really? That's cool!"

Darek rolled his eyes. "Dude! It's not! The adults are all worked up about the store. They want to close it down."

"It just opened!" Clinton said. "Why's everyone all worked up about it?"

"Opened five days ago," Darek said. "You know what's happened since? You heard about the junior high?"

We all shook our heads. Darek continued: "It's been basically shut down 'cause none of the kids are showing up. Everyone's sluffing school. Same at our school. Didn't you notice it today? Half my fifth period class was out. Probably seventy percent sixth period. It's a ghost town. You didn't notice?"

I honestly hadn't noticed, but then when you are as fascinated by learning and education like me you don't spend much time observing the common rabble.

Clinton nodded. "Yeah, I did. Figured everyone had the flu or whatever."

Sidney said, "I don't get it. Sorry, I've been at the hospital since Dad was brought in. What's going on?"

Darek told about our experience last night—all the activity around the once-abandoned theater. He wisely omitted mention of dead bodies. He then related what he'd learned from his brother and several other completely unreliable sources.

"The place is apparently totally cool. They've converted the entire theater area into a massive multiplayer game-cave! I guess half the town is inside there playing the games. It's totally unique. They don't sell any regular games there. Nothing for PlayStation or Xbox or any normal system."

"Well, that sucks," Clinton interrupted. "No *Call of*

Duty? No *Madden*? Sounds dorky. Probably low-quality knockoffs."

Darek shook his head. "Aren't you listening to me? Freak, Clinton! You *are* as dumb as Carter says!"

"Thank you," I said, tipping my glass of Cherry Coke toward Darek. "I've been saying it for years."

"Why's everyone skipping school, Clinton?" Darek asked. "Why have some kids gone, like, totally missing? Not because the games are lame! Because they're so cool!"

That seemed to penetrate Clinton's concrete head. He nodded and smiled in excitement. Sidney, however, was frowning.

"Wait a minute!" she said. "Kids have gone missing? What's that mean?"

Darek shrugged. "It's nothing, just normal parent paranoia. What I heard is that Jordan McInerny went totally AWOL, like no one knows where he is. Parents are saying it's a kidnapping."

"So what's that got to do with the store?" Sidney asked. "Maybe it really is a kidnapping!"

Darek shook his head. "Maybe. But it's not just Jordan. Kenyon Martin didn't come home from school yesterday. Parents didn't even miss him until today, but I guess now they're all freaked out."

"Kenyon's an idiot," I said. "He could have drowned in an inch of water. He probably ran off to join the circus or some religious cult. Became a monk. Who knows?"

"He's not an idiot! He's the senior class president! Like the most popular kid in town!"

"I'm the most popular kid in town," I said. Sidney rolled her eyes at me.

"Kenyon was last seen headed to the game store," Darek said.

"Could be total coincidence," I said. "Maybe our Russian friends got him."

"Maybe," Darek said. "But that's not all of it. There's also the crowd all sick and dying."

"The what?" Clinton asked. Even Chambers looked up from his smartphone at this comment.

"There's a bunch of kids at the hospital, dehydrated and starving, like they haven't eaten for days. From what I hear it's because the games are so addictive the morons forgot to eat. Isn't that cool?"

I nodded, grudgingly agreeing. That *was* cool. If only I could create an *app* that cool!

"My dad would be freaking out about this," Sidney said. "He would be all over this if only he wasn't . . ."

She swallowed and looked away. I could see moisture glistening in the corner of her eye. I said, "Hey, don't worry about it. I'm sure my dad's taking care of things while your dad's . . . uh . . . out of commission."

"Hey," Darek said, smacking the table. "That's right! What's your dad saying about this? He's a cop too!"

"No kidding," I said. "Brilliant. You just figure that out? We've been friends since first grade."

Clinton, who must have felt a bit out of this conversation, said, "Dad's in charge now that Sidney's dad is brain dead or whatever you call it."

I smacked Clinton on the arm. "Nice, bro," I said. "Really sensitive of you."

Sidney waved it off. "It's okay. Even brain dead, my dad's still smarter than yours."

I laughed. Ah, now that's the old Sidney! I saw a real smile on her face for the first time since the shooting. It lit up the whole room.

"So what's your dad saying about all this?" Darek asked. "What's the official police line?"

I shook my head. So did Clinton. I explained, "Dude, this is our *father* you're talking about. You think we actually have conversations with him?"

"He had to say something about the store," Darek pressed.

Clinton said, "No, Carter's right. Dad's never around. When he is, we try not to be. Not that it matters. He'd never tell us anything. We're just snot-nose punks."

"This doesn't sound too good, you have to admit it," Sidney said. "About the store, I mean. No wonder the parents are protesting if all these bad things are happening."

"But it's crap!" Darek said. "What are they protesting? That someone actually made a game so cool we all want to play it? Parents only want us to do lame things. Stuff that they want to do. Like go to school and church and have a job. Dumb stuff. They're just jealous we're having fun!"

"But we're not having fun, are we?" Clinton asked. "'Cause we haven't been to the store! Man, you're right, Darek. We really *are* the biggest losers in town."

Darek nodded. "Yes, my point exactly."

Chambers shifted in his chair. "Guys, this isn't good. Not good at all. I can't let this get out. If the girls think I'm hanging with the loser crowd, I'll lose my street cred. We gotta do something about this."

"I'll tell you what we're going to do," Darek said. "We're going to the store right now. Let's go see what this's all about."

"I can do better than that." I pulled the video card from my pocket and placed it on the table.

As my friends—including Sidney, I'm happy to add— stared in open-mouthed, wide-eyed wonder, I said, "I can get us a private tour."

CHAPTER FOUR

I went to the Lazarus Game Shop expecting to give a secret handshake just to enter the place—guards at the door, guns mounted beneath tabletops, surveillance cameras everywhere. Inside, I guessed it would be dark and menacing, the smoke-choked haze of a gambling hall or one of those shady showrooms for door-to-door vacuum salesmen. Instead I found it as sinister as the Disney Store.

We rode in Chambers's new blue Volvo, the "top-rated car for safety in its class" as Chambers's mom so often reminded him. The real reason Chambers had the car, we all knew, was his secret infatuation with *Twilight*. Not that I could mock him too much. At least he had his driver's license and a car. On my dad's pathetic police department salary, I'd be lucky to drive a pogo stick.

Cars and pickup trucks jammed the streets around the theater. We had to park four blocks away to find an open spot, so far we could have almost walked there from the IHOP. No one ever has to park four blocks from anything in Merewether. Our mayor once started a local city transit bus but no one rode it. There's just no place to go in our armpit town.

The theater marquee glowed like a lighthouse beacon from four blocks away. I walked quickly, fearful the store would close before we could get inside. My friends labored to keep up. At three blocks away I could see lines of people out the front doors. At two blocks I could hear the excited chatter of the crowds. At one block I found myself entirely surprised by whom I found in line.

The crowd didn't just consist of kids and teenagers; there were tons of adults in line. Yes, there are always the loser adults who hang out at video game stores, the guys with ear gauges and black-dyed beards who work at Starbucks or Barnes and Noble. There are the thirty-year-old weenies still living with parents. But that's not what I saw in line. I saw normal, ordinary, respectably boring adults. I saw whole families, as if they were going to Build-a-Bear Workshop. I am a genius, but I couldn't figure this out. What were they all doing here? Aren't they supposed to be protesting the place?

Clinton, the dolt follower that he is, queued up in back of the massive line. I pulled him out and gestured my little gang forward. I marched right up to the door where two beefy men in black sunglasses and black suits stood guard. As I approached, they gave me the same ornery scowl I get from my grandmother every time I'm forced to visit her. Before they could speak or shoot or scold me for not visiting more often, I flashed my video business card at them.

The men reacted in obvious surprise. One of the men bent down to examine the card. He lifted a sleeve to his mouth and said something, either speaking into a microphone or talking to his arm hair. He tapped a hand to the wire at his ear, listening, and then waved us through the front door.

My friends were all very impressed by my VIP treatment, even Sidney. I'll just never understand girls. I risk my life to capture Dmitri, the Russian mobster who shot Sidney's dad after a botched burglary attempt, and I get nothing. I get her inside a store and she wants to throw herself at me. Go figure.

The inside lobby had been completely transformed. Gone were the long low glass cases of overpriced candy. Gone were the popcorn machines, drink dispensers, ticket stands, and "coming soon" movie posters. The suffocating 1930s-style plush red carpet, sticky from soda pop and chewing gum, had been ripped out. Gone, too, were the gaudy fake crystal chandeliers. The room bore no resemblance to the old theater I used to haunt. It now looked like an Apple Store, only even more modern and cool. It reminded me of the deck of the starship *Enterprise*.

Three-dimensional video images danced from every square inch of wall. I'm not talking about monitors or flat-screen televisions. I'm not talking about some lame video projection shooting flat images on the wall. I mean true three-dimensional video objects, like holographic images, moving and running and flowing across the walls. It took a few moments for my eyes to adjust, to even track the movements, let alone discern outline and context and shape. It was as though my eyes lacked the sophistication and biological technology to comprehend what I saw.

Once I finally adjusted, I realized the images represented what had to be characters from video games. Dozens of games played out on the walls, on the ceiling, even on the floor where I stood. The entire room convulsed in video imagery, as though I had stepped out of the real world and into the digital guts of a hundred video games.

My friends muttered various expletives as they gazed at the imagery on the walls and ceiling. My attention, however, had shifted to the moving display of games. Amazingly, the displays—the little shelves that hold product—actually *moved* around the room.

Each "stand" appeared to be about four feet tall and maybe as thick around as Clinton. The stand had three sides, a perfect pyramid, with shelves holding plastic DVD-sized game cases on all three sides. The stands must have had wheels attached to the bottom, for they rolled this way and that, pivoting, twirling, moving everywhere—just like little R2-D2 units.

I watched as a little girl, maybe seven or eight years old, gazed up at the wall next to her. Horses galloped across the wall. As she gazed in rapt wonder, a display stand—about the same size as the girl—rolled up to her. The little girl plucked a game off the stand and held it up to her mother. I observed the behavior in dumbstruck awe, perceiving the purpose of the moving display stands.

Spinning about, I surveyed other customers in the room. I watched long enough to see similar action and reaction time and time again. It was truly astonishing.

The games came to the customers! Somehow the computer technology running the showroom identified the interest of each customer and brought the relevant game right to them. If a customer lacked interest in a particular image that game stayed far away. If the customer showed interest, the game moved quickly toward them. It was cool and scary at the same time.

I turned to the images speckling the wall beside me, curious to see what kinds of games I could find. I had only just started to study one of the games when I heard a voice behind me.

"Ah, Mr. Chance! I wondered if I would find you here! I guess it's no surprise, given your penchant for technology."

Mr. Elton? What is *he* doing here?

I shook the hand suddenly thrust near my eyeballs. Looking up, I saw the principal of Merewether High School smiling down at me. Mr. Elton once played basketball at some famous university like Duke or Kentucky or the California State Penitentiary. Apparently that qualified him to be both basketball coach *and* principal at our high school.

"Amazing place, isn't it?" the principal asked. "I just can't even begin to understand all this technology! Heck, I still remember when Pong came out! And we all thought *that* was cool!"

Oh, sweet gods of mercy, I prayed, *please don't let Elton start reminiscing about the good old days.* If I have to hear again how he played against Michael Jordan in the McDonald's High School all-star game back at about the time of the Civil War, I'm going to kill myself.

Fortunately, he asked a question instead: "So what do you think, Carter? You're our resident genius. What do you think about all this?"

"It seems like an evil place designed to ensnare impressionable minds through addictive entertainment for the purposes of financial gain at the expense of the mental, social, and emotional health of our children."

Elton nodded, a sagacious look on his face.

"That's what I think too. Just amazing."

Huh?

I tried again: "I believe that responsible adults should demand the closure of this store before we become desensitized to violence, have our core values twisted, and have our brains turned to mush."

"Technology's wonderful nowadays," Elton said, a grave, pensive look on his face. "No doubt about it. Where would we be without technology? I'd still be playing Pong, that's what. Ha!"

I considered asking what medication he'd stopped taking, but before I could, a strange-looking man interrupted us. The newcomer was nearly as tall as Geoffrey Chaucer, but paper-thin. Had the guy turned sideways he might have disappeared. He was dressed all in black except for a silver tie and a shimmering diamond necklace. He wore a near-identical sideways figure eight necklace as Chaucer, only not quite as large, the diamonds more like dimes instead of quarters.

"Mr. Elton, I have your gift bag. If you would permit me?"

His voice sounded gravelly and pitchless, like an old washed out rock 'n' roll singer with his voice box blown out. More striking than the man's voice, though, was his ghastly pale appearance: luminously white skin, colorless eyes. His hair lacked any shading—not white, not gray even, just . . . nothing. The hair appeared translucent, as though each strand were made of glass. The hair, skin, eyes, voice—it all gave him a macabre, deathlike appearance. He looked awesome. He looked like a living ghost.

Ghost Man handed a tote bag to Mr. Elton. "This is a small gift of appreciation for visiting us today. My name is Thomas. If there is anything you need, please let me know."

Elton accepted the bag without comment, eyes hungry, hands groping the bag. I watched as he rummaged inside. A bundle of hundred dollar bills fell from the bag to the floor. Elton didn't even notice. From the way he dug about the bag, it appeared there were *dozens* of bundles of hundred dollar bills. Elton grunted in satisfaction and tucked the bag over his shoulder.

I blinked in surprise. Bundles of money? Gift bags filled up with cash? What's going on here?

I gazed about the room. I noticed that all the adults had black tote bags in hands or over shoulders. I could see bunches of cold hard cash peeking up from the tops of the bags. There had to been hundreds—no, thousands of dollars in the bags! Every parent had one of them. I knew at once what it meant. The store was paying off the adults! He was bribing them so they wouldn't close down the store. Geoffrey Chaucer was flooding the whole town with cash.

I needed to get some of that action!

I turned to find Sidney but instead found myself staring at a sideways figure-eight diamond necklace. Stepping back, I saw Geoffrey Chaucer looming over me. The dark-haired monolith seemed to nearly reach the ceiling. He smiled down at me.

"Ah, Mr. Chance, so good of you to come. I knew you would not be able to stay away for long. Not a young man of your intellectual curiosity. So what do you think of my little operation here?"

"It's okay," I said, shrugging. The smugness in his voice irritated me. "It's not like you've opened another Smithsonian. It's just a store."

Chaucer appeared amused. "Just a store?"

"Might as well be another Walmart," I said. "Except you lack the old geezer door greeters."

"Is that so? Well, perhaps I can change your opinion of what we're doing here. But first, please, introduce me to your friends."

He nodded toward the group of teenagers standing

behind me. Each one of them—including Sidney—gawked as if Tom Cruise had just walked through the door. Okay, maybe Chaucer looked all big and tough and cool, and yes, he did have a great car, and perhaps he could throw ninja stars so hard he could split handguns, and yes, he had created this store and all the amazing technology, and maybe he had a diamond necklace the size of a small poodle around his neck that was likely worth the total value of the state of Delaware, but that didn't mean my stupid friends had to act all fawning and obsequious. They were in the presence of a genius every day!

"This must be Sidney Locke," Chaucer said, holding out a hand to Sidney. "I've heard that there is one exceptionally beautiful young woman in town, and surely you are she. It is an honor."

She raised a hand to shake his, but of course Chaucer took her hand to his mouth and kissed it. What a loser. As though girls cared for such stereotyped rubbish nowadays. Sidney blushed and smiled and muttered something incomprehensible. I swore under my breath.

"Carter, this must be your brother?" Chaucer asked as he sized up Clinton. My brother's mouth hung open. A trickle of spit escaped the corner of his mouth.

"Adopted, not natural," I said. "We found him floating down the river in a basket."

Chaucer laughed. "Sorry, Carter, but the family resemblance is unmistakable."

I reeled from the insult. I didn't have to stand here and take this kind of abuse!

Chaucer turned to Darek. He asked me for Darek's name. I shrugged as though I didn't know him. Sidney supplied the names for Darek and Chambers. Chaucer greeted them with a show of great civility. He even asked them questions about their interests and hobbies, as though either of them actually had any. Chaucer appeared genuinely fascinated as Darek explained some of the mechanical contraptions he'd invented. Chambers talked about his job as debate team lead and glee club president and all the rest of the stupid things he did. It all grew quickly tiresome.

"So what about this private tour?" I asked, interrupting Chaucer just as he started asking my brother questions. "You said you'd give *me* a private tour."

I put great emphasis on the *me* part of my question, but Chaucer didn't seem to get the hint. He smiled at all of us and motioned toward a door at the back of the showroom.

"Yes, yes, of course! Please, all of you, follow me. I'd love to show you Alexandria Hall. This is where the real magic happens."

The real magic . . . I shook my head. Rubbish, indeed. What, is he taking us to Disneyland? Will there be talking birds and singing flowers? I better at least get a Dole Whip afterwards.

Chaucer led us through a swinging door. We walked down a long hallway that led into the massive theater room. The theater once held about two hundred red-upholstered chairs in front of a wall-to-wall screen. The carpet had once been plush and gaudy, with intricate mosaic patterns, and real honest-to-goodness chandeliers hung from the 1930s era art deco ceiling. Like many of the old-school theaters, it had a full stage just in front of the projection screen. I guessed the place once had live entertainment as well as movies. In my days the stage served simply as the collector of spit wads. The theater always seemed ridiculously out of place for a town like Merewether—like lipstick and pearls on a pig.

As we walked, Chaucer regaled us with the background to the name "Alexandria Hall." For my friends' benefit, Chaucer explained that Alexandria, Egypt, held the largest and most famous library in the ancient world. Not only did it house the world's greatest treasures of knowledge, but also all the great scholars resided there, sharing ideas, scribbling on papyrus, and basically wishing they had iPads.

"Today we are constructing a virtual Alexandria," Chaucer said as he led us down the hallway toward the closed theater door. "We're building an online community that will not only store the world's knowledge but serve as a catalyst to achieve the next stunning breakthroughs in human achievement. We are on the verge of unlocking the great secrets of the universe, and it is largely through the gamification of ordinary everyday people. Come, let me show you."

He opened the door and stepped inside. My friends disappeared behind him. Sighing, irritated that this had become a school field trip, I wandered along after the common crowd.

I walked into Alexandria Hall and lost my ability to breathe. I felt the air knocked out of my lungs. My mouth opened, my eyes stared, my brain lost its ability to reason. Synapses stopped firing. Neurochemical signals halted. All I could do was gaze in dazed, stupefied wonder.

Now, let me say here for the record that I am not easily impressed. I have been to the White House. I've been to Sony headquarters and jointly developed the world's first and only PlayStation Artificial Intelligence device. While kids my same age were learning to add and subtract, I built a smartphone app that did my homework for me. I've done more and seen more in my short fifteen years than any thousand regular people put together. Yet I had never seen anything like this.

At first I saw nothing physical at all, no walls, floor, or ceiling. I had walked into a kaleidoscope of color—swirling, churning, roiling, weaving, and dancing all about me, snaking through my fingers and coiling through my hair, caressing my skin and blanketing me in light, motion, and energy. As my eyes adjusted I discerned corporeal pattern and physiology. Shapes darted through the air, prancing over and above me, crawling over my shoulders, flitting between my legs. I saw familiar images in the light that played all about me: animals, people, water, machines, buildings, trees, mountains, entire galaxies. All this swirled around me like leaves caught in a twisting tornado.

I took several more steps, somehow managing to move. As my eyes continued adjusting, I discerned that these images played on the walls, on the floor, along the ceiling, in the very air all about me. The holographic imagery I had observed in the showroom lobby appeared a weak two-dimensional sham compared to the intense reality of the digital world I had entered. I fell from the physical tangible world through an Einstein-Rosen bridge wormhole into a digitally hypnotic fantasy.

In the real world, digital images do not live and play in the very air about your head. In the real world, teenagers do not sit in elliptical pods with small electronic headpieces attached to foreheads while hands wave and fingers trace invisible nonsensical patterns in the air. In the real world, teenagers do not manipulate digital enzymes that are floating overhead and play god with amino acids to re-engineer new strains of proteins.

The real world, however, did not apply inside Alexandria

Hall, for this is exactly what I saw in front of me. Eight teenagers sat back to back to back, shoulder to shoulder, small mechanical devices attached to heads, while their fingers jabbed at the air. Above the teenagers floated a massive 3-D image of an enzyme. As the teenagers waved their hands, the enzyme rotated in the air, amino acids exchanged and interacted, the enzyme morphed and convulsed, and new shapes and strands appeared. I knew exactly what the teenagers were doing. I had just never seen it take physical form.

Gene folding. They are playing a game of gene folding!

This has been done online, of course, in a crude manner over the Internet in a controlled environment. Yet what I saw before me was alive and interactive, the enzyme growing and transforming in front of my very eyes. The teenagers controlled the enzyme. Their "game" was to create a new biological catalytic reactor.

This was just the first "pod" of teenagers. As I stumbled through the room, I discovered ten similar pods of players, some of them kids, some adults. Each sat in a rough circle, backs and shoulders touching, as though forming a larger symbiotic brain. None of them held a game controller or sat at a keyboard. All of the "play" occurred in the air, as though the participants could see and manipulate images that were not visible to my eye. The boy nearest me shaped an invisible substance with his hands, and suddenly a dinosaur sprang from the boy's empty hands to lumber across the room.

I shuffled further into the room. One pod conducted military war games. I could see missiles launching, battleships in the oceans, submarines diving and tanks rolling. One pod appeared to be constructing a visual history of the Egyptians—I saw pyramids built, tombs dug, a sphinx carved out of stone. With another I saw the Milky Way explored, planets appearing, comets blazing, supernovas exploding. Everywhere I saw motion, energy, knowledge, and power.

I don't know how long I wandered about the room. Time lost meaning inside the hall. I watched civilizations rise and fall. I explored galaxies, watching stars being born and die. I participated in the evolution of new species. How could normal time apply in a place like this?

It was some indefinite period later when someone took my arm, causing me to jump. I heard laughter. Chaucer stood at my side. He was alone. My friends had vanished. I saw only Chaucer's mountain of a body teasing the air above me. He grinned with obvious pleasure.

"Impressive, wouldn't you say?" he asked. "Not exactly Angry Birds on your smartphone, is it?"

I shrugged, giving my best nonchalant "I've seen it all before" dismissal.

"No big deal. You've got some 3-D technology. You're working with artificial reality headsets. You're doing the same kind of modeling work that's been on the market for five years now. And I've seen more impressive visual effects at the World of Color."

Chaucer nodded and rubbed his beard with his hand.

"Ah, I see. I haven't shown you much, is that it? Well, perhaps you're right. You see, this is the education section, the Alexandria Initiative. Maybe this isn't all that exciting for you. The real, uh, *cool stuff* is back there behind that curtain."

His words startled me. I turned to follow his gaze. He motioned to the curtain that draped across the theater stage. Six large men, all as pasty white-skinned as Thomas the Ghost Man, stood at the front of the curtain. A line of teenagers stood in front of the curtain and men.

I studied the line, trying to determine if I knew any of the kids. Through the haze of color in the room, I could just barely distinguish their features. I thought I could see Jordan McInerny at the front of the line, the kid who hadn't been seen in days. I frowned, puzzled. The Jordan I knew had been a bit chubby. This kid appeared to be a poster child for Weight Watchers, all thin and scrawny.

"What's back there?" I asked. "What are those kids waiting for?"

"Their wildest fantasies to come true," Chaucer answered, smiling. "It's our beta test area. But more on that later. All in good time. For now, we need to talk about your job interview."

"My what?"

"Your job interview! I need your help. My games are wonderful, yet there's much more to be done. I have a vision for the future of this company, and I need your help to get there."

"My help?" I asked dumbly, as though confined to speaking only two words at a time. I added, just to keep up the momentum: "Why me?"

"I am recruiting geniuses from all over the world to come work with me."

"Looks boring," I said.

"You can make a real difference, Carter."

"Who cares?"

"You can truly change the world. Our technology could eradicate cancer, find new sources of clean renewable energy, solve the great problems of our world."

"Big deal."

"I can also make you filthy-rotten rich."

"Okay . . . maybe."

"Then are you ready to take the test?"

"What test?" I asked. I felt like asking a long question, but I was getting pretty good at this new form of two-word communication. I could revolutionize the world by reducing the amount of wasted sentences and unnecessary conversation. Women would hate it! Just consider that all really important messages can be contained in two words: *Go away; drop dead; more food; clean this; give me; you suck.*

"The aptitude test," Chaucer said. "To see if you qualify to work for me."

"Me . . . qualify?"

"I have lots of geniuses at the Lazarus Corporation . . . whole bags of them. I can replace them like changing a light bulb. Maybe you don't have what it takes."

"Of course I have what it takes! I can pass your little IQ test or computer engineering quiz or whatever ridiculous scenarios that you throw at me. Do you know that I have never missed a question on a test in my entire life? I'll take that test and shove it down your arrogant—"

"Okay, okay." Chaucer laughed. "So you'll do it?"

"Of course I'll do it! Where is it? Behind the curtain? I'll go back there right now and—"

"It's not here. It's at our headquarters. We'll go there tomorrow. I'll pick you up. Agreed?"

I nodded. *Of course I'll take that stupid test, and I'll pass it, and I'll get a better score than any of his other supposed geniuses, and I'll be the best employee they ever had.*

And it was only much later that I recognized that I signed up as an employee of the Lazarus Corporation without even realizing it.

Boy, did Geoffrey Chaucer make me—the great genius—look like an idiot.

CHAPTER FIVE

From the way my friends acted on the way home, you'd have thought we just came from church instead of an awesome new video game store. Everyone acted mopey and depressed.

"So," I said, "pretty cool place, huh?"

No one answered. Sidney stared out the window as though finding the shabby houses and dirty streets of Merewether the most fascinating thing she'd ever seen. Darek bit his fingernails. Chambers drove without speaking. Clinton looked as depressed as the time I used his pet rat as a science experiment.

I wouldn't normally waste any time worrying about what Clinton thinks or feels. If he wants to get all miserable and depressed, that's his business. But I figured I could score points with Sidney if I acted charitably, so I inquired after Clinton's delicate state of mind.

"Dude," I said, "what the freak's up with you? Why so mopey?"

Clinton scowled at me but said nothing. Sidney didn't seem to notice our exchange. Sighing, more out of boredom than anything, I asked: "Bro, what's up? Didn't they have the game you wanted? All out of My Little Pony or whatever?"

"They had it, all right," Clinton said. "Not My Little Pony. But they did have the perfect game."

I blinked. "Really? When'd you have time to find a game?"

"When you were off pow-wowing with that Chaucer guy for an hour. We had tons of time."

Darek and Chambers muttered an agreement. Even Sidney glared at me, eyes accusatory, as though I'd wasted a huge chunk of her valuable time. This made no sense. I talked to Chaucer for about ten minutes, max. What were they talking about?

I asked them. Darek said, "You were in the Alexandria Hall for about an hour. We got the quick tour, then that weird white guy, Thomas, ushered us out. Then you and Chucky had a nice little chat."

"Chaucer," I corrected. "But that's insane. I swear it was only a few minutes."

"Carter, it really was about an hour," Sidney said. "You know I needed to get back to the hospital. You really shouldn't have made me wait that long."

I rubbed my face, thinking hard. This couldn't be true. My whole discussion with Chaucer lasted no more than ten minutes. I know, because my two-word answers made the whole thing so darn efficient. So how long had I been wandering about the pods? Could it really have been an hour?

We rode in silence for a few moments while I grappled with the time twist. I mean, it wasn't a huge deal, right? It's not like in that stupid *The Lion, the Witch, and the Wardrobe* book when five minutes is worth a lifetime on the other side. That whole thing drove me nuts. What was the big deal of helping defeat the evil queen if you could just go get lunch, use the toilet, and then come back three thousand years later and everything you really cared about was long dead and gone anyway? I mean, what's the point of doing anything at all if nothing really lasts? If everything you care about will be gone in a blink of an eye?

I hated that story. You fight and bleed and sacrifice, and all for what? You leave for a minute and come back and it's all gone. Just like with people. People you love are here one minute, gone the next. One day Mom and Dad at home, then not. Nobody stays. Nothing lasts.

I really, really hated that story.

"We need to go back," Clinton said at last, breaking the silence. "I *need* to get that game."

Something in the way Clinton said *need* bothered me, like the way a druggie needed his next hit.

I shrugged. "I've got a bundle of cash, if that's the problem. You can always owe me."

Sidney shook her head. "I've got to get to the hospital, Carter! I should never have left Dad!"

What's the big rush? The guy's a turnip right now, I thought. But I decided to play nice.

"Come on, guys. I'm sorry, all right? I didn't mean to be in there so long! What's the matter with all of you? Mr. Chaucer just wanted to talk to me about—"

"Going to work for him," Clinton interrupted. "Yeah, don't act all surprised. Even me, the big dummy, could figure that out. That's why they kicked us out while you talked to the big shot. You, the boy genius, get all the perks, while the rest of us get nothing? Not even the game I want."

"Hey, it's not my fault Chaucer wants to hire me," I said. "It's not my fault I was born smart."

Clinton turned violently in his seat. His face flushed red. He swore and smacked the dashboard with his fist so hard that Chambers cursed at him in return.

"I'm so sick of hearing that!" Clinton shouted at me. I seriously think my brother planned on hitting me. He raised his fist and waved it at me. For the first time in my life, I actually felt afraid of him.

Fortunately for me a car came screaming past us, swerved, and nearly hit our Volvo. The speeding car, a large black Chrysler 300, nearly forced us off the road. Chambers jerked the steering wheel to avoid hitting the 300. Clinton pitched sideways in his seat, smacking his head against the window. Sidney fell into my very lucky arms.

"You idiot!" Chambers shouted as he fought to steer us back to the middle of the road. "Could have killed us!"

We were driving on city streets, heading toward the hospital. It was a twenty-five-per-hour zone: there could be kids in the streets and bikes lying around and old people using strollers. Not the kind of place to be speeding, even at night. But this moron must have been traveling at least sixty miles per hour.

"Good thing you got a Volvo," I muttered as Sidney remained prostrate across my lap, unable to pull herself back upright. I did nothing to help her. "Safety first, right?"

Darek shoved me off his shoulder and released several very choice words. After a quick litany of cursing, he said: "And just where is a cop when you need—HOLY CRAP! LOOK AT THAT!"

Darek pointed excitedly at the front windshield. I pushed Sidney upright and leaned forward, trying to see what caused Darek such excitement.

"What?" I returned. "What is it?"

"On the car! On the roof! There's a dude up there!"

"A dude?" I echoed. "Wait, I can't . . . Chambers! Speed up! He's getting away!"

"Of course he's getting away!" Chambers returned. "He's going sixty and we're not!"

"But I can't see if . . . . Darek, what did you see? A guy on the car?"

"I swear there's a guy dangling off the top of the car! Right on the roof! It's the coolest thing ever! Chambers, quit driving like your grandma and catch up to him! We've got to see this!"

"Guys," Sidney said, "I really need to get to the hospital."

"Not now!" Darek shot back. "Not when there's a guy about to fall to his death! We can't miss that! Chambers, really, I could run faster! Step on the pedal, man!"

Chambers cursed but finally put his foot down. The motor roared and the car accelerated. Just then I heard the wail of sirens behind us.

"Oh, great!" Chambers cried. "You see! You see what I get! My mother's going to kill me!"

I spun around in my seat. Sure enough, I could see the whirl of blue-and-red cop car lights coming up fast behind us. I knew that cop car.

"It's Dad," I announced. "We can't get busted by my dad. Kyle, you've got to outrun him."

Mentioning our father revived Clinton from his game-envy doldrums. He cursed and nodded vigorously. "Carter's right. No matter what it takes, you gotta get us away from our dad!"

Chambers looked horrified. "I'm not going to run from the police!"

"It's my father!" I snapped. "He doesn't even count! Come on, move it!"

But my father's Crown Victoria gobbled up the distance between us in about five seconds. By the time Chambers stopped whining about his precious Volvo, my dad's car was right on our bumper.

"I've got to get over!" Chambers said. I swore.

But Dad's car veered around us, swerving into the opposing lane of traffic. The cop car barreled right past us. I could see Dad in the front seat, some other loser in the passenger side. Both men's necks craned forward, their attention fixed on the Chrysler 300.

"They're past us!" I shouted. "They're going after the other guy! Speed up!"

Chambers shook his head and muttered something, but I did feel the car accelerating again. We hit fifty on the speedometer. Chambers flew right through a stop sign—I was very proud of him—and a few seconds later we careened through an intersection, left the city streets behind us, and got up on to the highway leading out of town.

"Go faster!" I cried.

The Volvo hit sixty-five without breaking a mechanical sweat. Up ahead I could see Dad's cop car and the 300. The police cruiser tailed it by only a few feet, colored strobes lighting up the back of the black Chrysler. In the eerie red-and-blue spotlight, I could see a human figure astride the top of the 300, riding the top like a cowboy in a rodeo.

"There's really a guy up there!" I exclaimed. "He's right on the roof!"

"He's on his belly!" Darek said. "How's he holding on?" Somehow the man perched to the top of the roof as the 300 sped at sixty miles per hour. His arms wrapped around something in the roof, a handhold that gave him purchase on the slick metal surface. The man's legs swung back and forth like a pendulum over a pit.

"He's holding on to something," Clinton said. "It looks like . . . hey! We know him!"

"It's Hobo Warrior!" I cried. "The guy from the alley! What the crap is he—that's it! It's the axe thingy! Look at that! He stuck the axe thingy halfway through the roof of the car!"

Hobo Warrior rode the top of the 300, gripping what remained of his wicked four-foot-long axe. The handle protruded out of the top of the metal roof. The rest of the weapon stuck down through the car like a sword slid inside its sheath.

"Hobo Warrior stuck that axe right through the metal!" I yelled.

"That's so cool!" returned both Clinton and Darek. Even Chambers muttered agreement and nodded, though carefully, not to upset his driving concentration. Only Sidney said nothing, though I noticed she craned forward trying to see around my backside.

My father pulled his cop car to the side of the 300. The window came down. A hand came out, finger pointing at the 300. I could hear a muffled, electronically amplified voice booming, my father on the loudspeaker, telling the driver of the 300 to pull over.

Hobo Warrior moved atop the car. He shifted his weight, rolling to his right side. I watched him release the blade with one hand, keeping his grip with the other. My father's car came closer, as though they would ram into the 300 and force it off the road. Hobo Warrior's hand went to his waist, then extended toward the cop car.

"GUN!" Clinton cried.

Hobo Warrior held a gun in his left hand. He pointed the gun at Dad's car.

At that moment headlights flashed in the road ahead of us. A car came toward us. Some poor idiot chose the wrong time to be driving down the highway.

"CAR!" Chambers cried.

My father veered away from the oncoming car. At the same time I saw three bright bursts erupt from atop the 300, shots fired from the handgun.

Too low, I thought, seeing the trajectory of the gun, the angle Hobo Warrior held it. He aimed too low. He'd hit the ground. He'd miss the car completely.

The Crown Vic fishtailed in the road. I saw a blur beneath the passenger door and then rubber fragments exploded across the highway. Metal screeched on pavement and a hubcap bounced three feet off the ground. Hobo Warrior had shot the front passenger tire. The police car careened out of control.

The oncoming driver panicked. The car angled into the right lane, heading right for the 300.

"They're going to hit!" Clinton yelled. "Look out!"

The cop car skidded to a stop at the side of the road. We passed the Crown Vic. I glanced to my right, seeing my dad pounding the dashboard in frustration.

The 300 shot to the right, heading toward the highway shoulder as the oncoming car swerved the opposite way. I thought the two cars would miss each other. The 300 is a big car, however, with a big butt. The oncoming car clipped the back bumper, causing the 300 to spin as it careened off the road. The other car kept moving, safely clearing the 300 and the cop car and continuing on down the road.

The 300 hit the guard rail and slid along it like an

Olympic bobsled riding the side of an icy track. Hobo Warrior's legs flew off the metal roof, yet somehow he held on. He flailed around like an astronaut in zero gravity. Sparks spit in a fiery shower as the 300 grated against the rail. Then, at last, the 300 came to a smoking stop.

Chambers brought the Volvo to a halt a few yards behind the 300. Before I could move, Hobo Warrior leaped from the car, feet on pavement. He held the axe in his hands, yanked free from the car roof. He moved toward the door.

"Get out!" I screamed, shoving at Darek who sat beside me. "Go! Move!"

Darek kicked the door open. From the front seat Clinton shoved his door open and jumped out. I followed Darek through the open door, my feet churning. I ran toward the 300. Clinton and Darek sprinted beside me, none of us stopping to consider what we'd actually do when catching up with Hobo Warrior. Adrenaline—not brains—pushed us forward.

My feet pounded the pavement. Clinton ran past me, his longer legs propelling him like a Jamaican sprinter. Hobo Warrior didn't notice us or didn't care. His tattered, frayed trench coat waved in the breeze as he came around the car to the driver's door.

That'll slow him down, I thought as I ran, lungs burning with exertion. *Surely that door's locked!*

Hobo Warrior didn't reach for the door handle. He hefted the axe above his head and hacked it right through the window. Glass erupted as the axe pierced the window like a pin through a balloon.

Hobo Warrior reached one hand through the opening, grasping the driver by the collar. He pulled the driver out of the car and tossed him to the ground. The big man raised the axe, ready to kill. I recognized the driver who now lay prostrate on the ground: Thomas the Ghost Man.

Clinton hit Hobo Warrior with a flying tackle, shoulder to back, the big seventeen-year-old hitting the poorly dressed assassin with two hundred pounds of muscle and bone. I'd seen that tackle snap the collarbones of quarterbacks. I'd seen that tackle snap a perfectly healthy femur in half. I knew that tackle could have earned Clinton a football scholarship to Oregon . . . had he wanted it. My brother may be a moron mentally, but physically he was a freakishly fine specimen of human brutality.

Hobo Warrior staggered forward a couple of feet, as though a five-year-old had bumped into him on a tricycle, a minor annoyance. Impossibly, Hobo Warrior kept his feet, stumbled briefly, and whirled around. My brother's missile-like propulsion made him bounce off Hobo Warrior and crash to the ground.

My feet skidded on the asphalt as I put on the brakes, trying to stop myself. Darek slammed into me from behind. Our legs tangled, and instead of stopping I tripped and fell headfirst right into the chest of Hobo Warrior. I bounced off him, landing on my back. I stared up at the homeless hit man.

"Idiot boy!" Hobo Warrior growled, fury burning in his eyes. "What are you doing?"

"I'm sorry, I was just . . . crap! Look out!"

Hobo Warrior spun around just as the driver rose up from the road, white skin glistening in the headlights. Thomas the Ghost Man stood behind Hobo Warrior, his face as pale and ghastly as a corpse. He looked so emaciated the breeze might pick him up and carry him away.

The man rose up from the ground like a wraith levitating out of a crypt. In his hand he held the largest pistol I have ever seen. Thomas lifted the silver revolver to chest level. The gun looked like something out of an old Western, the kind you would see in a Billy the Kid shoot-out, a dusty tumbleweed-blown-High-Noon duel. The barrel looked to be about three feet long, like the man held a silver rifle in his hand. Thomas's finger already touched the trigger. I watched the hammer pull back.

The battle axe was already moving. The axe sliced through the air, razor-sharp metal humming and singing. The blade slashed across the barrel of the pistol, slicing it in half. The gun fell useless to the ground.

Hobo Warrior reversed the blade, yanking it back hard to his right. The edge of the blade cut upward, catching Thomas in the chest and impaling right through the man's body.

I screamed as the blade punctured Thomas's chest. Hobo Warrior slid the blade out of Thomas's body. Blood coursed down the axe, turning the metal red. Thomas staggered and wheezed. He slid off the blade, took a single step backward, and fell to his knees.

Hobo Warrior raised the blade, positioning it at Thomas's neck, placing the edge right against the sickly white skin. Hobo Warrior's muscles tensed, knotting his neck, shoulders pivoting, blade pulling back. Another a swing of the blade would sever Thomas's head from its neck.

I dove for Hobo Warrior's ankle, trying to trip him. Darek sprang forward at the same instant, grabbing the other leg. The disheveled man stumbled. He couldn't get sufficient leverage to swing the blade. I heard him cursing as he tried to kick me loose from his right leg. I tightened my grip.

"Stupid boys!" Hobo Warrior cried. "Stupid foolish boys!"

I grimaced, realizing that while the man couldn't swing at Thomas, he could plunge that blade right down on top of me. I loosened my grip, ready to let go and roll away.

Before I could give in to my cowardly side, my brother sprang to action. Clinton swung a heavy right hook at Hobo Warrior's face. Clinton's fist smacked the guy right on the chin, snapping his head back. It was a textbook jab.

Hobo Warrior might have fallen, but Darek and I held his feet fast to the ground. He reeled back. Clinton swung his left fist. The man somehow caught Clinton's fist in his open hand. Holding Clinton in place, he swung the blade at my brother's head. I screamed a warning.

But Hobo Warrior didn't use the sharp edge of the blade. He swung the axe like a baseball bat. Clinton rocked backward as if struck by a two-by-four. I didn't fear for my brother. I knew his head was thick enough to withstand a hundred such blows.

Voices rang out from behind me. I could hear feet pounding pavement. My father and his deputy approached in a slow, wheezing jog. Hobo Warrior noticed it too. He gave a mighty kick that sent me tumbling away.

When I rolled to my knees I saw Hobo Warrior holding Darek by the collar of his shirt. He lifted Darek three feet off the ground. He shook him roughly, then tossed him four feet away. He lifted his axe thingy and brandished it at Clinton and then at me. I raised my hands in the universal sign of surrender.

Hobo Warrior gazed at me and scowled, shaking his head like a disappointed teacher.

"I know you, Carter Chance! I know all about you! If you knew me or anything about what is really going on here, you'd have let me kill that man. In fact, you'd help me!"

"You, man with the sword!" called my father as he approached. "Freeze right there!"

I rolled my eyes. It wasn't a sword! Trust my father to embarrass me in front of an assassin.

Hobo Warrior glanced my father's direction. I could see my father coming, but it was slow progress. My father was not exactly Usain Bolt. Hobo Warrior leaned toward me.

"Listen to me, Carter Chance. You have to listen to me! Don't trust Chaucer! Get away from him now, while you still can. He's not what he seems! He's a—"

"DROP THE SWORD OR I'LL SHOOT!"

Hobo Warrior sighed and stood up.

"My name is Logan Pierce. We will meet again. When we do, you'll be on my side. Believe me. You'll be on my side . . . or you'll already be dead."

With that the big man turned and ran. He darted around the still-smoking 300, jumped the guard rail, and disappeared down the embankment.

My father ran to my side. He pulled me to my feet and started checking me over as though I had lice or some nasty skin infection. I swatted him away.

"Forget about me!" I cried. "There's a dead man behind me!"

My father glanced over my shoulder and frowned. I heard Clinton swearing. Darek echoed it. At that moment Sidney and Chambers decided to join us. They had been holding back at the Volvo. They walked up to me, but they were looking past me. I could see from the expression on their faces that something was very wrong.

I climbed to me feet and turned, expecting to find a very dead white-skinned man and a pool of very red blood.

I found neither.

Thomas the Ghost Man had vanished.

CHAPTER SIX

I stood in the parking lot of Merewether High School the next morning waiting for my ride. Chaucer promised to pick me up for my job interview. I wandered about the lot, wondering when Chaucer would come, curious about the interview, eager to take the stupid test. I sat on the curb, threw rocks at an alley cat that prowled across the street, and refused to think about my family squabble of the previous night.

I don't want to think about my so-called family. Because I don't like thinking about it, I don't want to write about it, either. So I'm not going to tell you anything about it. It's really none of your business that my dad is a jerk and my brother an idiot and my mother an irresponsible runaway who . . . never mind. I'm not going to talk about it. You'd just be bored to tears anyway.

This is a story about the Lazarus Game, a story of action, adventure, and mystery. This is not a story about my personal feelings, family relationships, personal growth and self-discovery, or any of that kind of crap. If you want that sort of nonsense, you can pick up a Newbery Award Winner or just go watch just about anything on PBS.

I promised at the beginning not to bore you with technical details and mathematics or anything remotely scientific. I did this because I know that no one really cares about education. All anyone wants is mindless entertainment. Along those same lines, I won't trouble you with my family issues, particularly not what happened last night.

Except that I'll tell you this much: it's all so frustrating! Being surrounded by imbeciles, I mean. If I lived with intelligent, successful people, it might be different. I might be able to enjoy a significant, meaningful relationship. But I live with morons.

My father, now there's a real winner. He's a cop. Okay, maybe in some cities this is cool, helping people, chasing down criminals. But not here. Not in Merewether. If your priority is keeping Clara's Diner and Donut Shoppe safe, then my dad's a freaking hero. He has that totally covered. Plus he took his parenting skill class from Genghis Khan. It's tough love or no love. His idea of care and nurturing is to drop off a cold Little Caesar's pizza once a night.

It's not just my father, of course. I come from a family of losers. I have two older sisters, neither of whom went to an Ivy League university. One is a nurse, the other an elementary school teacher. As if those were real jobs. And of course both are divorced, because nothing lasts in my family. No relationships. No amount of Hollywood-type "romance." Not even family fortunes. Apparently we had a great-grandfather who was a big-time capitalist and made millions of dollars. But none of that is left, because nothing lasts in my family. We're all losers.

Then, finally, there is Clinton. By now you should know his worthlessness. I think every day that I have found the absolute depths of his loserishness. But then he goes and surprises me.

The latest example was that when we got home from the car chase and near axe-murder my brother opened up his stupid mouth and actually tried to talk to our father. What an idiot. Both of them.

The sighting of our mother's Toyota Corolla pulling away from our house instigated Clinton's attempt at normal communication. The white Toyota drove past us without slowing. My mother didn't screech to a stop at seeing her two sons. She didn't slam on the brakes all excited and eager and desperate to see us. She didn't even hesitate. She drove right by. She kept her eyes straight ahead, pretending she didn't notice us.

My father—in a rare act of intelligence and wisdom—also pretended not to see her. He chose instead to comment on the near-death activities of the past hour.

"You shouldn't have been chasing that criminal," he said as he steered the police cruiser into our driveway. "I know you fancy yourselves vigilantes, particularly after that stunt with the Russian gang. But you've got to leave the criminals to the professionals."

I wanted to argue with him about the car chase, but Clinton spoke first. Of course he brought up the least important subject imaginable.

"Why was Mom here?" he asked. What an idiot. Why did he have to bring *her* up?

"Just picking up a few things," Dad said. "She called me earlier. She also said she wants to come see you two."

"She does?" Clinton asked, his voice just brimming with ridiculous hopefulness. "She really does want to see us?"

"That's crap," I said, nearly spitting the words out of my

mouth. "If she wants to see us, she could have stopped! It's total crap."

My father killed the engine but stayed in the car. I put my fingers on the door handle, eager to escape. Before I could, my father said, "It's me, you know. She just doesn't want to see me. It's not you two at all. She truly wants to see you."

"Oh, yeah, right," I said, rolling my eyes. "She's making a real effort."

"She asks about you every time I talk to her," he said. "She heard about your SAT score. She's really proud of you."

I swore and kicked the door open. Before I climbed out, I paused and said, "No, she isn't, she's . . . she's . . . well, okay. Maybe she is. I mean, maybe she *could* be proud of me. But she isn't, and it's all Clinton's fault."

Clinton reeled back as though slapped across the face.

"What? *Me*? How's it my fault?"

"Carter!" my father growled. "How can you say that about your brother?"

"She spent all her time at your stupid games, Clinton, and you know it. Football, baseball, soccer. It's all she did. You took over her whole life. She didn't care what *I* was doing. She didn't have time for me. She didn't have time for Dad. All she could do is drive you to this game and that tournament. Then you go and drop out of all of it. Just like that. Cold turkey. She goes from Soccer Mom to Soccer Mom Reject."

"I quit to help her out!" Clinton shouted. "I quit because I thought it would help! I wanted to give her more time to—"

"You broke her heart!" I interrupted. "You were just another disappointment to her! Just like Dad! She couldn't take that much disappointment, so she left."

Clinton slumped in his seat, head bowed, shoulders and arms slack. My father pounded his fist on the dashboard.

"Carter Chance! That's stupid! It has nothing to do with you! Either of you! It's about me and her. About a grown man and a grown woman and our relationship! It's about—"

"Relationship!" I cried. "Oh, please. Relationships don't last. Love doesn't last. Nothing lasts. It's like in that stupid book. We had our three minutes as a family and now it's gone. Everything gone in a blink of an eye. One minute you're fighting to survive, the next it's all gone. Nothing lasts."

"Carter, what's gotten into you?"

"Nothing. Nothing at all. I'm just honest. I'm the only one who will speak the truth. If you two can't deal with it, that's just tough."

That pretty much ended our little heart-to-heart. Don't get impressed by the depth of our discussion, the "real-world" issues we face. That was the longest talk we've all had in about six months, and I'm sure it won't happen again for at least another year. I feel good about that too. Now I could go back to ignoring my dad for several more months.

Clinton ran off to cry in his pillow or whatever. My dad acted like he was going to get emotional, which was a huge farce, as he has the emotional depth of a lawn mower. I just wanted to get something to eat. It had been several hours since IHOP. I left my dad and went straight to the kitchen.

Okay, now, swallow back the vomit. I'm sure this whole mushy narrative got you totally sick to your stomach. If you want to burn this book right now, I can't blame you. I really shouldn't have dragged you through such a sappy topic. I hadn't planned on it, honestly. It's just that Chaucer took so darn long to pick me up I couldn't help but think about it. Don't worry, it's all behind me now. I won't give my parents and their sucky relationship and my brother and his huge disappointment of a life and my two sisters and their mediocre jobs and broken marriages another thought. I really won't worry about Sidney and how she will never really want to be my girlfriend because she knows deep down that I can't handle relationships because I'm a Chance and nothing lasts forever in the Chance family. Certainly I won't trouble you with any of that.

Most important of all, don't go feeling sorry for me. I don't need your pity. It's not your fault or mine I was born into a family of idiots.

Besides, Chaucer showed up just a couple minutes after I started thinking about all this. He came in style too. Not the Lamborghini, this time.

He came in a helicopter.

CHAPTER SEVEN

Was it the great German philosopher and poet Goethe or the Grinch that stole Christmas who so famously said, "I'm going to die! I'm going to die! I'm going to throw up, and then I'm going to die!"?

The helicopter—which looked so cool when it descended in a hurricane of wind into my school parking lot—ascended back up into the morning sky with me inside it, going up, up, up just like the breakfast in my stomach was coming up, up, up my throat. I gripped the seat, I gripped my throat. I felt the chopper pitch, I felt my stomach roll. The Blackhawk military grade helicopter hurtled 180 miles per hour through the sky, my Egg McMuffin hurled three hundred miles per hour up my throat.

"A little bit afraid of flying?" one of the copilots asked, pivoting in his chair to smile at me. He sat well away from me, fortunately for him, or he'd be wearing my tossed groceries.

I shook my head. "A little bit afraid of dying."

He smiled. "We're perfectly safe up here. Just relax. We'll be to Lazarus headquarters soon."

I managed a weak smile. "You don't have to hurry or anything. You can take it nice and slow."

"Mr. Chaucer's expecting you. We can't leave him waiting. Sit back, think happy thoughts, and we'll be there before you know it."

Chaucer hadn't, in fact, come. He sent the chopper for me. He may as well have sent a mass murderer. This helicopter was going to kill me.

Think happy thoughts. Yes, that's it. Happy thoughts. Only happy thoughts.

Sidney. Sidney at my side. Sidney holding my hand. Sidney talking gently to me. Sidney CRASHING TO THE GROUND IN A FIERY EXPLOSION OF AGONY AND DEATH!

No, no, no. Sidney's not up here, is she? Sidney can't crash to the earth. It will be okay.

Yes. That's right. No Sidney. Only Carter. Only Carter left to CRASH TO THE GROUND IN A FIERY EXPLOSION OF AGONY AND DEATH!

Focus, Carter, focus. You are a genius. You are a rational, logical person. The chances of this helicopter crashing are less than one percent, right? One percent. That means one out of every hundred flights. Very low odds. Except that some unlucky loser will be the one percenter, and then that person will CRASH TO THE GROUND IN A FIERY EXPLOSION OF AGONY AND DEATH!

"So you're the boy genius, huh?" called the copilot, I presumed to be conversational, maybe to keep my mind off impending death.

"I guess so," I croaked, my voice barely working.

It's okay. Focus on the fundamentals. Breath. Inhale. Exhale. Swallow. Puke. No, no, don't . . .

"Sorry!" I managed after discovering I had a bit of McDonald's hash browns inside me—or at least I used to have it inside me. Now it dangled from the back of the copilot's chair.

"Don't worry about it. Happens quite a bit with the Lazarine."

"The what?" I asked. "Did you say *Lazarine?*"

"Yeah. You know, Mr. Chaucer's employees? The employees of Lazarus Corporation? The Lazarine. You want to get hired, right? That would make you a Lazarine too."

I said nothing. He said, "So . . . you must be excited for your interview, right? It's a big honor, huge. We haven't had a new employee in, what is it now, Charlie? Forty, fifty years?"

The pilot glanced at his copilot and frowned. The copilot laughed.

"I meant in *four* or *five* years! That's a long time, you know, in the software business. Mr. Chaucer takes only the best. We get quite a few applicants, but very few survive the application process."

Something in what the man said bothered me, but I couldn't quite put my finger on it. I might have, had I not been pressing my finger over my mouth to stop another upchuck.

"Does everyone get the helicopter service?" I asked. "You could have sent a car."

"Hey, count yourself lucky!" the copilot said, laughing. "Sure beats the times back when we'd pick 'em up in horse and buggy!"

The pilot muttered something. The copilot coughed, recovered, and said: "Yeah, well, the company's been around a long time! Can you imagine back in those old days? Whew! Not me!"

Horse and buggy. Yes. That sounded nice. A nice slow old plow horse.

"There's the office," said the copilot a few minutes later. "That new shiny skyscraper. Isn't she beautiful? Landing platform right on the top. Mr. Lazarus spared nothing for our new headquarters."

I leaned to the window and peered out. I could see the Portland cityscape gleaming in the morning sunlight. Following the copilot's gesture, I identified the Lazarus Headquarters building. It wasn't hard to find. It truly did sparkle in the light. I hope my poor splattered, bloodied, mostly disintegrated body wouldn't mar it too badly after we crashed on top of the building.

"Let's start the descent," the pilot said.

I closed my eyes. The chopper lost altitude. I lost my cappuccino.

We touched down on top of the building. I unbuckled my seat belt, wiped the last of the chunky spittle from my chin, and prepared to climb out. I took a deep breath.

That went well, I thought. *Glad I was able to hold myself together.*

The door opened. Mr. Geoffrey Chaucer stood on the landing platform, ready to greet me.

So I'm guessing that some of you think you've been to some pretty cool exclusive places. Maybe you've been to the Dr. Seuss House in Alaska, or the Star Wars Archives at Skywalker Ranch, or inside Club 33 in Disneyland. Perhaps you've spent time at Googleplex and thought the place was all high-tech and futuristic. It could be you've descended into Carlsbad Caverns or hiked the Grand Canyon and thought these were amazing natural wonders. You may have seen and experienced many interesting places in your lives, but here's the thing, and you've got to trust me on this.

You've never seen anything like Lazarus Headquarters.

After exchanging various inane pleasantries with Geoffrey Chaucer—who looked quite stylish in a light-colored James Bond–style suit—I followed him off the landing platform, through a sliding glass door, and into a television commercial.

It must have been a long straight corridor (because I never ran into anything in front of me), but I never saw the floor, walls, or ceiling. Holographic video images washed over me as I walked, a baptism of continuously swirling color, motion, and sound. Children ran and played and laughed alongside me as a tall beautiful woman explained how Lazarus Corporation is curing genetic disorders. Hale, beefy, bicep-rippling old men appeared around me, jogging, volleying tennis balls, playing golf, relating how the Lazarus Corporation is eradicating the diseases of age and extending the quality of life. Scientists in white lab coats demonstrated myriad experiments while praising Lazarus Corporation for funding breakthroughs in all aspects of science. I walked through fields of waving wheat in desert climates that should have never supported agriculture; I witnessed energy harvested from ocean waves, sufficient to illuminate entire cities; I observed environmental damage reversed and life rejuvenated. I saw all this while walking down this long corridor, a talking, moving, breathing, *living* advertisement for the wonders and accomplishments of Lazarus Corporation.

I came out of the corridor into what appeared to be the heart of the skyscraper. The ceiling above me opened up into a cavernous space, the vast core of the structure.

The center of the towering building was a hollow throat extending from floor to ceiling, a massive open-air atrium. Looking up I could see a distant glass rooftop. Looking down I could see all the way to the lobby. I could see the edges of each of the seventy or so floors, each one running like the spoke of a wheel to the center open hub. Each floor of the building emptied at the central core and then continued on again in the opposite direction. People walked the halls on the floors below me, bustling this way and that, some in business suits, others in white lab coats, others in the dowdy unicolor uniform of mechanical workers and industrial staff. Everywhere was motion, energy, and purpose.

"Welcome to Lazarus Corporation," Geoffrey Chaucer said. "Before we get to the interview, I'd like to give you a brief tour. You need to know the type of work we do here before deciding if you want to join us. We'll descend a bit first. Ready to go?"

I nodded. "That's why I'm here, isn't it?"

He smiled. "Of course. Now, you'll probably want to watch me go first. This can be a bit unsettling the first time."

He stepped to the glass partition that protected us from the gaping abyss at the center of the building. Chaucer pressed a red button and the partition slid back. He grinned at me like a kid about to show off his favorite toy.

"The first step is a leap of faith, Mr. Chance. You may consider it a metaphor for the journey ahead of you. If you're not a literary type, then think on the technology required for something as simple yet astonishing as *this*."

With that Geoffrey Chaucer stepped off the edge of the precipice.

What?

I rushed to the edge, watching in horror as Chaucer plummeted hundreds of feet to his death.

Only he didn't plummet to his death. He hovered in the air just below the lip of the floor where I stood, arms neatly folded across his chest, mouth smiling, eyes twinkling in amusement. His body floated in the air like a Ping-Pong ball on a vent of air, like an astronaut floating through space. He levitated in the air like a Las Vegas-style magician. He stood right in the middle of the vast open pit without falling as though it were a simple and pedestrian a thing as walking down a well-paved street!

How is he doing that?

"Come on out!" Chaucer called, waving to me. "This is the only way down!"

There is no freaking way I'm going out there, I thought. *They must have injected me with a chemical, a hallucinogen, a pathogen, a make-me-dopey virus! I've been bedazzled, be-drugged, be-stupefied! This can't be . . . yikes!*

That was when I noticed that Chaucer had plenty of company in the wind tunnel or whatever the crap it was. Dozens—no, hundreds!—of people floated around in this open core. They went up and down, they went this way and that, they went fast and they went slow, they fell off one floor to be carried to the next. I watched a woman applying mascara to her eyelashes while levitating up from the main floor. People talked on cell phones. One guy chomped on a sandwich. Two men carried on a lively discussion. It was as exciting to these people as an elevator.

"There's absolutely no danger," Chaucer said as he beckoned me. "Have you heard of the Casimir effect?"

"No," I replied, "but I've heard of gravity. Gravity

means I step off this ledge and die like a squashed bug. Newton had it right a long time ago. I suppose you've heard about him?"

Chaucer laughed. "Newton? Isaac Newton? It's funny you should mention him. Actually quite ironic. Carter, I'm talking about quantum mechanics and the force that sticks things together. We've simply reversed the Casimir effect so that instead of sticking us together, instead of gravity pushing us down, it keeps us up!"

Quantum mechanics? Casimir effect? Anti-gravity? What's next? Money growing on trees? The Fountain of Youth?

Shrugging, I stepped off the floor and into nothingness.

I didn't fall. My feet didn't touch anything, my arms waved in the air, yet I felt supported, not from a surge of wind like in an air tunnel, just, well, nothing. Chaucer laughed and we started to descend.

We floated past several floors. I bit my tongue to stop from wild maniacal laughter. What kid didn't want to fly? To float in the air? To manipulate quantum mechanics and spit in the face of scientists for the last three hundred years? Okay, well, I'm probably the only kid that wants to insult the memory of Newton and Einstein . . . but you have to admit it, this was cool!

Chaucer walked out of the Pit of Reality-Twisting Doom as though stepping off an escalator. I followed his lead. Once I decided to walk I found I could move right across the open air, my feet finding some sort of leverage in the anti-gravity force. When my shoes touched actual carpeted floor I felt heavy and sodden.

"You have to understand," Chaucer said as we walked down the hallway, "that a tour at Lazarus Corporation is a very rare honor. Nobel laureates have begged and presidents of countries have pleaded, yet very few of these ever come inside our walls. You are afforded this great honor, but it is entirely warranted. You have great potential, Carter. Today, I am the one honored that you should be here."

Chaucer rapped his fingers into a keypad outside an imposing metal door. The vault-sized door swung open, and the tour commenced.

I cannot relate all that I saw and heard and experienced on the tour. There was so much to consume, to comprehend, to really *grok* that even a genius like me couldn't take it all in. I can't even attempt to make a common person like you understand it all. I'll have to settle on a few examples.

The first half of the tour was the "museum" portion. Chaucer guided me through the astonishing collections the Lazarus Corporation had acquired over the years. Have you ever been to the Louvre in Paris, the Metropolitan in New York, or the British Museum in London? Trash heaps in comparison.

First off, let me admit here that I know a bit about art. My mother—before she decided to flip out and run off and abandon her family—had a thing for art. Being the genius that I am, I absorbed her teaching and continued on by myself, becoming a bit of an expert in fine art. Thus, when I saw the Lazarus collection, I could appreciate the artistic wonder of it. More important, I could also instantly appraise the monetary value! Holy mounds of dollars, Batman!

They had Monet water lilies that the art world didn't even know existed. They had Van Goghs beyond anything I had ever seen. There were Rembrandts and Picassos and—get this—a version of the Mona Lisa where she was portrayed in full-belly laugh! I'm talking Leonardo *Freaking* Da Vinci paintings that the rest of the world didn't know existed! And it wasn't just paintings. Sculptures from Michelangelo. Grecian urns and Incan jade. Pottery and statuary and tapestry and artifacts from every culture and people. I couldn't calculate the cost. I couldn't fathom how they had acquired any piece of it.

We wandered through a library of such astonishing books, scrolls, and papyri that I wanted to abandon all other interests and ambitions and simply spend the rest of my life immersed inside the walls in ravenous reading. Yawn, you say; who cares about old books? Okay, you like money? These suckers were literally priceless. You want an original signed copy of the Declaration of Independence? Check. You want the first ever printing of the Gutenberg Bible from 1451 (for roughly the price of the state of Utah)? Got it. How about the only handwritten copy of *Hamlet* with a note from Shakespeare identifying himself as Sir Francis Bacon? Lazarus Corporation has it. How about really ancient stuff? They had a portion of the Dead Sea Scrolls no archeologist has ever seen! Chaucer said that once it was translated it would revolutionize what we know about the original Christian church. But that's not much of a big deal, right? La de da, who cares, just a bunch of boring old books . . . .

So if that doesn't impress you, there was the car "museum." I'm not talking about a lame collection of old rusty Model-T Fords, I'm talking about the Lamborghini Veneo that hits sixty miles per hour in 2.8 seconds. You can't even buy this car—they only make three a year for very elite customers who can pay the 3.9 million dollar price. Lazarus Corporation? They have four of them. Then there's the three Bugatti Veyrons that can reach 267 mph at a bargain price of two and a half million dollars. They have an original Lunar dune buggy, the kind the astronauts rode around in on the moon. If none of that is interesting, how about the 1957 Ferrari Testa Rossa that sold at auction for eight million dollars. Heard of that? Yep. They have it.

I'm sure you're not into old pop culture stuff, so this next portion of the museum wouldn't have interested you. I mean, I kind of rushed through it myself. Original Elvis leather pants? The guitar and drum set the Beatles played on their first American Ed Sullivan show? The black vest Harrison Ford wore when filming the 1977 *Star Wars*? There was lots of celebrity junk like that, but it was all pretty boring so I didn't pay attention. I'd never even heard of a band called One Direction, so why did I care if they had a CD full of unreleased songs that no one has ever heard before?

After an hour wandering through all this fairly commonplace stuff (ha ha), Chaucer took me back to the antigravity air tunnel. We levitated to a floor high up in the building. Chaucer led me through another key-padded vault door.

"That's what I consider the historical section of Lazarus Corporation," Chaucer explained as I walked beside him. "It's a bit of a tribute to the past. I've spent many years collecting all of that, Carter, and I'm very proud of it. But let me be clear about something. All those artifacts? Those priceless works of art? Trivial compared to what I'm about to show you. What you'll see next is the heart of our work. It's why we exist. It's why I have created the Lazarus Game."

Over the next couple of hours Chaucer toured me through dozens of different "labs." Each of the so-called labs inhabited an entire floor of the building. Now I understood why Chaucer needed such a huge skyscraper. The scope and scale of the place was astonishing.

Chaucer led me from lab to lab, floor to floor. Each of the so-called "labs" was a hive of activity: computer engineers writing code, scientists in lab coats running around performing various experiments, technicians and mechanics fiddling with wiring and machinery, assistants scurrying around with tablet computers making notes, filling coffee pots. None of this seemed all that odd or out of place in any big computer company—I should know, I've had backstage tours at Google, Microsoft, and Apple, to name a few. That kind of thing happens to people who create artificial intelligence apps sold to the FBI at age thirteen and consult on Department of Defense war-game simulations at age fourteen. Point is, I know what a big technology company looks like. They're all about the same.

Not here.

Because in addition to the engineers and technicians and assistants, each lab contained "pods" of teenagers and adults playing video games. They sat side-to-side in a vast circle of *Star Trek Enterprise*–like captain chairs, each person hooked up by wires and monitors, each person with a device strapped to their forehead. It was just like at the Lazarus Game Shop back in my hometown. Regular common teenagers and run-of-the-mill adults, all average-looking people, probably teachers and accountants and Walmart workers, sat in the chairs, waving hands in the air, playing video games.

Tall, thin, pale-skinned men hovered around the game players. In each lab, at each pod, I saw the same type of men. They were different from the engineers and technicians, different from the players. They had the same colorless eyes and white skin as Thomas the Ghost Man. It was as if Lazarus Corporation had hired a gang of albinos to supervise the operation.

What had the copilot called Chaucer's followers? His little gang?

Lazarine. Yes, these must be the Lazarine. Chaucer's boys. They really needed to get out into the sun a bit more.

Chaucer offered no explanation of these strange men. I didn't ask. I had too many other things to absorb. In fact, I saw so much that I can't even begin to describe it all. I can only give a sampling.

There were what I consider the "medical floors." In these labs the Lazarus Corporation apparently had solved the great diseases of humankind, such as cancer, Alzheimer's, and teenage acne. I watched scientists engineering molecular biology to create perfectly healthy babies. Chaucer explained how all genetic disorders would soon be a distant memory, as would disease of any kind. As the scientists hunched over microscopes and tubes and petri dishes, a pod of gamers played on.

There were the "environmental floors." Experiments here included plants that only needed to be watered once a year—even my father could keep this kind of geranium alive. I saw 3-D models for synthetic icebergs that could naturally reduce global warming by lowering the temperature of entire oceans. I inspected trees that could grow a hundred times the normal rate. Trees grew, icebergs emerged, and a group of teenage gamers played on.

There were the "social floors" that had some very strange things going on. I saw computer "learning games" that transformed what appeared to be backward Idaho potato farmers into Google-worthy computer engineers. I witnessed a room full of allegedly violent criminals playing a game that turned them all into YMCA volunteers. I even saw computer modules that could transform Boston Red Sox and New York Yankee fans into best friends. Three men in business suits, a woman in an evening dress, and five punk skateboarders in skinny jeans reclined in chairs in the center of the room, fingers punctuating empty air. Their video game playing on.

There were "art" floors filled with odd people singing and dancing and painting, but I'll skip that entirely. Modern art is a bit strange to me. This was like futuristic modern art, meaning only a drugged blind crazy man with a master of fine art degree could appreciate it. There was a sign advertising nude models on floor 53, but Chaucer wouldn't let me go up there.

My favorite section by far was the "technology floors." Here I found myself right at home. Not just because all the people working there were clearly nerdy, *Star Trek*– loving, math weirdos like me, but because all the coolest stuff was there. They had honest-to-goodness flying suits—sexy tight-fitting Spandex suits that allowed the wearer to soar around the room. Harry Potter–like cloaks that rearranged quantum matter to render the wearer completely invisible. There were gadgets to make James Bond jealous, and my personal favorite device, a Star Trek–like food replicator that transformed a small, sugar cube–like object into any food imaginable. I ate three double fudge brownies, a Disneyland Dole Whip float, one Ghirardelli's hot fudge sundae, and a Big Mac. Hey, I had to try it out!

I ate, scientists invented, and the video games continued without pause.

As I stuck a funnel cake in my gullet, Chaucer said: "So, Carter, what do you think?"

"Very good. Just like I got at Six Flags, only you need a bit more powdered sugar."

"Not the food, Mr. Chance. This place! Our inventions! The technology! Are you impressed yet?"

I chewed and considered. Well, let's see. Priceless artifacts. Sixteen-million-dollar Ferraris. Cures for cancer. Red Sox and Yankee fans living in harmony. Uh, yeah, impressive.

I nodded. But I also scratched my head.

"How is it done?" I asked, voicing the question that had been troubling me the past hour. "How can you do all this?"

Chaucer smiled. "It just takes a whole lot of brainpower."

"What?"

"It's all about crowdsourcing. Think what could be accomplished if you could harness together the brainpower of thousands—even millions—of people around the world. A single human brain is many times more powerful than the most advanced computer. What if we could utilize the processing power of not just one human brain, but thousands, millions even! If we could link all those brains together, just imagine what could be accomplished!"

The funnel cake tasted like sand in my mouth.

"That's what you're doing? Yes! The games! It's gamification, right? You use the games to link up and access the spare brain processing!"

Chaucer nodded. "Correct. Now you understand why our games are so important. We use the games to tap into the power of the human brain! This is why we need you to help us! It's only as we work together that we can accomplish these breakthroughs."

I shrugged. "Do the people know? The gamers? That you're stealing their brain power?"

Chaucer laughed. "Steal it? We hardly steal it! We tap into the 98 percent not being actively used! They don't even know the difference."

I said nothing, thinking about the revelation. It sounded pretty cool, but something bothered me. I never had much problem with ethics or morality. I didn't spent much time worrying about burning in Hades or whatever. But there was something vaguely troubling about what Chaucer said.

Perhaps reading my expression, Chaucer said, "This is how it's always been done. Think about it. All the truly momentous achievements in human history have come by joining together the labor of thousands, of entire communities. Think of the pyramids of Egypt and South America. Think of the Great Wall of China. It is always the same."

Interesting examples, I thought, given that the thousands of people who built the pyramids and the Great Wall were slaves.

Chaucer, who seemed to be able to perceive my thoughts, said, "It is about the common good, Carter. The little people who play our games would never amount to anything on their own. They have no true genius, no ability to create, no talent to invent. But when linked together, when tethered to an intellect like yours, then anything is possible! Look at what we are accomplishing!"

I nodded. I had to admit it. It made sense. I thought of Clinton. My brother will never amount to anything on his own. But if we could leverage some of the raw processing capacity of his brain, then maybe that gray matter between his ears could be used for good.

"There is no limit on what you could accomplish here,

Carter. This is the place for geniuses. This is where you can truly make a difference. You want to eliminate poverty? You want to eradicate crime? You want unlimited riches? No problem. You can have it here."

I sat silently, staring at my hands. I considered his words, what I had seen. Geoffrey Chaucer and his Lazarus Corporation were changing the world. They were making a lasting difference. Something permanent. Something real. I could be part of that.

Again, as though reading my mind, Chaucer said: "All great men want to be remembered. All great men want to leave a lasting legacy. Some think that by military conquest they will be forever memorialized. Men like Caesar or Napoleon. Some believe it is through audacious acts of terror, like John Wilkes Booth. But then there are those few, like my coworkers here, who know that true immortality is through fundamentally changing the human condition. You can do that here. You can gain immortality."

He paused, gazing at me. I stared back at him, the food forgotten, my past life in Merewether a distant memory, my old boring normal fifteen-year-old life a thing of the past.

Nothing lasts forever, I heard a voice inside my head taunting. Everything fades. Relationships end. Moms leave. Parents divorce. People die. Nothing lasts.

Except, possibly, here. I could do something here that could last forever.

I leaned forward and extended my hand. Chaucer smiled and shook it.

"I want in," I said. "I want to join the Lazarus Corporation."

CHAPTER
EIGHT

I saw all sorts of bizarre and wonderful things during my tour. Yet the most astonishing of all came right at the end while I was wolfing down a Belgian waffle. Chaucer was calling someone to prepare my little "test" while I tried out another food item from the replicator. I had just stuffed the last piece of maple syrupy goodness in my mouth when the lab door slid open. I gagged and choked and spit bits of waffle all over the stainless steel counter.

Thomas—the guy who had been skewered like a fish on a hook—walked through the open door. He handed Chaucer a tablet computer and waited while the big man read something on the display screen. I watched with mouth agape, breath held. The ghost-man regarded me silently.

"You're . . . you're . . . *dead*!" I cried.

"Obviously not," Thomas said with a dismissive shrug.

"No one could have survived that!"

"I think you're exaggerating things," Thomas answered, voice raspy like an unoiled hinge. "I have barely a scratch."

"Hobo Warrior stuck an axe thingy right through your gut! I saw it!"

A sneer creased Thomas's face.

"You must be referring to Logan Pierce. It was a flesh wound. Nothing serious."

Chaucer set the tablet on the table and smiled at me.

"We have the world's leading medical doctors on staff, Carter. It's just one of the many privileges of working here. In fact, we'll get you so healthy, you may just live forever."

I kept shaking my head at Thomas. The guy had been struck clean through, yet here he stood, sneering at me as though nothing happened. He looked no worse for wear. In fact, he looked better than the last time I saw him. His eyes gleamed light blue, whereas before they had been colorless and dull. His hair, once colorless, was now light blond. I must have remembered him wrong.

"You are lucky to have survived your encounter with Logan Pierce," Chaucer said. "He's a very dangerous man. A murderer. A terrorist! I'm surprised he didn't try to kill you too."

I thought of the strange blade-wielding Hobo Warrior. What had he said to me, when was it . . . just last night? He warned *me* about *Chaucer*. But it wasn't Chaucer chasing people around with guns and blades trying to kill people.

"You must stay away from him, Carter," Chaucer said. "He's a very evil man. He wants to destroy everything we've built here. If you see him again you must call me. We will take care of him."

"Who is he?" I asked. "What's his deal?"

"Logan is a former employee of mine," Chaucer said. "One of my best, actually. But he grew greedy and power hungry. He wasn't content that I wanted to use our science only to advance the good of society. He wanted power. He would have used our technology and innovations to topple governments, to prop himself up as a dictator. I fired him. You have seen what he has become. A killer."

"He wants to destroy us," Thomas added, his voice a low gravelly bass hiss. "To do this he terrorizes all who are associated with us, even the innocent children who play our games. "

"What?" I asked. "He's killed children?"

Chaucer nodded gravely. "Slaughtered them. It has happened several times. He has killed dozens, hundreds."

"I can't believe it. How have I not heard about this? It would have been all over the Internet."

"He didn't kill them with a blade or gun!" Thomas said. "He poisons them as they play the game. He's trying to turn the public against us! You know the old story—video games are harmful, they rot your brain, they turn you into desensitized zombies, all the rest. Pierce wants the public to believe this is true about our games!"

"But you've seen what we are doing here," Chaucer argued. "You know the truth. Logan Pierce is poisoning the public as surely as he poisons those poor innocent children. He's a cold-blooded murderer and must be stopped."

I shrugged. "I still think I would have heard about this. Kids poisoned?"

"The news is out there, all over the Internet," Chaucer said. "I can show you if you'd like. But it's not obvious. A child dead in one town. Two in another. A handful in a different place. Mysterious ailments. Flu-like symptoms. It looks like a virus, something deadly but natural, part of the unfortunate cycle of nature. I assure you it's not natural. It's Logan Pierce. He's a genius, just like you. Only a dark, twisted genius. He doesn't care how many innocents he has to kill to take us down."

I said nothing. I didn't know what to say. I wasn't exactly planning on going out for cappuccinos with Logan Pierce. I shrugged again.

"Okay," I said. "I won't join his fan club. Now, this test. Is it going to take long? My dad's not the parent of the year, but if don't get back sometime today, he may send out the police looking for me."

"Yes, yes, the test," Chaucer said, smiling. "That's why Thomas is here. He will administer it to you. Is everything ready?"

Thomas nodded. Chaucer waved me toward the door.

"Follow Thomas. He'll take you to our test center. Oh, feel free to ask him anything you'd like about our antigravity air lift. Thomas invented it."

Thomas waited for me at the door. I regarded him silently, fighting back a surge of irritation and resentment. This cold fish invented the coolest transportation device in the history of mankind? This guy? I sighed. I guess geniuses are a dime a dozen around here.

"Let's go," I muttered as I walked toward the pale-skinned genius. "Let me get my hands on your little test. I'll show you people a few things about acing tests."

Thomas laughed soundlessly. His deep blue eyes—weren't they light blue just a few minutes ago?—gleamed with a strange hunger.

"I'm sure you will, Mr. Chance. I'm sure you will."

———

The test center turned out to be a small room with padded walls. I'm not joking. For a moment I feared Thomas would pull out a straightjacket and strap me in. He explained that the padding is for sound proofing, so I could have the optimal environment for concentration.

He seated me at a small desk. Near the desk was a captain-style chair with a gamer headset resting on the leather-upholstered seat. I had seen similar chairs in each of the gaming pods throughout the building. A tablet computer rested on the desk, in the center. A bottle of water, a single sheet of paper, and a ballpoint pen occupied the corner. Other than that the room was empty.

"So, about this test," I said as I followed Thomas into the room. "Anyone ever get a perfect score?"

Thomas smiled, a thin smear across his alabaster face. "It's a pass or fail kind of a test."

I nodded. "Okay, I see. Thing is, I always get perfect scores. Not that I'm bragging or anything, but it's just that . . . I've never missed a question. Seriously. Not even once."

Thomas didn't seem to hear me. He walked to the desk and picked up the paper without reacting to my statement. He probably just didn't understand me.

"Even on the SAT," I said. "I got a perfect score. I don't make mistakes on tests."

He nodded as he scanned over the paper. Didn't this guy get it?

"All I'm saying is, don't feel bad if I destroy your previous record, or whatever."

Thomas handed me the paper. He appeared completely clueless at what I was trying to tell him. Maybe he wasn't so bright after all. *Don't say I didn't warn you*, I thought. *I hope you didn't write it, Thomas. I'll make you feel pretty darn foolish.*

"What's this?" I asked, taking the paper.

"Legal disclaimer and waiver. Read it carefully. We are a responsible company, Mr. Chance. We put all warnings up front. We don't want any surprises for you. If you're afraid to take the test, that's not a problem. I'll take you right back home, no questions asked."

I laughed. "Afraid to sign it? What, do some people get cold feet about taking a test? A little bit of test anxiety? Don't worry. I eat things like this for breakfast."

He did not smile. He nodded toward the paper.

"Just read it carefully. If you sign it, leave it on the desk and tap on the tablet. The test app will take it from there."

He strode to the door. Pausing, he looked back and said, "I'll return in a few hours to see if you've made it."

I grinned. "Don't you mean to see if I passed?"

He considered me for a moment, frowned, and nodded. "Yes. Of course. To see if you passed. Good luck, Mr. Chance. I do hope you'll be able to work for us."

He closed the door.

I gave the paper my usual speed-read. My eyes darted over the paper, rapidly consuming the relevant points. There were phrases like *proceed at your own risk* and *Lazarus Corporation cannot be held liable* and *make every reasonable effort to notify your next of kin* and that sort of thing. Standard legal mumbo jumbo. I scribbled my John Hancock at the bottom and shoved the document to the edge of the desk. I plopped down on the chair and put both hands on the tablet, eager to begin.

A square box popped up on the screen. Fifteen numbered tiles filled up the box, numbers 1–15 in seemingly random order as though the box had been shaken and the tiles mixed up. The first tile was 3, then 10, then 6, and so on, four tiles across, four tiles down. The board contained one empty space the exact size of a missing tile. The objective of this game would have been obvious to a preschooler. Arrange the tiles by moving them up, down, or sideways using the space provided by the missing tile, until you had them in ascending number order from one to fifteen. Sound easy?

Hardly. I knew this puzzle. It was sometimes called the Mystic Square, more commonly the 15-Puzzle. It was often used by computer scientists to model—if you'll excuse just a tiny insertion of technical jargon here—certain types of algorithms when speed and approximation is more important that absolute precision. It was once thought that half of the starting positions—the open space on the board—were impossible to resolve. It was thought an unsolvable puzzle, the most difficult in the world. But that's for normal people. The famous world chess champion Bobby Fischer would dazzle live crowds by solving the puzzle in twenty-five seconds. It was just one more evidence of his freakishness.

I put my finger on the tablet and started moving tiles. Fifteen seconds later I solved the puzzle. Take that, Bobby Fischer.

I took a deep breath and stretched. That was easy.

The tablet screen refreshed. Instead of another puzzle box, I saw a large block of text. I leaned forward to study it. The title above the text said "The Hardest Logic Puzzle Ever." It was from some philosopher dude name George Boolos. I'd never read it before. I saw that it had been published in the *Harvard Review of Philosophy*. Huh. Don't know how I missed it.

The puzzle was as follows: "Three gods, A, B, and C, are called, in no particular order, True, False, and Random. True always speaks truly, False always speaks falsely, but whether Random speaks truly or falsely is a completely random matter. Your task is to determine the identities of A, B, and C by asking three yes/no questions. Each question must be put to exactly one god. The gods understand English, but will answer all questions in their own language, in which the words for *yes* and *no* are *da* and *ja*, in some order. You do not know which word means which."

Okay, so this one took me a bit longer than the Mystic Square. I had to think for a while. I probably spent a good fifteen, twenty minutes. Maybe a whole half hour. After that enormous pause I started typing. I composed my answer and hit "enter." I stood and stretched, pulling my arms behind me, breathing deeply. I didn't bother to check the app to see if my answer had been accepted. There was only one way to answer the puzzle. My way.

I smiled at my success. I had to give it to these guys. This was not your typical computer engineering test. This was sort of difficult. Probably only a handful of people on the whole planet could have solved those two puzzles. Of course I was one of them. But was Chaucer? Thomas? The other dudes I saw in the building? I couldn't believe that many people could solve these puzzles.

The app refreshed again. The following text appeared: "Every simply connected, closed 3-manifold is homeomorphic to the 3-sphere."

Crap. Oh, this is not good. I knew at once what this meant. The Poincaré Conjecture. Every self-respecting mathematician knew about this, but only one man in history had proven it. It took more than a hundred years before a Russian guy solved it. I'd read about it in *Science* magazine. A few math freaks had verified it, and by now several people (by which I mean maybe the top dozen math weirdos in the world) now could replicate it, but I'd only read about it. I had never actually solved it. Crap.

Let's see . . . think, think, think. Remember. Let's see. Algebraic topology. What was it? Five-dimensional space. Smooth out the rough spots. Yes, the Ricci flow. Now, how . . . ?

I worked. I thought. I paced. I literally bounced my head of the padded walls. I sweated. I struggled to remember everything I'd ever read about this stupid conjecture. Finally, after what seemed like hours of effort, I had it.

Using the tablet stylus, I scribbled the solution. I can't replicate it here using words. Don't worry about it, though. You wouldn't understand it anyway.

I sagged back in the chair, exhausted, stinky, hungry. I checked the time on the tablet. Three hours had passed. I felt hammered but also exhilarated. I hadn't put my brain through that kind of workout in a very long time. I felt like a marathon runner just after finishing the race.

The door opened. I smiled, excited to receive the congratulatory praises. I stood and turned, expecting to see Chaucer with a medal or flowers or at least a piece of cake. Instead I found Thomas. He didn't look all that impressed or even very happy. He did, however, offer me another bottle of water.

"I see you completed the warm-up," he said. "That is very good."

"Warm-up?" I laughed, appreciating his keen sense of humor. I chortled, I snickered, I downright guffawed. A warm-up! How funny is that?

Thomas did not join my jocularity.

"Do you need a break before starting the test? Something to eat, perhaps?"

Laughter froze right in my throat. I started choking. What did he say?

"Mr. Carter?" Thomas asked. "Are you okay? Can you continue?"

"The test. Did you really say . . . I mean, didn't I just take the stupid test?"

Now Thomas laughed. He had poor comedic timing.

"Test? This? Really! This was a mental warm-up, just to

get the juices flowing. Of course we expected you to complete the puzzles, naturally. You wouldn't be here if you couldn't complete these basic warm-ups."

Warm-ups. My butt hit the chair without my even realizing it. I found myself slumped over the desk. I thought I'd just graduated college here, only to find I was really still back in kindergarten? What's going on here?

"You don't appear well," Thomas said. "Perhaps it's better if we reschedule for—"

I snapped upright, my spine straight, spirit restored.

"I'm ready. I'll do it! Come on, bring it on! Let's do this thing!"

Thomas nodded. "Very well. Please take a seat on the chair over there. If you'll place the headset just over your forehead like . . .yes, that's right. Close your eyes. The game will start momentarily."

"Game?" I asked.

"The Lazarus Game. It's the test. Beat the game, pass the test."

"That's it? All I have to do is beat the game?"

"That's it. Now, it will make it easier if you close your eyes."

"Wait! I need to know my odds. How many people beat your game this year?"

"None."

"Okay . . . the past two years? No? Five years? Really? Not one?"

"None."

"Crap. How long since someone beat this thing?

"Let me think . . . ah, yes. 1955."

I swore. I closed my eyes. I heard the door close behind me. The Lazarus Game began.

CHAPTER NINE

Two Secret Service agents bustled me into the elevator. The hulking men—more than six feet of bone and muscle—practically carried me through the door. My feet barely touched the ground as the men herded me down the hall and into the waiting lift. A grizzled, uniformed African American man waited for me inside the elevator.

"Carter! Thank heavens you're here! The president is waiting for you."

As the elevator lurched and dropped, I realized I knew this man. General Barry Earl, Chairman of the Joint Chiefs, one of the most powerful men in America. He regarded me with obvious anxiety.

"The situation is worse than we imagined. I cannot speak of it outside the Situation Room, not even here. The National Security Advisor will brief you and the president."

I knew this elevator. I had been here several times before, dozens of times. I descended below the main floor of the White House to the secret bunker nestled far below, the Situation Room used by presidents of the United States at times of great national crisis. Unfortunately, lately, this was a room used far too often.

The elevator door slid open and again the agents took me by both arms and hefted me off my feet into the room. Once we reached the long conference table, the men released me. A man in a trim blue pin-striped suit sat at the end of the gleaming black table. He stood as I entered the room. The other thirty or forty people jammed inside the Situation Room scrambled to their feet. When the president stood, you followed.

"Carter!" President Ellison cried as I gained my own feet, thankfully set free by the Secret Service agents. "Once again you come to save us!"

Calmly, as though I'd done this a hundred times before, I walked around the table to a chair at the left side of the president. Secretary Bradford, the Secretary of Defense, stood on the president's right side. The National Security Advisor, Emily Bonhoff, drummed her fingers on the table as she hovered at Bradford's side. She looked as though she hadn't slept in days.

President Ellison waved us all to our seats. My backside had no more than touched the leather chair than Bonhoff started talking. She pointed to one of a half-dozen massive flat screen monitors that covered the opposite wall.

"This is the Eagle Nuclear Missile facility in Colorado. At 1830 hours Eastern Time an unidentified source infiltrated the computer network in this facility."

"Wait a minute. Are you saying someone hacked the computers?" Secretary Bradford interrupted.

Bonhoff nodded. "This seems to be another terrorist cyber-attack. Somehow all of our security protocols have been overridden. We cannot contact the facility. Landlines, computers, even mobile phones are inoperative."

A series of satellite images appeared on the monitors.

"At 1845 hours Eastern Time we detected a heat signature in two launch tubes inside the facility."

"Heat signature?" the president asked, leaning forward in his chair. "Do you mean from the rockets? Are those missiles preparing to fire?"

"Yes, Mr. President," Bonhoff said, her face grim. "We have no way to stop it."

"Do we know where they will land? Do we have any way to intercept them?"

Secretary Bradford put his hand on the president's arm.

"No, sir. Because we have no idea their target, we cannot realistically launch countermeasures. They could be headed here. Or New York. Or Moscow. This could start World War III."

"Thermonuclear holocaust," the president breathed, eyes wide in fear and dismay. "What are we going to do? Is there no way to override the launch? Can't anyone stop this?"

I was hoping the President was going to say that.

"I can," I said, raising my hand. "That's why you brought me here, right? To save your sorry hides?"

"Carter, of course!" the president exulted. He slapped me on the shoulder. "Our savior! Can you do this?"

"We cannot access the servers," the National Security Advisor said. "We are helpless."

"You may be," I said. "But I'm not. Get me to a computer terminal and give me space."

I stood. The president followed me to his feet. Everyone in the room stood.

"And get me a Dr Pepper."

"Dr Pepper!" President Ellison shouted. "Get the boy a Dr Pepper!"

I strode to the computer terminal as three men and one woman shoved Dr Peppers at me. I took one of them and sat down at the desk.

"And a Big Mac."

"Big Mac!" went the cry from the president, the National Security Advisor, and the Secretary of Defense.

"We have no Big Mac here!" called one of the Secret Servant agents.

"Then go commandeer the nearest McDonald's!" yelled the Secretary of Defense. "Get a chopper in the air! Seize the whole building if you need to. I want Big Macs here in five minutes."

"Four," I muttered as my fingers began dancing on the keyboard.

"FOUR MINUTES!" screamed Secretary Bradford. "MOVE! MOVE! MOVE!"

Agents, military officers, and staffers sprinted toward the elevator. I heard one soldier shouting into a cell phone.

"Break down the door if you need to! No, he doesn't want the Happy Meal toy! Wait, do you?"

I shrugged. "The boy toy. Don't get me some stupid pony or Barbie."

The man barked commands, but I had turned my attention to the nuclear missiles. My fingers pounded the keyboard. Adrenaline coursed through me. On the launch pad, the missiles continued to warm.

"Sixty seconds to launch!" cried Emily Bonhoff.

I found the hacker's backdoor and piggybacked on the signal, penetrating the firewall. Now I had to override the override, hack the hacking, outthink the devious terrorist thinking.

"Fifty seconds!"

I almost had it. Then a big fat body plopped down on the desk, blocking my view of the monitor.

"Excuse me? Stupid person! I'm trying to save the world!"

The man leaned down, sticking his bearded face in my line of sight. I jerked back. Geoffrey Chaucer sat on the desk, blocking my view, grinning at me.

Geoffrey Chaucer. Owner of the game store. President of the Lazarus Corporation. He sat on the desk, diamond necklace swaying in front of him. He smiled and drummed his fingers.

What was he doing here?

"Having fun, Carter?" Chaucer asked.

"What are you doing here? Never mind. Can you just move?"

"Don't you want to come back? To the real world? Out of this game?"

I shoved his face out of my way with my open palm. I kept typing.

"I know it's exciting to save the world, but wouldn't you prefer your real life? Back in your armpit town. Living with your loser father. Separated from the mother who doesn't want you. Your brother. Your friends. You can have all that back."

"BIG MAC INCOMING!" boomed a voice behind me. Three boxes of Big Macs landed on the desk beside me. The soldiers must have tossed them from the door. A moment later a pink My Little Pony toy landed on top of the Big Mac boxes. I cursed.

"Twenty seconds!" blared the National Security Advisor. On the big screen I could see steam spewing from the bottom of the rockets.

"Can we talk about this later?" I growled at Chaucer. "I'm sort of busy."

He nodded amiably. "No problem. Stick around as long as you like."

Geoffrey "Stupid Person" Chaucer moved his fat head and let me finish my work. Bonhoff shouted "ten seconds" while I flipped open the Big Mac box. I took a huge bite of double meat patty goodness. I hit the enter key on the keyboard.

"Five . . . four . . . three . . . wait! It's stopped! Engines have deactivated!"

Spontaneous applause rippled across room. Soldiers and agents cheered and hugged each other and slapped hands to backs. A woman I'd never seen before kissed me on the cheek. Secretary Bradford would have kissed me, but the Secret Service held him back. A chant of "Carter! Carter! Carter!" went up around the room.

"You've done it again!" said the president as he shook my hand. "You saved us all!"

I shrugged. "No big deal. Just doing my job."

"If only I had an entire staff just like you!" the president glowed. "If only you were my son!"

I laughed and tried to appear modest. It was more difficult than defusing the missile launch.

"Is there anything at all I can do for you?" President Ellison asked. "You name it, it's yours."

"I'd like California."

"The whole state?"

"Just the good parts. Disneyland for starters."

"Yours. Anything else?"

I thought about it. "There is this girl . . ."

President Ellison laughed. "Ah, I know just who you mean. Are you talking about her?"

He gestured behind him, waving his arm dramatically,

like a used car salesman showing off a shiny Camaro. Behind the president stood Sidney Locke. She smiled at me in a way that said she really wanted to be kissed right now. I started toward her. I couldn't let her down.

Geoffrey Chaucer stepped in front of me, blocking my way. I tried to get around him but could not. His big broad body was like a cement barrier.

"Sure you don't want to come back?" Chaucer asked. The big idiot was all that stood between me and Sidney's plump pink lips. "This isn't real, Carter. You know it's not real. Why not come back?"

"Who cares? It looks real! It feels real! That's good enough for me. Now get out of my way!"

He stepped back. I rushed into Sidney's waiting arms, feeling the warmth of her body as she wrapped her arms around my back, my neck. My lips met hers. I closed my eyes.

My eyes opened, then widened. I stared at my mom and dad. They sat across from me. My mother wore a flowing red dress, very fancy, low cut, and frilly and glamorous. She wore a dazzling diamond necklace, a figure eight turned sideways. She had matching diamond earrings. She looked stunning, more beautiful than I'd ever seen her. My dad sat beside her. I barely recognized him. Gone was the police uniform, the week-old whisker stubble. He wore a tuxedo. He was clean shaven. His hair was slicked back. He looked like a tough-man version of Tom Cruise. My mom looked like a sexier version of Gwyneth Paltrow. They looked amazing.

I sat on a long leather cushioned seat. Gazing about me, I realized that I was inside a limousine. The automobile rolled through the brilliant city streets of downtown New York City. My parents reclined on a bench across from me.

"We're so proud of you, son," my mother said. She leaned forward and patted my hand. "To be on our way to the awards ceremony with you. What an honor! A Nobel Prize at your age! What parents could be prouder?"

The touch of my mother's hand. Her gentle smile. Real affection in her eyes. How long since I'd seen it? She was here with me, right now. All of her attention was on me.

"I love you, Carter," she said. "I'm so proud of you."

She loves me? No, she left me! She abandoned me! She ran away from us!

But here she is! Sitting right here! Her hand on mine. Her eyes fixed on me. Her smile of love and affection directed at me. At me! My mother. She loves me!

"We're here with you tonight," she said, her eyes luminous, her smile dazzling. "And I'm never going to leave you. I'll always be with you, my son. Because that's what love is, don't you know? It's forever. It lasts. It endures. Some things really do last forever."

I felt a wave of peace and comfort wash over me. Anger and bitterness flowed out of me, seeping out of my very pores. I felt my sarcastic, prideful heart melting. Had Clinton been there with us, I doubt I could have thought of an insult. All of my thoughts and all my emotions had turned positive.

I closed my eyes, letting this absolute happiness envelope me. When I opened them again, Geoffrey Chaucer sat beside me. My parents didn't seem to notice him.

"It's not real," Chaucer said. "It's only in your head."

"It feels real," I said, all my peace and happiness shattered by the sound of Chaucer's voice. "It looks real. It smells and tastes and sounds real. What's the difference? If I think it's real, then isn't it?"

Chaucer shrugged. "Certainly. Of course it can be, if you wish it. You could stay here forever. Your mind would accept it as truth. You would never have to leave."

"Then why would I?" I asked. "This is the life I want!"

"Of course," Chaucer said, his voice mild, reasonable. "Of course it is. You don't crave power. You don't want to control the dreams of others, do you? No, not you. Not Carter Chance. You have no ambition for greatness. You are content in your own delusion, just like all the other common people. Just like your friends."

He paused. Then: "Just like your brother."

I blinked, and when my eyes fluttered open again I saw a hundred thousand people around me. I stood at the fifty yard line inside Lambeau Field football stadium. I was on my feet, voice raw from screaming, hands numbed from clapping. Sidney stood at my side, hands in a cup around her mouth, her voice shrill from screaming. We both wore heavy coats. It was cold outside in Green Bay, Wisconsin.

A whistle blew. A black-and-white-clad referee brought the two football teams back to the field from the time out. The Packers ran to the eighteen yard line. They were in the red zone now, ready to strike. Eleven players from the Chicago Bears ran out opposite from the Packers, bending into defensive position, dancing back and forth near the end zone, crouched over near the receivers. The Packers quarterback led his team to the line. The massive offensive linemen bent down, hands on the ground. The quarterback squatted over his center, barking an audible.

The ball hiked. The quarterback took it, scrambling backward. Receivers sprinted toward the end zone. The halfback burst toward the quarterback, who first seemed to hand the ball to the running back, but then pulled it back.

Play action fake! Both defensive safeties froze; the linebackers inched forward. The quarterback hurled the ball, a tight spiral that flew with guided missile–like precision, striking the receiver in the hands in perfect stride.

"TOUCHDOWN!" blasted the announcer over the loud speaker. The crowd went crazy.

I screamed the quarterback's name.

"Clinton!" I shouted. "Clinton! Clinton!"

"He did it!" Sidney yelled, grabbing me in a bear hug. "Your brother did it! He won the game!"

"Of course he did!" I returned, laughing, yelling, pounding my hand on Sidney's back. "He's the MVP! He's the best quarterback in football!"

People around me were high-fiving each other as if old friends. I called to them.

"That's my big brother!" I cried. "That's Clinton Chance!"

"You must be so proud!" said an old woman in front of me, the top of her head covered with a yellow foam block of cheese. "You must be the proudest brother in the whole world!"

"I am! That's my big brother!"

I turned to high-five the guy beside me. Geoffrey Chaucer stood there, a foam "number one" finger over his fist. He chomped on a hot dog. Between bites he smiled at me.

"Great game," he managed through a mouthful of polish dog. "Your brother did it again."

"He's the best," I said. "All that practicing paid off. You know my mom would run him around to practice all week long, right? She went to every single game."

Chaucer nodded. "Must have been quite a sacrifice."

"We all sacrificed for Clinton. But why not? Look at him now! That's my big brother out there!"

Chaucer finished his hot dog. He wiped mustard from his mouth. He said: "But it's not real, Carter. Your brother isn't a football star. He quit the team, remember? He quit the team because of you. You blamed him for Mom leaving home, because all she ever did was run him around to practices and games. So Clinton quit. He gave it all up, just for you. To please you. Now he's nothing. Just one more in a long line of Chance family losers. He'll never amount to anything."

"He's the quarterback, Chaucer!" I returned, frustrated at his constant interruptions. "Can't you see it? He's happy here! I'm happy here!"

"But it's only a game. The Lazarus Game gives you your fantasy. The Lazarus Game is unique to each player, just as each person's fantasy is totally their own. My game taps deep inside the innermost desires of each player, translating those fantasies into a virtual reality. My game makes it all perfectly real. You can see it. Taste it. Smell it. Touch it. You could live your whole life here. You could grow old and die here and forget the real world. Isn't that a miracle, Carter? You see the good we do for people?"

I said nothing. Sidney stood frozen at my side, like a statue, like a mannequin. I just wanted Chaucer to shut up. I wanted him to leave me. Why did he have to interfere?

"Can I stay here forever?" I asked. "Do I have to go back?"

"No, you don't have to go back. You can live out your life right here. But you have to agree to sacrifice your real life—your physical life—in order to stay here."

I nodded, smiling. This is what I wanted. This is all I ever wanted. Here I have my family. I have Sidney. I have success. I saved the world. I won a Nobel Prize. People love me. What else could I want?

"Or you could come back," Chaucer said. "You could sacrifice all this and come back."

"Sacrifice my family? Sacrifice Clinton? He's happy here!"

"Yes, sacrifice Clinton."

"Sacrifice my mother? She loves me here!"

"Yes, sacrifice your mother."

"Sacrifice Sidney? My Nobel Prize? All of it?"

"Yes. All of it."

"Why? Why would I come back?"

"Because this is not real power. You are being controlled, Carter. Some people want this. They want to be controlled. Manipulated. Brainwashed. This is a drug. A hallucinogen. But people want that. They want unrestrained happiness."

"Yes! I want that!"

"Do you? Or do you want to control others? Do you want to be the one trapped inside a dream—even a glorious dream like this one—or do you want to be the trap maker? The game master or the game player? The zookeeper or one of the animals? If you join me you can create games that control the brainpower of millions of people. Or you can be controlled. It's your choice."

The football game played on, but it seemed distant, remote, the players wooden and fake, like pawns on a chessboard. Chaucer's voice taunted me, mocked me.

"You would have me sacrifice everything I ever wanted?" I asked.

"That's correct. But it's not a sacrifice at all. You think of sacrifice because you've never felt the power of the Lazarine! It is like asking a child to trade a penny for a hundred dollar bill. Once you become a Lazarine with me, your vision will change. Your dreams will grow. You will no longer be satisfied with the love of a parent or the infatuation of a girl.

You won't care about your brother's dreams. You will have true happiness. You will have power."

I looked at Sidney. She loved me. It was obvious. I looked down at the football field, seeing my brother carried on the shoulders of his teammates, the game-winning hero. I thought of my parents. I thought of the president. I thought of all the happiness I could have here with my family and friends. I turned back to Chaucer. He extended his hand.

I took it.

My eyes opened. Bright light stung my eyes, blurring my vision, making tears well and flow. I tried to sit up. Cords tangled my arms. Blinking, my sight cleared enough to see tubes running down my arm, a needle stuck into my hand, clear liquid pumping into my veins.

"You're awake," came a familiar voice. Looking up, I saw Thomas staring down at me. He didn't seem pleased to see me. He appeared . . . surprised.

"What's this?" I asked, yanking my arm against the tubes.

"Intravenous fluids," he explained. "To keep you hydrated. You've been asleep for some time."

I blinked several times, trying to clear my vision, hoping to clear my head.

Thomas reached down and yanked out the IV. I swore at the sting in my hand. Thomas wiped my hand and arm with a cloth. He stood upright and appraised me.

"So, you choose to be a Lazarine?" he asked.

I took a deep breath. I released it. I said, "Obviously."

He shrugged. "Mr. Chaucer believes you will help us make the Lazarus Game perfect. It is time to transform the game, take it to the next level. With your help, we can extend the game all over the world. Is this what you want?"

I nodded. "I'm here, aren't I?"

"Indeed. Yes. Indeed. Good. Tomorrow we begin."

"Tomorrow? Why not right now? Let's get started!"

Thomas shook his head. "You were inside the game only a short time . . . minutes, actually. But afterward you slept for a long time. A very long time. Your body is not yet accustomed to handling the rigor of the Game. It's late now, later than you would guess. It's time for you to return home. Tomorrow we begin."

He left the room, presumably allowing me to get myself back together. I sat in the chair a long time without moving. I felt an odd pang in my belly.

It had all been a game, I told myself. Just a game. A fantasy. None of that was real.

But it could have been real. I could have had the family I always wanted. The life I wanted. To me at least, it was real!

Now all gone. Worse than gone. Because I knew the truth. The sacrifice inside the game was as real as the sacrifice in the real world.

I chose this job over my family. Over my dad. Over my brother. Over even Sidney. I would sacrifice everything just to work for Lazarus Corporation.

I sold my soul to the devil.

CHAPTER TEN

didn't mope around very long. I shook off the depressing thoughts and self-doubts. It had only been a game, after all. Just a game. I didn't *really* sacrifice my family, you understand. I mean, no matter how real it felt at the time, it still was just a game. All I did was choose to come back to the real world. Why should that be so bad? I simply wanted to work for this amazing corporation and make life-changing video games. Nothing wrong with that.

Then why did I keep feeling so darn—what? Sorry? Regretful?

Guilty.

I shook off the unfamiliar, stupid, meaningless emotion. I forced myself to think about my bright future, all the revolutionary things I would do while working with Chaucer. By the time I was leaving the office building I felt much better. My genius brain could overrule my foolish heart any day.

Besides, by the time I had been bundled back inside the helicopter for my trip back home, all my doubt and hesitation had been replaced by sheer excitement. I couldn't wait to get started with this new job. More than that, I couldn't wait to show off the place to Sidney and Darek! I knew they'd love it. Especially Darek. He loves all sorts of mechanical inventions. I knew he'd have a kitten when he saw the anti-gravity lift.

The chopper ride back home didn't bother me one bit. I didn't get the slightest bit motion sick. I barely even noticed the ride. I spent the trip gazing at my new diamond necklace, a sideways figure eight, courtesy of the Lazarus Corporation.

Thomas presented it to me just before we lifted off. He attached it around my neck like I was getting an Olympic medal, like Princess Leia giving Luke and Han those "you just saved the universe" medals.

"You are one of us now, Carter Chance," he said gravely, as though I'd just be inducted into the Freaky White Albino Guy Hall of Fame. "You are a Lazarine."

Chaucer didn't bother showing up. Thomas said he'd already gone back to Merewether, back to the store. At least I knew where to find him when I got back home.

I rubbed my thumb and finger over the necklace as the chopper started its descent toward Merewether. I could see the town spread out below me, as glorious as a bed of fungus. Soon I'd be away from this place. I'd be rich. Famous. Powerful. I could leave this town for good.

I knew the symbolism of the diamond sideways figure eight. Of course I did. I'm not Clinton. In math, it is known as the lemniscate. It is the symbol of infinity. Some olden time people (weirdos, obviously) saw the symbol as an ancient snake eating its own tail, a never ending double loop, the worm Ouroboros. No beginning. No end. Infinity.

Chaucer has quite the ego, I thought as I rubbed the diamond symbol. What had he told me? That I could gain immortality working for him? Create something that will last forever? I will do that. But not as just some employee of Chaucer. *Someday*, I told myself, *he'll work for me.*

The ground grew large in my sight as we descended rapidly toward Merewether. A voice crackled inside my flight helmet.

"You having some sort of celebration in town?" the pilot asked me. "Merewether Days or Tree Days or something like that?"

We had no community celebrations in Merewether. What was there to celebrate?

"No," I called back. I tried to be funny. "Not unless they've started up Deodorant Days. Why?"

"Looks like a parade's about to start. Police have all the major roads blocked off."

There are two main roads that go through Merewether, one that goes north-south, the other a nearly perfectly perpendicular east-west. The two roads meet up at a county courthouse in the exact center of town. Merewether is a neat little Old West pioneer city, a platted community in a perfect square. The two roads were the only ways in or out of town, four entrance or exit points.

Looking down, I saw that there was no getting in or out of Merewether. Police cars parked crossways at each point. Cement barricades had been dragged into the middle of the road. The town had been blockaded.

"What's going on down there?" I asked.

"How should I know?" returned the pilot. "It's your town."

You'd have thought a descending helicopter would have attracted some attention, but the cops appeared rooted to their positions at the barricades. I thought one of the cars would break away and come meet us, but no one moved. I guess they had orders to "stay there!" or whatever. Common people don't often think for themselves.

We landed in the deserted high school parking lot. I figured it must be about six o'clock Saturday evening. I left town about eight in the morning. There were no cars in the school lot, as usual on a weekend. We touched down in a cyclone of wind. Pop cans and trash flew across the lot. I threw off my helmet, unbuckled, and exited the chopper. The chopper lifted off as I huddled near the ground, the wind shear about taking my head off. I waited for the helicopter to gain altitude before standing up.

I stood, stretched, and turned to head for home. I ran right into the chest of the Russian gangster.

"Ouch!" he cried as I stumbled into him, knocking both of us several feet across the parking lot. "That's my . . . oww . . . hurt . . . arm! Care! Take! Take, care! Care-full! You hurt hurt arm!"

I managed to stop myself from tripping to the pavement. I shoved the gangster away from me. He clutched a heavily bandaged right arm while hopping up and down on one foot. He looked pathetic, and not just because of the way he cradled his bandaged arm. He hadn't shaved in several days. His hair was greasy and tussled; clothes creased, dirty. He looked like he just crawled out of a hole in the ground.

"This is hurt arm!" the man shouted. "Arm of hole! Hole arm! Holy arm! Arm that big man stuck with knife! You care take with holy arm!"

Chaucer had thrown a ninja star right through this man's arm. The little blade pinned his arm to the side of a car. I sort of thought that would be the last I'd see of this guy. His persistence and poor grammar surprised me.

I sighed. "Dude, learn to speak English, okay? You're killing me, here."

"Your fault!" the Russian shouted. "All fault yours!"

"Now you just sound like Yoda. Look, it's not my fault you tried to kill me. Sorry you got a hole in your arm and all, but that's not my problem. I thought you'd clear out of town by now. What are you even doing here?"

"My men dead! All men dead! Your fault. You and Big Man."

I had thought of making a run for it and leaving the gangster in my dust, but his words made me pause. The Russian gangsters had a few cuts and holes, but that was it, right?

"What do you mean? They're dead? Your four goons? I mean, your four friends? How?"

"Big Man did it. Killed them dead. At the store. At Big Man's store. They go there. Now all dead."

I laughed. I probably shouldn't have. It wasn't really funny, and the guy's friends were dead, and that is usually not a time for a lot of levity. But I laughed because I knew the truth. It wasn't Chaucer. It was Logan Pierce! *He's still here, trying to make trouble!* It was just like Chaucer said. *Logan is trying to destroy Lazarus Corporation by terrorizing its customers.*

"I know who killed your friends," I said. "It wasn't Big Man! It's was a different big man. I mean, not the guy who stuck you with knives, but the guy with the axe thingy! He's got a big time knife, and he stuck it right through the hood of a car! So it's a big man with a blade, but not Big Man with the knives. Do you see what I'm saying? DO YOU UNDERSTAND ME?!"

"Now who can't speak English?" the Russian muttered. "You no sense make. My guys die at store. It your fault. You work with Big Man. It Big Man store! Now I kill you!"

"Whoa, wait! What?"

The Russian pulled a gun from his jacket. Last time I saw a gun pointed at me Chaucer split it neatly in half with one of his throwing stars. At this moment I didn't see Chaucer around. Russian gangster's finger went to the trigger.

"You get Dmitri arrested. You get my men killed. Now, you the die!"

I heard a car door slam. I jumped in fright. I thought the gun fired. I grabbed at my chest.

The Russian hadn't shot me. In fact, he spun around, also startled by the car door. The man had only barely pivoted when two hundred pounds of seventeen-year-old flesh slammed into him. My brother took down the gangster with a perfectly executed tackle.

Clinton rolled off the man, lithe and quick to his feet. The Russian tried to stand. Clinton smashed his fist into the man's face. The Russian hit the ground again. Clinton grabbed a tuft of hair and dragged the man's head up into the air, just high enough that he could smack him again with his hammer-like closed fist. When the Russian hit the ground for the third time, he didn't move.

I glanced past my brother and the unconscious Russian to the car idling at the curb. Chambers's Volvo sat on the curb, my friend in the driver seat. The window was down. He waved at me. I gave him the "head nod" gesture of universal male greeting.

Clinton jumped up and grabbed me. I think he was trying to hug me, or maybe steal something out of my pocket, or invade my personal space, or whatever, but I shoved him away before he could wrap his big arms around me. He looked a bit stressed out.

"Carter!" he cried. "There you are! We've been looking everywhere!"

I rolled my eyes. "You knew where I went. The job interview, duh! I just left this morning."

"That was on Saturday! You been there ever since?"

I sighed. Being gone a few hours hadn't done anything to improve my brother's intelligence. "Dude, it's only been a few hours."

Clinton looked at me as though *I* were the moron.

"Few hours? It's been three days! It's Monday night, Carter! Not Saturday!"

Monday night? Monday night! Could this be right?

"You're joking me," I said. I yelled at Chambers. "What day is it, Kyle?"

"Monday! Dude, where've you been?"

I swore. Monday! Three whole days? How is that possible? How long was I asleep? Thomas said I was inside the Game only a few minutes, right? Then I took a nice long nap, isn't that what he said? That I slept a long time, my body all weak and wimpy and flabby and unaccustomed to the "rigors" of the Game, whatever that meant? But three days? What am I, Rip Van Winkle? This is nuts! Three days of sleep! I thought that only girls could sleep in that long!

"I've been worried about you, Carter," Clinton said, interrupting my mini panic attack. "We've all been worried. Dad's going crazy. Mom came back home when she heard you were missing. She's been here ever since. We've all been freaking out."

Irritation flared in me. I can be a real jerk at times, I know. Sometimes I can be a nice guy, I really can. Just usually not around my brother. Right now, hearing all the condescension in his voice, I got angry. Why was he worried about me? Who was *he* to worry about *me*? Mentioning Mom didn't help matters either. What right did she have to be here?

"Well, that's sweet of you and all, Clinton, but I really don't need your help. As you can see, I'm just fine. You and Dad and especially *Mom* can just leave me alone!"

Of course there was an unconscious Russian lying face down on the pavement that would have killed me without Clinton's help, but I chose to ignore that fact. Before Clinton could point that out to me, I said, "Don't tell me you've wasted the whole weekend looking for me! You've really got to get a life, bro! I didn't give you a single thought. I was having a great old time."

"Carter, wait!" Clinton called. "I need to ask you something!"

I reached the front passenger door and flung it open.

"Carter!"

Clinching my teeth, I turned to face Clinton.

"What?"

"I've been looking for you 'cause I was worried about you, you know. But . . . but also 'cause I wanted to show you something I got in the mail. Something addressed to me."

I tapped my foot impatiently.

"Well? What is it?"

He paused. He wiped his palms on his pants. He pulled a paper from his pocket.

"You went to the company headquarters, right? Of the Lazarus Game? You know all about it?"

"Yes! You know that! Freak, Clinton, we just talked about it! What do you want?"

Clinton's jaw clenched. I could see the muscles tightening around his neck and face.

"Nothin'. I just thought maybe you'd know about this letter. It's about the Lazarus Game."

I sighed. "Look, can we talk about this later? There's a

bit of an emergency going on here, and you want to talk about a stupid letter? I'm going to the hospital. You coming or not?"

He shook his head. He crumpled up the paper and threw it at my feet.

"No. Forget about it. Go on."

I threw up my hands. What was his problem?

He took off. I watched him jogging away. He jumped right over the Russian and kept running. I wondered if I should do something about the unconscious mobster. I shrugged. I could deal with him later. I had to stop Logan Pierce! But, just to be on the safe side, I did pick up the Russian's handgun. I stuck the gun beneath my belt. I felt a bit like Jason Bourne with the gun at my waist. I hoped I wouldn't accidentally shoot something important down there.

I stepped into the car. Before slamming the door I cursed and slapped my hand on the dash. Stupid Clinton! Why did he have to make me feel this way? There it is again . . . regret? Anger?

Guilt. Ugh. What a pointless emotion!

I jumped out of the car and grabbed his precious letter. I picked it up and stuffed it in my pocket. I climbed back in and slammed the door.

"Take me to the hospital, Chambers," I said. "I've got to stop Logan Pierce from killing every kid in town."

—

The scene at the hospital was pure pandemonium. As we drove into the parking lot, an ambulance came careening to the hospital entrance. While I climbed out of the car, two paramedics pulled a gurney from the back of the ambulance. I could see a girl on the gurney, long dark hair spilling over the top of the table. One of the paramedics held an oxygen mask over the girl's face while the other pushed the gurney toward the open door. By the time I reached the curb of the parking lot, the paramedics had the girl inside the hospital.

The sidewalk and hospital entranceway were packed with people. I saw parents and young children, teenagers, old people. Nurses ran from the front door as another ambulance approached. I walked quickly toward the hospital, shocked by what I saw. I noticed that many of the people in the crowd wore white cloth masks over their faces, surgical masks. This is what people wore when a deadly virus had infected their town.

Three police cars waited at the front of the building. Eight police officers stood in a line in front of the main entrance. I saw reporters, I saw our town mayor, I even saw Mr. Elton, our high school principal. Dozens of people pushed toward the hospital doors. The cops held everyone back.

I knew the police officers. The whole force had been at my house at one time or other over the past several years. Jim Folkman was the senior officer among the group. He held a megaphone in his hand. He was trying to calm the crowd.

"For your safety, we cannot allow you inside the building! The virus is spreading too rapidly to control."

"My son's in there!" cried one of the men in the crowd.

"My daughter's in there!" shouted a woman.

"We are working with the hospital staff on a protocol for parental visits, but right now we just have to remain calm! Please, we have to let the doctors work in there! No one enters the building until we get clearance. Please just try to be patient."

I paused at the back of the crowd. This was hopeless. I'd never get through that door, not if they wouldn't even let the parents inside. I went back to the Volvo.

"What's going on, Chambers?" I asked, once seated back inside the car. "The town's gone nuts!"

"It started Saturday afternoon," Chambers said, "right after you left. Remember how we were at the store on Friday? We saw Jordan McInerny there, right? I guess he went home not long after us. His parents found him in his room Saturday afternoon. He hadn't come down for breakfast or anything. When they finally got around to checking on him, it was too late. He was dead. He was the first one. Kenyon Martin—senior class president, remember him? Remember he went missing a couple days back? He's dead too. Killed by this mystery virus. Rumor is at least three more are dead, though no one's giving out names right now. School closed today, so we're all trying to figure out who's dead and who's alive, if you know what I mean. It's crazy, Carter."

I pounded the dash. I knew what was happening! *Logan Pierce! He's here, right now, doing this!*

"Have you seen Hobo Warrior around?" I asked Chambers.

Chambers shook his head. "No. But then I've been out looking for you. Clinton hasn't slept since Saturday. Dude, you were pretty harsh with him."

"He can handle it," I said, distracted, thinking. "Where's Sidney? Crap! Is she inside the hospital? Is she still up there with her dad?"

"They kicked her out. When all the kids started coming in sick. They won't let anyone else in."

"Where is she now?"

"With Darek."

"Where are *they?*"

"Looking for you. Like we've all been! You could have at least called."

I sighed. "It's a long story. Tell Sidney and Darek to meet me."

"Where?" Chambers asked.

I didn't answer. I sat staring at the hospital. I watched the parents and siblings and teachers and police milling around. I saw panic on the faces of the parents. I saw confusion and fear on the faces of the kids. I saw frustration on the faces of the cops. Right now they thought this was all a disease, a virus, like the Spanish Influenza. But they would soon think different. They would start to blame it on the Lazarus Game. Logan Pierce's lies would infect the town as surely as this mysterious illness. The citizens would turn on the store and burn it to the ground.

The diamond necklace seemed to bite against my skin. I tucked it under my shirt just before the chopper set down. Now it felt icy hot against my chest. Thinking of the symbol galvanized my plan.

I was an employee of Lazarus Corporation. I was a Lazarine. It was my responsibility to stop Logan Pierce. I couldn't let him destroy the store. I couldn't let him destroy our game.

"Take me to the store," I ordered Chambers. "See if you can find Sidney and Darek after dropping me off. I've got to see Chaucer."

CHAPTER ELEVEN

Strangely enough, the flu epidemic did nothing to lessen the crowds at the Lazarus Game Shop. A line of customers still extended out the front door. It seemed horrifying that parents would let their kids hang out at the store when friends and neighbors were dying. Chambers pulled to the front curb, idling the Volvo. Teenagers and adults packed the front entrance, a human wall blocking the door. I could hear people yelling and swearing as tempers flared, the long wait causing a mob scene. Shoving broke out as one kid tried to move up in line. I watched him get slammed to the cement and kicked over the curb to the street. The kid climbed back to his feet and limped to the back of line.

I saw no one going out of the store, only people trying to get in. I could see no employees anywhere near the entrance, no one controlling the crowds, no one that could help me skip through the line. It could take me an hour to get inside, or I could get my face smashed in while trying to elbow past people. The crowd didn't seem in the mood to let me by them.

"Good luck getting in," Chambers said as we sat

observing the crowd. "Hope you don't mind waiting a couple hours."

"This is stupid," I returned. "This won't work. Let's go around back."

"Back?"

"Take me around the block. You can drop me on Forest Street. I'll go through the back alley."

Chambers drove me around the block. We drove east on Forest Street, driving toward the narrow alley I'd used with my friends just a few days before. My plan was to use the alley to gain access to the service road, then walk up to the loading dock behind the Lazarus Store. If the dock was open I could slip through without incident.

To my surprise, I found three big black Cadillac Escalades parked at the curb right in front of the alley. I could see the silhouettes of four or five heads through the tinted glass of each SUV.

"Looks like someone's keeping an eye on the alley," Chambers observed.

"Keep going. Take me around the corner. Maybe I can walk up the service road."

We rounded the corner, heading south toward the service road that split the block from east to west. We'd barely turned the corner when I heard Chambers cursing softly. He nodded forward.

"Same thing up ahead," he said. "Can't get in that way. More SUVs."

Sure enough, another three matching black Escalades parked right in front of the service road, completely blocking the entranceway. As we neared the big trucks I peered at the windows, trying to spy the occupants inside.

"There's no one in there," I said as Chambers drove past the Escalades. "Pull over in front."

Chambers aimed the Volvo to the curb ahead of the last of the three Cadillacs. I opened the car door. Chambers called to me as I stepped outside.

"You still want Sidney and Darek to come here?"

I shook my head. "Tell them to hang out at my house till I get back."

"What about Clinton?" he asked.

"What about Clinton?"

"What do you want me to tell him?"

I shrugged. "What do I care?"

I slammed the door shut. I set off at a brisk jog down the service road. I didn't go far.

My trot reduced to a walk which turned into a very deliberate inching crawl as I neared the back of the old Capitol Theater. I hugged the brick wall of Gus's Gun and Pawn Shop. Ahead of me I could see a large group of black-clothed men standing in a circle in the middle of the service road. The men closest to me had their backs to me, eyes fixed on something happening inside the ring. Those on the opposite side of the circle could have spotted me easily, yet they also appeared to have their attention on whatever was happening inside the ring. Not taking any chances, I ducked behind a blocky green garbage dumpster that sat beside the back door of the pawn store.

The dumpster had been dropped about two feet from the pawn store building, leaving a narrow crawl space between metal and brick wall. I jammed my body into the space, scraping and shoving my way along the brick. I think I stepped on a rat or cat or something like that. Something scurried out from under my feet. Gritting my teeth against

the wildlife and terrible smell, I made my way to the edge
of the dumpster where I had a clear but protected view of
the back of the Lazarus Game Shop.

Twenty or thirty men stood in a large circle. White faces
gleamed in the dying autumn sunlight. My breath caught
in my throat as I studied the men. They all looked like
Thomas—alabaster white skin, pale eyes, metallic silver
hair. They stood tall and thin, wraithish and gaunt, yet
also wiry and strong. Sunlight sparkled in reflection from
diamond necklaces, and at once I knew them. These were
all Lazarine. All men like Thomas. Employees of Lazarus
Corporation.

Sunlight faded quickly, shadows crawling over the tops
of red brick buildings. I watched the tall groping shadow
fall over the men, yet the glistening whiteness of their skin
did not lessen. The more the sky darkened, the brighter the
whiteness of skin on exposed faces and necks and hands
intensified, until each man glowed in the gloom. The skin
of the men radiated with incandescent light, rippling in
texture and pattern as the men shifted and moved at the
edge of the circle. As the light failed, the black clothing
blended into the blackness of night, leaving only the shining skin visible to my eyes. It was like watching a conclave
of disembodied ghosts. I shivered at a sudden chill.

Two men stood facing each other at the center of the
wide circle of Lazarine. Both wore long black coats. Both
had dark beards, both stood well above six feet, both had
broad shoulders, powerful barrel chests, lanky arms. One
man looked disheveled and tussled, as though he'd just
fallen out of bed. The other dressed immaculately, no hair
out of place, diamond necklace and diamond earrings dazzling even in the pale light. I knew both men at once.

Logan Pierce and Geoffrey Chaucer faced each other like duelists in an old Western, like gladiators in the Roman Colosseum. All eyes riveted on the two men, the group of Lazarine barely moving, barely breathing as they watched Pierce and Chaucer stare each other down. I could see tension in both men, arms close to their sides, hands hooked and ready for action.

I caught what sounded like the middle of a conversation.

". . . gone too far now, beyond any point of reasonable compromise," Logan Pierce was saying. "There is but one choice now, only one recourse. It must end now."

Chaucer laughed, an odd, heavy sound in the still autumn night.

"Listen to you, Logan! Speaking in absolutes! There is no such thing as black and white, right and wrong! You know that!"

"The world has changed," Pierce said. "You have changed it. Now there is right and there is wrong. You are wrong, Geoffrey. "

"And I suppose that makes you right, my old friend?" Chaucer scoffed, laughter turned derisive.

"It ends now," Pierce said, voice calm, cold. "I cannot allow you to continue."

Chaucer threw up his hands in feigned surrender.

"Oh, yes, well, of course! If you say so! If you were any other man, I'd think you merely naïve, simply misled. Any other man could not comprehend the significance of what you imply. Yet you are not any other man. You do know better. Which makes me conclude only one thing about you, Logan. You must be mad."

"I am mad for allowing this to continue so long. I will end it. I will kill you and your precious game."

"Kill me? You can't kill me, dear friend. Now, come, let us put this all behind us! Why not give up this anger and come back. I welcome you back with open arms, the prodigal son returned home."

Pierce reached inside his jacket. He pulled out the axe thingy. The blade shimmered in the fading light, flickering and rippling with color. I could see marks on the broad blade and on the axe heads, strange characters like Asian writing, blocky, bizarre. I was enough of a Tolkien nerd to recognize them as ancient runes, like magic incantations etched into the blade.

Logan Pierce lifted the blade in front of him, tipping it to his forehead, the flat of the blade resting against his unwashed skin.

"You can die, my old friend," Pierce said as he held the weapon before him. "You fear death as no one else could possibly fear it."

"Not for long," said Chaucer. All amusement and condescension had gone out of him. Chaucer's voice had gone cold, seething with rage. I thought I heard a trace of fear as well.

Pierce extended the blade.

"This is why I will kill you now," Pierce said. He took a step forward.

I emerged from behind the dumpster, incredulous that the men around the circle weren't doing anything. Why didn't they grab Pierce? Why didn't they just shoot him?

I felt something digging into my waist. My hand reached for the object, feeling the heavy outline of a handgun tucked beneath my belt. The mobster's gun! I had forgotten it in all the excitement. My fingers wrapped around the handle. I pulled the gun clear.

Chaucer's coat billowed back, a flowing inky wave of fabric. Radiant silver light burst from within the folds of dark cloth, and a blade emerged from the sheath of darkness. Chaucer brandished an axe as well, long blade and axe heads with jagged runes cut into the metal. The big man swung the blade in a swirling pattern around his head. My little geek heart about burst with joy as he arced the blade above his head, axe-end tip extended toward Pierce. With his free hand Chaucer beckoned to his adversary, a gesture that had only one possible meaning: come get some.

I lost my opportunity to shoot Pierce. For several long moments he stood fixed in place, watching Chaucer twirl the axe thingy around his head. He was an easy target. I probably should have taken a shot, only I'd never shot a man before, not even a murderer like Logan Pierce. He stood there, not moving, observing Chaucer. Then he moved. From that moment Pierce became a blur of motion.

My eyes could not follow him. He became an element of nature, a wave of light. It was like trying to detect a gamma-ray or x-ray with your bare eyes. You could not possibly focus on the frequency; it was beyond the human capacity to see such matter. Pierce moved at a rate beyond my perception, so fast I could discern only movement back and forth across the alley. I saw an occasional flash of arm, a glimpse of black cloak, and a reflection of light on metal. I knew as I watched him that Pierce could have killed every Lazarine in the circle before they took three steps back. He tore across the alley like a supersonic missile.

Yet Chaucer moved just as fast. Pierce erupted in a tornado across the road only to be matched by the hurricane force of Geoffrey Chaucer. The two seemingly superhuman forces clashed against each other, shadow on shadow, elemental force against elemental force, hot and cold alternating currents of air causing claps of ear-shattering thunder. Sparks erupted from metal clashing against metal, some shooting a hundred feet into the sky. The clang and crash of blade on blade sheared the night like metal claws on a hundred blackboards, a tearing, sundering, roaring sound that made my ears ring until I felt half-deafened, half-numb. I shrank against the wall and shoved my hands against my ears.

Back and forth across the street they raged, two swirling patterns of color, motion, and sound. I had witnessed the slightest example of Chaucer's deadly speed only a few days earlier when the big man saved my life. I had watched him slice and dice the Russian gangsters with his throwing stars, and I knew the big man had speed and accuracy. But I had no idea he could do something like this.

Bursts of fire streamed from the cyclones that defined the two men. Sparks spat like artillery rounds against brick, glass, and asphalt. A spark caught a wood pallet behind the Eats and Greets diner and at once the dry wood erupted in flame. Smoke spewed from the dumpster beside me. I jumped out from behind the metal just as six-foot-tall flames leaped into the night air. Lazarine milled about me, seemingly confused and disoriented by the fire and smoke. They paid me no heed.

I heard a tremendous crash. Peering through the rising smoke, I saw a truck smashed against the back of the theater like a pop can crushed under a heavy steel-tipped boot. The careening blurs stopped, and I saw Logan Pierce sprawled three feet deep inside the twisted metal frame of the truck. Chaucer stood six feet away, his hand extended as if he had just pushed something away from him.

I gasped as I saw it. Chaucer had pushed Pierce against the truck with such force it shoved the vehicle over the curb and up against a brick wall. Pierce pulled himself out of the steaming wreckage. He appeared annoyed but unhurt. He brandished his weapon.

"You're getting slow, Chaucer," Pierce said, smiling at the big man who had just used Pierce's body as a battering ram against a two-ton truck. "You must not be getting enough nourishment."

"I'm about to rectify that," Chaucer said. He lurched forward, and again I lost them to a blur.

While I stood there I figured out how to take the safety off the gun and get a bullet in the chamber. In the past few moments I'd lost all inhibition and moral anxiety over shooting Pierce. If I got the chance, I'd just do it. The guy could slice off my manhood before I could sing Glory Hallelujah. Shooting Pierce would be preemptive self-defense.

I waited for the Lazarine to do something, but they stood around, gasping and coughing, shuffling their feet, doing nothing at all. Perhaps there was a rule about interfering in this clash between titans. Or maybe they were just all cowards. I didn't care. I couldn't wait. I had to do something.

I got my chance a minute or two later when all at once the two men solidified back into real physical form. By that time, the smoke had grown so thick, I choked and coughed and tried to cover my nose with my non-gun hand.

I ignored the smoke, pushing closer to the two men. To my horror, I found Chaucer on the ground, gaping wound in his neck, blood streaming from a cut all across his forehead. Logan Pierce stood over him, blade extended, face triumphant with bloodlust.

"You will die once and for all, Geoffrey," Pierce said. "This time, you'll stay dead."

"You can't kill me," Chaucer said. "It's already too late."

"No, you lie. The boy can't help you yet. You and I both know you can't do it on your own. I'm sorry, old friend, but this is the end."

He pulled the blade back for the killing blow. I stepped forward. I pulled the trigger three times.

Pop. Pop. Pop.

Pierce staggered forward, pummeled by the blinding hot chunks of metal spewed from the Glock handgun. He took two steps, steadied himself, and turned around.

I stopped dead in my tracks. Pierce looked suddenly very angry. Not hurt. Not dead. Not bleeding with gaping holes in his back. He just looked pissed.

"CARTER CHANCE!" he roared, his voice booming over the hiss of flame and shout of Lazarine racing to Chaucer's aid. "WHAT ARE YOU DOING?!"

I held up my hands in a show of complete innocence.

"What? Me?"

His eyes fell to the gun. I shrugged my shoulders and tossed the weapon into the road. Pierce's eyes narrowed and he frowned, but luckily he didn't chop off anything important. He shook his head at me with the same kind of disappointment I get from my Bible class instructor. I kind of felt bad that I shot him. But I felt even worse that he was still living.

My little diversion had succeeded in one thing: it gave Chaucer time to get back on his feet. Before Pierce could turn around, Chaucer hacked his blade through Hobo Warrior's right shoulder. I saw the crown of the axe peeking out through Pierce's black coat. The axe thingy had sliced through muscle and bone just below the collar bone. Chaucer yanked the blade free and took a mighty Paul Bunyan like swing right at Pierce's exposed neck.

The neck vanished. Actually, all of Pierce vanished. He jumped away from Chaucer, sprinting by me at the speed of one of Chaucer's Ferraris. Pierce barreled through a group of Lazarine who had been running toward their fallen leader. The white-skinned men fell back like pins before a bowling ball.

Pierce ran down the service road the direction I had come. I watched him with great pleasure, knowing that three Cadillac SUVs had the exit blocked. Pierce would be trapped against the Escalades until Chaucer and the Lazarine could regroup and go . . . darn. Well, never mind.

Pierce didn't get trapped at all. In fact, he didn't even slow down. He jumped to the top of the nearest Cadillac like a cat springing to the top of a fence. He leaped off the opposite side and disappeared into the street beyond. Just like that he disappeared into the night.

I started really swearing at that point, but a hand on my shoulder stopped me. Turning, I saw Geoffrey Chaucer—my boss—smiling down on me. He had wiped the blood from his face. A piece of black cloth had been tied about his neck, bandaging the neck wound. He looked perfectly healthy.

"Nice work for the first day on the job," Chaucer said.

I laughed. I really couldn't help myself.

"Is it always this exciting?"

"No," Chaucer said, shrugging. "Most days it gets even better."

CHAPTER TWELVE

The Lazarine—who had been standing around uselessly during the fight—used extinguishers to douse the flames. Chaucer swatted dust from his coat and straightened his necktie. The Escalades were moved away from the service road. The rest of the Lazarine returned to the game store as if coffee break had just ended. Within five minutes the area cleared and life returned to normal.

"You want to explain to me why this guy hates you so bad?" I asked as Chaucer finished grooming himself. "What's Pierce's problem?"

Chaucer sighed. "It's an old grudge."

"Grudge? Seems like more than a grudge. Do you know he's killing people? I was just at the hospital. Everyone thinks it's some sort of virus, but that's not true, is it?"

Chaucer shook his head. He rubbed at a streak of dirt on his hand. "I warned you about him. Told you he'd stop at nothing to hurt me, hurt my company. This is what he does. You cannot imagine the hundreds of innocent people he's killed."

"Why don't you stop him?"

Chaucer laughed, a short incredulous bark.

"Stop him? You mean, why don't I kill him? You saw him, didn't you? He's not exactly the easiest guy to kill."

I had seen Pierce. I witnessed how fast he moved, how lethally he fought. Chaucer moved pretty quickly himself, though. The two seemed very similar. Old friends, Chaucer had said.

"How does he move so fast?" I asked. "How do *you* move so fast? It isn't natural. No one can do that. No one can survive three bullets to the back, either."

Chaucer shrugged. "It's all about genetic engineering, Carter. You've seen what we can do back in my laboratories. If we can eradicate disease, we can also improve the human body. If we can engineer cells to never turn cancerous, don't you think we can alter our muscles to move faster, be stronger? Don't you think we could engineer the body to heal itself almost instantaneously? The human body is still evolving, you see, and it has a long way to go yet. I've simply sped up the evolution process. Pierce and I, we are, how shall I say it? Our bodies are simply superior to the rest of you."

I said nothing for a long time. I considered Chaucer's words. I guess it made sense. It was no crazier than anything else I'd seen.

"So why does he hate you so much?" I asked at last.

"He blames me for stealing his technology. He thinks the Lazarus Game is his own."

"Why? Why would he think that?"

"He was my partner, long ago. He did help me, it's true. But the technology was mine. Logan wanted to twist the game in monstrous ways. He wanted to sell it to the military. Imagine what this could do in the hands of the military! I wouldn't allow it. Since then he has done everything in his power to destroy me and the game. He'll stop at nothing. Including killing these innocent children."

"But why? What good does that do?"

Chaucer rubbed his face, wiping dirt or tears from his eyes.

"Pierce is very effective. He has done this many times, in town after town. At first it seems like an infection, but over time he will convince the citizens that our game is responsible for the deaths. The poor grieving parents turn on us. They drive us from town. It has happened many times."

"And he's doing it again here, right? In Merewether."

"Soon your friends and neighbors will drive us out. It's only a matter of time."

"That's crazy. How can you run a business like this? You've got to stop him!"

Chaucer smiled. "I will. You will help me."

"Me?"

"Yes. You will help design versions of the game Pierce cannot infect. Come, let us go to my office where we can talk more comfortably."

I followed Chaucer through the dock door and into the darkened interior of the old theater. We stepped inside the main theater hall. Gamers packed the room, as many as the last time I visited. Chaucer led me past the pods of teenagers and adults, the gamers staring vacantly ahead of them, eyeballs moving but focused on nothing visible. Hands waved in the air. I knew now what they saw. I had my own taste of the Lazarus Game.

We walked toward an office at the edge of the theater. As I trailed behind Chaucer I noticed a line of kids near the theater stage. Two Lazarine stood in front of the curtain that separated the main hall from the stage. Gamers were admitted one at a time through the curtain.

"What's behind the curtain?" I asked Chaucer, hurrying to catch up to him.

"It's one of our test games," Chaucer explained. "Those kids have volunteered as beta testers."

"A new version of the Lazarus Game?" I asked. "Is that what you're testing?"

He paused at the door to the office. He glanced at the stage and then at me.

"We are always developing new versions, Carter. We are always seeking to improve the game."

Improve the game? This amazed me. Was it not already the perfect game? Yet Chaucer had hired me to make it better. Better! Even my genius brain couldn't fathom how the Lazarus Game could be improved . . . or what I could do to improve it.

Chaucer opened the door. I remained outside, my eyes still on the line leading up to the stage. I recognized a few of the kids. Dunces, all of them. Why had they been selected and not me? I studied each of the kids, trying to find something redeeming about them, some reason why they had been chosen.

If the common denominator was genetic defects, then maybe they all had something going for them. I mean, Hunter Ries, there was a prime specimen. That moron had been suspended for bringing his pet python to school and letting it loose. Or how about Marco DiGuardia? Had Darwin met this idiot, he would have never believed humans were evolving. Marco's idea of a good time was to catch rodents, set them on fire, and release them inside the girl's locker room. This kid was a beta tester? They were all this caliber of loser. The only kid that even looked remotely normal was my brother.

My brother?!

Clinton stood at the back of the line. My stupid brother stood in the beta tester line!

"Carter, if we could step inside my office?"

I shook my head and pointed at the line. "That's my brother! What's he doing there?"

"He was invited," Chaucer said. "You should be happy for him. It's a rare honor."

I cursed again. I probably would have stomped my feet and thrown a baby tantrum had Chaucer not been standing behind me. Why Clinton? What right did he have to do this? Why was he even here?

Wait. The letter!

I reached inside my pocket, feeling the crinkled piece of paper. Clinton had been saying something about a letter he'd received. I pulled it out and unfolded it. I started reading.

Dear Mr. Clinton Chance,

Congratulations! You have been selected to test the latest version of the Lazarus Game! You are one of the lucky few teenagers in the country that gets this rare privilege. You may wonder why you have received this honor? It is because . . .

I stuffed the letter back in my pocket. I couldn't finish it. I wanted to vomit. Of all the injustices! Clinton picked for something over me? I ran through my entire litany of creative curses.

"Carter," Chaucer said, "I think you may be overreacting. Your brother is a tester, yes. But you will be a developer. You don't want to be a tester or a player if you can be a creator. True genius is in the creation, Mr. Chance. You want to be remembered forever? You want to do something truly significant? True immortality is in creating something that endures forever. This is what the Lazarine do. We change the world. This is what *you* will do. You are one of us."

I sighed. I couldn't argue with the logic. In fact, I felt pretty darn silly. I will create the games! Why should I care if Clinton gets to test them?

I took a deep breath. I followed Chaucer into his office. *Let's get this started*, I thought. *Let's change the world. I'm ready for immortality.*

CHAPTER THIRTEEN

The meeting with my new boss was a bit anticlimactic. He blabbered on and on about corporate strategy, mission statements, values, and company culture. He gave me a brief history of the company, something about starting with tarot cards and moving on to Ouija boards and then to Dungeons & Dragons–like role playing board games. Finally video games came along and revolutionized the Lazarus Game. He went on and on about it, but I wasn't really listening.

I was dead tired. I hadn't slept in three or four days. Yes, I was unconscious while playing the Lazarus Game, but that hardly counted as sleep. So while Chaucer talked I dozed. You can't blame me.

I woke up when Chaucer said: "And that's why I need your help, Carter."

Dang. I probably just missed the most important part! I sighed and stretched.

"We need to get started immediately," Chaucer said. "I need to get the second instance of the Lazarus Game up and running within the next week."

I yawned. I was feeling pretty hungry too. I would have

killed to have that food replicator about now. I made a mental note to get one of those written into my employee contract.

"Carter? Are you listening to me?"

"Uh, what? Oh, yeah, of course. So, get started right away, make the game, rule the universe. Did I leave anything out?"

Chaucer smiled. "You seem to get the general gist of it. Shall we begin tomorrow?"

I hemmed and hawed and fidgeted in my chair. I was ready to get going, no doubt about it. I was anxious to go change the world and all. But there was one little thing I wanted to do first.

"Uh, yeah, love to get started. But . . . um . . . well, there is this one little thing . . . ."

Chaucer tapped his fingers on the desk.

"Would it be too much trouble . . . I mean, if it is, that's fine . . . but . . . just wondering if . . . you know, if it doesn't slow down the progress of human evolution . . . if I could bring my friends to work with me tomorrow?"

"Your friends? The four teenagers I met at the store?"

"Four? Oh, no, not all of them. My brother doesn't count. He's here playing the game, right? And Chambers . . . Kyle Chamberlain, that is . . . his mother would never let him go. I'm talking about Darek Branderson and Sidney Locke. You know, the super-hot girl?"

He said nothing, sitting there in silence, brooding, thinking. After a pregnant pause he said: "Well, this is a bit unusual for sure. But I don't see the harm in it. I understand the teenage need to show off to one's friends. Especially to a girlfriend. I suppose this is what this's all about, right, Carter? To impress your girlfriend?"

I shrugged. "She's not really my girlfriend, not yet. But maybe this could help that along a bit. If you don't mind, that is."

"We'll call it your signing bonus. Just one day. Then it's to work."

I grinned and stuck out my hand. He shook it.

"Once again, Carter, welcome to the Lazarus Corporation."

CHAPTER
FOURTEEN

The chopper picked us up at seven o'clock Tuesday morning. School had been canceled due to the supposed virus. I thought our mayor or principal or church priest or someone would object to the three of us leaving town, but no one put up a fuss. I knew Logan Pierce was behind the deaths, but they all thought it was a raging virus. They barricaded the roads in and out of town. Yet they thought nothing of me, Sidney, and Darek flying out of town in a chopper, ready to spread this mysterious virus everywhere. I tell you, I live in an armpit town.

We arrived at Lazarus Corporation just after eight o'clock. Darek spent the first hour basically speechless, which was reward enough for bringing him. As predicted, the anti-gravity lift blew him away. He kept riding it up and down like a little kid just experiencing his first time on an escalator. He went on and on about the technology, the engineering, the physics of it all. He loves all things mechanical. He'll probably make a great lawn mower repairman someday.

I finally had to pry Darek out of the anti-gravity tunnel. I led Darek and Sidney off the lift on floor 60. Thomas met us there. Or at least I thought it was Thomas. He looked different than the last time I saw him. Less dead. More . . . colorful.

"Mr. Chance," Thomas said as I floated out of the anti-gravity tunnel. "Welcome back. This is Miss Locke and Mr. Branderson, I presume? You are all welcome here."

Thomas's hair had changed from dull silver to golden blond, a deep honey yellow. His eyes, once pale gray, had become deep mountain-lake blue. He also seemed to have gained twenty or thirty pounds. Only the voice truly identified him. Still that same gravelly monotone voice. Everything else was different.

"I have your ID badge for you," Thomas said.

He handed me a lanyard. A small blank plastic card dangled from the end. It had no name or picture. Maybe that came on Day Two.

"This will get you into every floor. Mr. Chaucer insisted you get full access. A rare honor. You've already moved right up in the food chain. He trusts you."

I shrugged. "Maybe because I scored so well on your test. Maybe because you're not used to dealing with real geniuses."

Thomas smiled. "Perhaps. Now, if you'll follow me, I'll show you to your office."

"You have an office?" Darek said, leaning in close, whispering over my shoulder.

I shrugged again. "I guess."

"Just like an old man," Sidney said, grinning. "You've gone all respectable. Part of the System."

I rolled my eyes. I hurried after Thomas. The man moved with the vigor of a teenager. No, correction. I am a teenager. He moved much faster than me.

Thomas took us to one of the corners of the building—couldn't tell what corner, my sense of direction completely lost inside the skyscraper. There was a tall, wood door. There was no gold name plate with my name neatly inscribed, however. I saw no secretary or *administrative assistant* or whatever you call them. No pot of coffee. No framed motivational posters on the wall. No file cabinets or typewriters or potted plants. It wasn't *that* old school, thank heavens.

Inside the office I found two walls of windows and a stunning view of the city. And a large reddish wood desk so polished and shiny I could see my reflection on the desktop. There were massive flat screen monitors. My desk contained a variety of electronic devices: tablet, smartphone, laptop, coffee maker. What I really needed was my PlayStation AI device. I didn't need any of this low-tech crap.

"Looks like an old man office," Sidney said. "It'll probably get pretty boring hanging out here."

I was a bit disappointed, to be honest. I thought it would be more like Google offices. Fireman poles dropping through the floor, everyone on Pogo sticks, and so on. I did have my own fridge, however. I popped open the door, finding it well equipped with soda and candy bars. I tossed a Snickers at Darek. Sidney took a Diet Coke. They seemed fairly impressed.

"You are free to tour your friends around the building," Thomas said as he paused at the door, about to leave. "There are only a few areas off limits, and these are well marked. Otherwise you are free to show off our many exciting innovations."

"The cars?" Darek asked. "Carter told us about the cars. Can we see the cars?"

Thomas nodded. "Of course. Although I'd suggest

you spend some time in our labs. Particularly you, Mr. Branderson, as I understand you have an affinity for mechanical engineering. You may be interested in our invisibility cloak. Miss Locke, you may find our spontaneous flowers fascinating."

"Flowers!" Sidney cried. "Why does everyone assume girls want to see flowers? You've got invisibility cloaks and you think I'd want to see flowers?"

"You're probably right," Thomas said. "This would probably bore you. I'm sure you've seen flowers that grow from seed to full bloom within seconds by only adding a drop of water? Think of how easy it would be to ship a dozen roses. Simply send twelve seeds. But you've seen stuff like this, right?"

Sidney's mouth hung open. I laughed. I said, "We'll check it out, Thomas. Thank you. You may leave now."

He opened his mouth to say something, thought better of it, and left the room.

"This place is amazing!" Darek exclaimed the moment the door closed. "You're the luckiest jerk in the world!"

"Just wait," I said. "You ain't seen nothing yet."

Sidney sat on my chair. She spun around in it. I grinned at her. It was good to see her acting normal again, not all mopey and depressed. And, of course, she looked stunning.

"So what do you think?" I asked.

She shrugged. "It's okay. I mean, it's a job. You really going to leave high school for this?"

I laughed. "Duh! Of course! Why wouldn't I?"

"Wait a minute," Darek said after helping himself to another Snickers bar. "You're quitting school? I didn't know that!"

"Graduating," I corrected. "Dude, I could have skipped the whole thing, remember? I only came for the social life."

"But now you're going to miss it," Sidney complained.

"Miss what? Drug deals in the locker room? The stimulating intellectual experience? What's there to miss?"

"Me," Darek said. "You'd miss me."

I snorted. "Oh, yeah, sure. I'll really miss doing your homework for you."

"You'll miss me," said Sidney. "Won't you, Carter?"

"Maybe," I said, heart suddenly pounding. I had to bite my tongue to stop myself from saying something really stupid and mushily sentimental. "I, uh, yeah. I'd miss all of you, I guess."

The mood turned downright somber in the room. Darek chomped the Snickers and stared out the window. Sidney studied something apparently fascinating on her fingernails.

"It's not like I won't be home sometimes," I said. "On the weekends, maybe. I mean, just because I'll be here doing all this important stuff doesn't mean I'll forget about you guys."

They didn't say anything, didn't even turn to look at me. I guess the hollowness of my words rang loud and clear. They knew, like I did, that once I left town I'd never come back. My father could get on without me just fine. My mom already chose to abandon me, so she couldn't care less. That left only Clinton. What would I do about Clinton? He'd probably end up in some state institution without me, or whatever. But is that really my problem?

Hmm. Once again I had my stupid brother to slow me down. What would happen to him?

I stood looking out the window for a time. Then I realized how stupid it was to sit around acting like someone just died when there was so much cool stuff to explore.

"Hey, come on. There's like the coolest stuff in the world here to check out. Grab another soda or candy or whatever you want, and then let's get going. You want to see that Lamborghini or what?"

My question jolted both of them out of their doldrums. We loaded up on junk food and headed off for our company tour.

———

We spent the next few hours touring through the science labs. Along the way we found some amazing stuff: giant robotic spiders being bred to replace humans on the battlefield; 3-D printers so powerful you could print your own car from your bedroom—simply fold it up and take it with you in your pocket; exercise equipment so advanced that all you did was climb inside, sit there watching TV, and a half hour later you emerged ripped and six-packed; and on and on.

Nowhere, however, did I see anyone working on the Lazarus Game. I saw those weird pods of gamers on every single floor, attached to every single lab. But I didn't see anyone programming the game itself. Chaucer said I had been hired to work on the next version of the game. He made it sound like there were lots of people working on it. Where they were, or what they were doing, I couldn't tell.

Darek spent forever inside the car museum. He had to sit in every freaking car. Sidney loved the museum of celebrity stuff, the Michael Jackson *Thriller* jacket, the Justin Bieber underwear collection. I grew quickly bored with it. It annoyed me that I hadn't found anyone working on the game itself, this game that would supposedly change the world and make me immortal in the annals of world history. If it was so darn important, why could I find no trace of it here?

Finally, just after Darek had discovered a whole show-room full of vintage motorcycles, I decided to find Chaucer. I had to ask him about the game. Now that I was here at Lazarus Corporation I wanted to get started. The "take my friends to work" day was growing quickly boring.

I left my friends inside the museums. They were content to stick around while I found Chaucer. I wandered from the car area through the modern art area, through the Impressionists, and past the da Vincis. I kept walking, trying to remember the location of the anti-gravity lift. I got quickly lost. The museum level in the basement of the sky-scraper was like a labyrinth. I had no idea where I was going.

After about ten minutes of wandering, I found myself outside the door to the Rare Documents library. This was the area with the Gutenberg Bible and Dead Sea Scrolls. I was excited to see the library, because I remembered that the entrance to the lift was directly through the other side.

I slipped quietly inside the library, as though worried I'd disturb a bunch of school kids in library study hall. The vast library was quiet, almost reverent. I wandered through the room, my fingers trailing over smooth glass cases, my eyes darting over priceless historical artifacts. As I stood studying the Shakespeare folio, I noticed a thick glass case set in the exact center of the room. The glass was slightly green, from bullet proofing, I guessed. All manner of little sensors and lasers and video cameras sur-rounded the display. I hadn't noticed it before, too over-whelmed by the Gutenberg and papyri and everything else. Yet this was clearly the most protected and guarded of any document in the library, more so than even the Dead Sea

Scroll fragments. What could be more valuable than that? Intrigued, I crept closer.

An ancient book lay open beneath the glass. I bent low to the case, studying the yellow pages. The displayed pages seemed more artwork than text, with sprawling, intricate patterns of red and blue flowers and leaves all about the margins and creeping into the book gutter. A strange fat man on a donkey had been drawn in the outer margin, perhaps a monk or priest. I knew enough about old books to realize that each page of this book would have been hand drawn, each page itself a work of art. It was truly beautiful—but I'd seen fancy books before. What made this special?

A small tag lay beneath the book, a helpful little explanatory note. It gave the book and author. I grinned as I read it.

The Canterbury Tales. Geoffrey Chaucer.

Ironic, I thought, *that my modern-day boss, Chaucer, had collected this book—perhaps an original—from his old namesake.* I stood there for a moment, trying to recall what I knew about the *Canterbury Tales.* My eidetic memory kicked in, and information flowed.

The Canterbury Tales was a series of stories, about twenty as I remembered, told from the perspective of medieval pilgrims walking to some sort of holy shrine. It was a contest, a literary duel, with the winner getting a Big Mac or slice of mutton or whatever they ate back then. My online Harvard literature class—I took this for fun in seventh grade—taught that Chaucer was a genuine genius, the first great English poet and author, a man who could pull even a modern reader back through time into the fourteenth century, his stories so real and compelling the vast gulf of time was erased for the reader, the era of knights and lords and serfs brought alive again. I also remembered hearing that the old author was a bit of a snob. Through his characters you got the sense that the author considered most people foolish, pathetic, and worthless. I laughed as I thought of this. Yep, that sure sounded like the Chaucer I knew!

Voices interrupted my dorky ponderings. I heard low talking coming from beyond a closed door on the far end of the room. Curious, I tiptoed across the deep carpet, quickly reaching the door. I could just make out the voices on the other side. Something in the tone of voice made me freeze. A sense of urgency, danger. Two men talked, hushed and tense. I recognized the voices. Chaucer and Thomas. I leaned in close to the door, listening.

"We can't wait any longer," Chaucer was saying. "You've got to deploy a game tonight."

"The boy's not ready," Thomas returned. "Carter is not ready to begin."

I sucked a mouthful of air in surprise. The sound of my breathing sounded like trumpets blaring. I cursed myself for such idiocy and tried to stand perfectly still.

"He'll be ready soon enough," Chaucer said. "The boy is perfect, as I knew he would be."

"Perhaps," Thomas said. "I do see the potential. But not now. Not tonight, at the very least. We need to properly orient him first. He is not yet ready for the truth."

A long pause. Chaucer must have been considering Thomas's words. Anger stirred inside me as I waited. Why didn't Thomas trust me?

"You are correct, Thomas, as always. We must give him a few more days. I need to open his eyes first. He has the hunger and ambition, but he is still emotionally connected. I was probably wrong to let him bring his friends today. I thought it might help him to say good-bye."

"So we will postpone tonight?" Thomas asked.

"Tonight? No. No! We cannot wait. We must have Isaac to get to the next stage. You'll have to go yourself, Thomas. We need Isaac to work with the boy. They will make the perfect team."

"You trust Isaac to work with Carter?"

"The boy can handle him. No, hold your objections. I have made up my mind. We start at once. Go with the trucks tonight. We have a factory full of trainees waiting for us. This should furnish us with all the power we need. Go there and bring Isaac back. Don't come back until he is with you."

"Why now? Why the rush? Why do it tonight if the boy is not ready?"

"Pierce grows bolder! Once we get to the next stage, Pierce will no longer be a threat to us. Until then, he poses a risk too great to ignore. Come, you have work to do. Meet John at the docks. You can ride with the convoy to the factory."

"What about the boy?"

"What about him? Take him home when you get back. I'm sure he'll find plenty to occupy his time. We should encourage his exploration here. The more curious he becomes, the better. It will make his orientation all the easier. Now, go. The trucks leave at six."

I stepped back from the door. I heard a chair scoot back across the floor. Thomas was about to leave. I couldn't let him find me here.

I retreated through the art galleries, moving quickly. I had a mission now, something to do. I wouldn't just sit around here, not after overhearing that discussion. I had to discover the meaning behind their cryptic message.

I had to follow Thomas on his mission tonight.

CHAPTER FIFTEEN

stood in front of the door that led to the loading dock of the Lazarus Corporation office building. I knew this because a sign above the door read: "Loading Dock—Secured Area." Not too difficult to find, that loading dock. My badge did not work on the card reader. This area was off limits even to me, newly hired employee of Lazarus Corporation.

Sidney and Darek stood beside me. It was about five thirty. The trucks would be rolling in a half hour. I had no idea where they were rolling toward, nor did I know what they would do once rolled there. All I knew is that Chaucer told Thomas to go on those trucks and do something so important and confidential that they couldn't trust me to come along. I had to know why.

I stood at the door, swiping my ID badge against the reader, going nowhere fast. I turned to Darek. If anyone could hot-wire a security door, it was him.

"Can you get me past this door?" I asked.

He studied the card sensor, a black box about four feet from the floor. You touched your card on the box and it triggered the lock to open. I seriously doubted Darek could do anything with it.

Darek yawned, rubbed his eyes, and nodded sleepily. "Yeah, no problem."

He pulled a screwdriver from his pocket. I have no idea why he had a screwdriver in his pocket. He jammed the flat-head screwdriver under the cover and popped it off. Piece of cake. There were a number of different wires and screws and metallic looking things under the cover. I may be a genius at most things, but mechanically I was about as smart as that screwdriver.

Darek went to work on the box. I expected an alarm of some kind to go off. Surely it can't be this easy. Not here at Lazarus Corporation.

Something clicked. Darek rattled the handle and the door swung open. Easy peasy. I frowned, a bit disappointed at the security of my new workplace.

Darek waved me through, all ceremonial. Sidney laughed and fist bumped Darek. I moved quickly through the open doorway, Sidney and Darek right behind.

There was nothing spectacular on the other side of the door. I guess I shouldn't have been surprised. We walked toward a loading dock, for crying out loud, not a nuclear missile launch pad. The most exciting thing I'd probably find was a stinky dumpster and a rat or two.

We jogged down a long hallway. White linoleum floors, white painted walls, long fluorescent light bulbs. There was nothing high tech down here in the bowels of the building. I passed a pallet of boxes with a big blue DELL printed on the side of each box, another pallet of industrial-strength toilet paper. Nothing even remotely interesting.

At the bottom of the hall, we came to a large swinging door. Noise filtered through from the other side. I motioned my friends to be quiet and inched the door open. I stuck my head through.

I spied a large roofed dock, open to the road at the far end. I stared into the gaping end of a large U-Haul type of a truck. Two more moving trucks parked on either side. Men bustled about the dock, transporting boxes inside the trailers. I saw no albinos. No obvious Lazarine. No Thomas.

I pulled back and whispered to my friends.

"They're loading the trucks now."

Sidney shrugged. "So what are we going to do? Climb aboard with them?"

I nodded. "Great plan."

I leaned back toward the door and inched it open again. About a dozen long crates had been arranged at the far end of the broad dock. Each crate looked to be about six feet long. I laughed.

"They've got more coffins," I said. "At least a dozen."

"Creepy," Sidney said.

"Cool," Darek added. "Just like we saw at the store? Any dead arms hanging out?"

"What?" Sidney croaked. "Dead arms?"

"The arms aren't dead," I said. "The people are. But, no, everything looks closed up."

Just as I said it, two men walked toward the coffin-ish crates. One of the two, a short, fat, beady-eyed fellow, scratched the side of his sweaty face while he gazed down on the boxes.

"Them look heavy," he said. "We gonna use a cart or what?"

"These are the empty ones," his partner said. "They already got the full ones on the truck."

I heard a large clang. A worker shut the rolling door on the trailer to my left. One man locked the gate while the other climbed through the driver's door. The truck roared to life. Another trailer clanged shut and a second truck rumbled and coughed. The trucks were leaving.

I cursed under my breath. I was too late! One of the trucks started pulling away from the dock. Only the middle truck, the one directly in front of me, had its trailer still open.

"I ain't moving no more full ones," said the fat man. "They give me the willies. You know what's inside them crates?"

"They don't pay me to care about that," said the other guy, a stout but strong-looking gray-haired man. "You're better off not caring too. You just don't let Mr. Thomas hear you speculating. He don't take to curiosity."

Right on cue, I heard Thomas's voice, somewhere to the right of my field of vision. I heard footsteps on the cement as the Lazarine approached.

"I don't take to curiosity, is that right?" came Thomas's voice. "Now what kind of thing is that to say? I am the father of curiosity. You could say that I invented the concept. It's not the curiosity that's the problem. It's the meddling that's the problem. Do we have meddling going on tonight, gentlemen?"

Thomas joined the men on the dock, standing right in front of the man-sized crates. I could see him clearly through the crack in the door. The two men made a show of vigorous head shaking.

"No, sir, Mr. Thomas, no meddlin' and no curiosity either," said the old guy. "We just move the boxes, that's all. You say move, we move. That's all."

"Good, good. Now, I have a particularly fragile crate for you back in the staging area. Get that loaded and then head out."

"You riding with us, Mr. Thomas?" asked the old man.

A sneer split Thomas's face. "I'm taking the helicopter. You best get moving. I'll meet you there at seven."

Thomas disappeared from my sight, walking off somewhere right of the dock. The workers left as well, presumably to pick up the fragile box that Thomas had told them about. I listened at the door until the footsteps faded. I turned to Sidney and Darek.

"Okay, let's go."

"Go?" Darek asked. "Go where?"

I pushed the door open and slipped through, not waiting to see if my friends followed. I rushed to the six-foot-long crates. I heard the clicking of Sidney's sandals behind me.

"Don't tell me this is your big plan," she whispered. "You've got to be kidding me."

"What plan? Kidding you about what?" Darek asked. "No, wait! Carter!"

I pried the crate lid off the box nearest me. It came off with little effort, the wood lid merely resting on top. The sight of the polished black coffin did nothing to reassure Darek and Sidney.

"I'm not getting inside that!" Sidney cried.

"We'll suffocate for sure!" Darek added. "Hey, there may still be someone inside there! I ain't lying down with some moldy old dead guy!"

"It's empty," I said. "You heard them. Come on, those guys will be back any minute."

Sidney shook her head. "Look, genius, you're missing something. How exactly are we going to close the lid from the inside? We can lower the coffin, but we can't get the crate lid on!"

Darek nodded. "Yeah, she's right! You see, this isn't going to work. Come on, let's just jump on board the truck."

"They'll see us in the truck," I answered.

I frowned. Sidney was right. We couldn't close the crate lid from the inside. I thought it over, considered my options, and shrugged.

"Well, looks like one of us is staying here. Someone has to slide the lid back on the top."

"We'll suffocate!" Darek said. "There's no air in there!"

"We'll keep the coffin lid propped open. Here, look, I'll stick my phone in the crack. It can't close all the way, see? That will give us enough leverage to push it off once the truck is rolling."

"This is the stupidest . . ." I waved Darek off.

"No more time. They'll be right back! Darek, you stay here."

"Me?"

"Him?" Sidney called.

I nodded. "He can hide out in the museum for hours. You can have all the time you want with the motorcycles. No one's going to come looking for you. I bet they've forgotten we're even here. Come on, if anyone can hide out in a place like this, it's you!"

Darek thought about it for a moment and then nodded. "Yeah, guess so. Okay, let's get you all nice and comfy! Just like Edward and Bella!"

"Nice," Sidney said, rolling her eyes. She pushed the lid off the crate nearest her.

"Remind me again why I'm doing this?" she asked.

"Something fishy's going on here," I answered. "It's my first day on the job and already they're excluding me? That stinks. Plus, this is fun!"

She shuddered at the sight of a long white coffin. I had

my coffin lid open, examining the soft plush padding inside. Looked kind of nice, actually.

Voices carried down one of the long hallway. I jumped inside the coffin and motioned to Darek.

"Come on, no more time! Let's do it!"

I lay down. From the corner of my eye I could see Sidney disappear inside the coffin. It was a bit unsettling.

"Going to be a bit cozy," Darek said as he leaned over me. "Cell phone?"

I handed it to him. He placed it on the edge of the coffin.

"If they end up burying you, it's been nice to know you. Oh, can I have your PlayStation?"

"Funny. Just don't get caught wandering around or I'll get fired."

"Don't you get caught or you might get killed," Darek parried. "Here goes. Don't say I didn't warn you how bad of an idea this was."

The lid started to close, shutting out the light. I felt a flurry of panic in my chest.

"Wait! Before you go let me make sure I can push it back up!"

"Hey, you can trust me!"

Great, I thought. *Putting my life in the hands of this guy! I really am nuts.*

The lid came down, shutting out all light. At once I felt the convulsion of panic, the basic human reaction against being buried alive. I jammed my hands against the lid. It swung open without effort.

"Better now?" Darek said. "Dude, I think those guys are coming. It's now or never."

"Do it."

The coffin lid closed. I submerged in total darkness.

No, not quite. A narrow slice of light filtered through the

coffin at my right. I could just see the dark outline of my smartphone stuck between the lid and the frame of the coffin.

I heard a muted, scraping noise. Darek must be sliding the wood crate lid back on top of the moving box. Good. If all goes well, I'll be on the truck in moments, completely undetected. If it goes poorly, then I'll suffocate and die.

I waited in the dark, trying to keep calm, keep my breathing even. Suddenly the coffin shifted, jostled. Through the narrow crack in the lid and through the loose crate lid I could hear the muffled sound of voices. I could just make out the words.

"This one's heavy!" said one of the men. "Thought you said these ones were empty!"

"Thomas said so!"

"We taking the wrong ones?"

"He said take them all. Come on, we can't be late. Let's just get these loaded and go."

I heard a grunting sound and then felt myself hefted higher in the air. The box pitched back and forth while the men carried me to the back of the truck. It felt like lying in the bottom of a boat. I hoped Sidney wasn't prone to sea sickness. Making her ride in a coffin of vomit might just end our relationship.

I felt a descent and then jarred a bit as the box presumably touched down on the truck floor. I heard additional commotion for the next few minutes, I guess as they finished loading the other crates. Then the truck fired up. I waited until the truck started rolling forward before pushing the coffin lid up a bit, giving myself more air.

I took a deep breath and settled back into the plush lining of the coffin. I stretched out. I took a deep breath. Relaxed, comfortable, I closed my eyes. I drifted off, sleeping like the dead.

CHAPTER SIXTEEN

I awakened in sheer panic. I banged my head against the coffin lid, gasping for air, mouth and throat constricted. I was six feet under the ground, crushed underneath a ton of dirt and rock, buried alive. I convulsed and smashed my hands and head against the barrier above me, frantic to get out.

The coffin lid pushed open. I heard wood scraping against wood above me. At once my memory returned and I went still. I didn't want to knock the crate lid off. I had to stay hidden.

I don't know how long I was out. Ten minutes? An hour? A day? It was impossible to tell. I had no bearing, no orientation. All I knew is when I dozed off the truck had been moving.

Now it had stopped.

I heard banging from somewhere around me, metal screeching. The truck door opening. The sound of voices. We had arrived at our destination.

I remained motionless, barely daring to breathe. I wondered at Sidney's condition. I had been a huge jerk to ask her to come. A million things could go wrong, and any one of them—including her death—would make my ongoing effort to win her heart much more difficult.

Why had she even come? I told her and Darek what I'd overheard between Chaucer and Thomas. I explained the desire to uncover what they were hiding from me. Yet those were pretty lame reasons to risk your life. Sidney had any number of reasons to tell me to take a flying leap, yet she didn't. She came. I could only think of one possible reason.

She likes me.

So there I was, lying in a coffin, risking my life, not knowing if I'd get buried or discovered or fired from my job, and I was grinning from ear to ear like a crazy man. When the guys picked up my box and slammed my head against the side of the coffin I just went on smiling.

She likes me!

I was carried for quite a long distance before being dropped. I hit the ground hard. The dudes were not exactly being gentle. I waited for a while after hearing the voices fade. They could be standing nearby, taking a smoke break or whatever, and I didn't want to go popping out of the coffin right in front of them. Although it would have been funny. I'd probably give those poor guys heart attacks.

After what must have been about twenty minutes I pushed the lid all the way open. I heard nothing in all that time since being dropped to the ground. I figured it was now or never.

The wood crate covering fell off. I sucked in clean cold night air. Early October in Oregon. A bit chilly. The crisp air invigorated me, filling me with energy and hope. I climbed out of the coffin.

I gazed around the place, trying to get my bearing. I

was outside, in open air. A massive wall loomed up in front of me, probably three stories high. I saw no windows, no exterior markings. It looked like the back of a huge factory. I could see a couple of large open dumpsters that sat against the wall, boxes and plastic and pieces of pipe and odds and ends of junk sticking out of them. A few broken crates leaned against the wall as well. A forklift, pickup truck, and two semi-trailer trucks were parked near a dark, quiet dock door. The name "StarWest Appliances" was plastered on the sides of the vehicles.

I counted twelve long coffin crates stacked on the asphalt at the back of the building. The crates had been placed near a solitary door with the warning "Emergency Exit Only" posted above. The entire area behind the building was deserted.

Where was Thomas? Why leave the crates out here? The bigger question is why Thomas needed empty coffins at all. Did he plan on bringing something back inside those boxes?

I had to get inside the factory, see what was happening. Chaucer was hiding something from me here, and I had to know what it was.

I studied the building, the dock, the door. Thomas had left the crates here. Would he give himself access through one of those doors? Most likely.

I walked to the emergency door. The handle dangled loose, broken. I pushed gingerly at the door, half-expecting an emergency alarm to squeal. The door swung open. The factory owners hadn't left that door open. It had to be Thomas. The thought sent another shiver through me. Something weird was happening here, no doubt about it.

I heard a scraping noise and jumped in surprise. The

dark, foreboding building and empty caskets made me edgy. I turned as a lid fell off one of the casket crates, clattering noisily on the pavement. I winced as the top of the casket popped up. The dead had risen! The dead would be pissed.

Sidney sat upright and rubbed her eyes. Then she lit into me.

"Why the crap are you just standing there, Carter Chance?! I'm suffocating inside this nasty old coffin while you're standing around taking in the sights? Were you planning on letting me out at some point or just leaving me in there? Carter! Were you born stupid, or did the lack of oxygen do it?"

I rushed to her side and held out my hand, offering to help her up.

"I'm sorry! I was just . . . uh . . . making sure . . . um . . . that the place was safe. You know. Before I let you out."

She swatted my hand out of her way and stood up.

"You forgot about me, didn't you?

"No! Me? Forget about you? How could I?"

She smoothed down her shirt and stretched. She flipped and tousled her hair. Once adjusted, she slapped me hard on the arm.

"Am I really that forgettable? Is that it? That hurts, Carter."

"You? Forgettable? I swear I can't stop thinking about you!"

She smiled. "Really? Are you a stalker now?"

"Not like that! I didn't mean it like that."

"So why are you thinking about me so much? 'Cause I'm so weird?"

"No!"

"Because I'm so ugly?"

"You? Ugly! Not even!"

"Because I'm so bad at math? You sit around laughing at me because I'm so dumb?"

"Who cares about math? Math means nothing! Nobody cares about math!"

"So you *do* think I'm dumb at math!"

I gritted my teeth in frustration. I opened my mouth to say something, thought better of it for once, and shut it again. Sidney laughed.

"I am dumb in math, so don't sweat it. So why're you thinking about me, huh? I want to hear it. You owe me for sticking me inside a coffin and nearly killing me."

I sighed. I groaned. I muttered. I shifted my feet. I checked my watch. I sighed some more.

"Well?" she asked.

"Okay! Because . . . err . . . you know!"

"No, really, I don't."

"Because . . . um, you know, because you're so . . . so . . . frustrating!"

She laughed. "Okay, don't hurt yourself! I'm just teasing you. You deserve it."

I nodded and smiled, relieved to be off the hook. She said, "So, we going to hang around the dock with the coffins all night or what?"

I said, "I'm just waiting for you to get done mocking me. You finished? Any more knives to twist in my back?"

"No, not for now. I'm feeling better."

"Good," I said, grinning. "Excellent. So here's the plan. The door there—the emergency door—it's open. We sneak inside. We find Thomas and figure out what he's up to."

She waited for more. I had nothing else to say. She said,

"That's it? That's the big plan? And exactly how are we getting back to the office?"

"Oh, that. I hadn't really thought of that yet. Don't worry about it. I'll figure something out. Come on, we'd better get going."

She waved me forward. "After you. Just don't forget I'm behind you."

I smirked. "Funny. Come on."

I pulled the door open, wincing at the slight creaking sound. I slipped through, holding the door until Sidney came behind me.

We stood inside a brightly lit but completely empty hallway. There was a double swinging door at the far end of the hall, nothing else. No stacked boxes or equipment. No windows or side doors. No people. There were two identical signs on the walls, one on the right, one on the left. The signs declared: "Hallway MUST be kept clear. DO NOT stack ANYTHING in this hallway!" Well, that explained it.

I moved quickly down the hall, making sure that Sidney followed behind. I didn't pause or slow down at the swinging door. I pushed right through.

We came into a massive room. The ceiling opened up to a huge expanse, at least three stories high, filed with all sorts of metal rafters and beams and big tubular vents and electrical lines and brilliant white flood lights. I could only see one portion of the room, but I could feel the bigness of the place. I could see how the ceiling extended without interruption far outside my vision, indicating that this one room likely took up the entire sprawling building.

I walked several feet through the door. Electrical panels and generators and computer servers and other unknown mechanical equipment stood ten feet high in long rows all along the back of the room. As I moved further into the room I could see strange mechanical arms dangling from the ceiling, robotic hands and metal jointed elbows, conveyor belts and computer monitors. I had seen similar rooms and equipment on television over the years. I knew where I was.

I had entered a manufacturing factory floor.

Sidney in tow, we moved past one row of the electrical equipment, padding quietly down a narrow alleyway between metal panels. Voices rang from deeper inside the room. I saw no one in this portion of the building. All the action must have concentrated in the center of the factory floor.

We crept from row to row, passing three more sections of blinking, whirling, humming electrical boxes. Voices came louder ahead of us. I stopped at the edge of one of the long rows, peering around, expecting to see the main portion of the factory ahead of me. I saw a final row of mechanical equipment. I started to move forward when a noise to the right froze me. I backed up, concealing myself again. I peeked around the corner.

I blinked several times, trying to clear my vision, certain my eyes had deceived me. From the sound of Sidney's inhaled breath and muttered expletive, I guessed my eyesight had it right. Opening my eyes, I repeated Sidney's choice cuss word.

"What are they doing?" Sidney hissed in my ear. "What are they doing with that . . . that . . . *mummy*?"

Four Lazarine squatted in the aisle between mechanical panels. White faces shone in the shadows. They huddled over an open six-foot-long crate. I could see the black paneled lid of a coffin propped open. A figure wrapped in dingy white cloth lay on the floor beside the coffin. It looked like an Egyptian mummy, all bundled up in strips of fabric. I shuddered at the sight.

Then the men started doing something truly horrible. I stepped back, bumping right into Sidney. Her breath came hot and insistent at my ear.

"No, no, no! Don't do it! Carter, why are they doing that?"

I shook my head, stunned and horrified. I mumbled something incoherent, some sort of curse or cry or prayer. Sidney continued swearing as she watched over my shoulder, both of us riveted by the macabre scene before us.

The white-skinned devils were unwrapping the mummy.

Strips of cloth fell away as the four men pulled and yanked and unraveled the fabric. I hunkered down against the floor to watch, Sidney following my lead, dropping low behind me. I held my breath as the cloth steadily unwound like a ball of string coming undone. Instinctively I knew I should turn away from this terrible scene. Yet I could not look away. I couldn't help myself. I had to watch!

I heard movement from beyond the four men. I tried to plaster myself even lower to the ground. Two Lazarine came around the corner. One pushed a hospital gurney; another pushed what appeared to be an IV stand. Electronic equipment had been stacked on top of the gurney. The driver parked the gurney beside the soon-to-be-unwrapped mummy and started unloading the equipment.

"Go get the wiring," said the gurney driver to the other man.

"They haven't even started yet," returned the other man. "I can't hook him up until Thomas starts the game."

"We can hook up on our end and be ready for when Thomas flips the switch. We're on a tight schedule tonight. No time to waste."

One of the four men who had been unwrapping the mummy called to the two newcomers.

"Here, help us get him up on the table. Wait, you got the wiring set up?"

The gurney driver shot an accusatory look at his companion.

"Just about!" he said. "Give us a minute. Thomas isn't ready anyway."

"Got to be ready for when he is," said the Lazarine still bent over the half-wrapped mummy. "On a tight schedule. Mr. Chaucer wants us back tonight. We leave the moment Isaac is up and running. Waking anyone else is just a bonus."

"That's what I was just saying," said the gurney driver. "Said we gotta get moving."

"So get that wiring over here, will you? But first let's get Isaac up on the bed."

I turned to Sidney. "Come on," I whispered. "We got to keep moving."

As fascinating as this was, I still needed to find Thomas. I meant to confront him directly, call him out. I would walk right up to him and demand to know what was going on. I am an employee of the Lazarus Corporation, after all! I shouldn't be sneaking around!

I led Sidney to the next row of panels, the final wall of concealment before the open factory floor. We crept to the edge of the panels where we could see out to the rest of the plant. Before I could see him I could already hear Thomas talking. It sounded like he was in the middle of an inspirational message, a sales pitch. I peered around the corner.

Thomas stood in the middle of a huge ring of people. What seemed to be a couple hundred people packed the middle of a sprawling factory floor. The people were dressed casually, denim jeans, T-shirts, sneakers, and so on, except they all also wore long blue aprons, hard construction-like helmets, and safety goggles. The factory workers, obviously. They stood in a loose circle around Thomas and another man, a tall, heavy-set, balding guy with huge perpetual smile-creases lining his eyes and mouth. The man had his hand on Thomas's shoulder as the Lazarine spoke.

". . . these practices made Toyota the model of lean manufacturing in the past two decades," Thomas was saying as I stuck my head around the corner of the metal paneling.

Thomas continued, "But today that's not enough! To remain competitive today you need that extra advantage, that extra boost of creativity and innovation to differentiate yourself from your competitors. And that's where the Lazarus Game comes in. Any of you heard of gamification?"

A few hands went up, mostly from the younger employees. College students, I guessed, working here while putting themselves through the local community college or whatever. They all nodded wisely as though already way ahead of Thomas and his silly little virtual reality technology. I grinned as I witnessed it. Little did these losers realize the incredible technology of the Lazarus Game.

"Industry leaders are using gamification in training, making the acquisition of new skills fun and enjoyable. At Lazarus Corporation we've taken this to the next level. Your company is rolling out a learning module for its new manufacturing protocols and standards. You know how this works?"

Several of the old-timers nodded and grimaced. I heard groans from many of them.

Thomas laughed. "I take it that the rollout of new standards has been a bit painful in the past?"

Assorted nods and grunts and "yes, sirs" from the audience.

"How long did it take to complete your training regimen?"

I heard three weeks, four weeks, and "I don't know because I was hospitalized after several weeks of it." Most of the employees laughed and nodded in agreement. Thomas had them in the palm of his hand.

"Are you saying you'd appreciate slimming down that training? Making it a bit more enjoyable?"

Universal agreement followed the question. He plowed on.

"What if I told you that not only could I reduce the training time, but I could guarantee 100 percent retention on everything you learn? Would that interest you?"

Again the crowd voiced approval.

Thomas turned to who I assumed must be the plant manager, the dude with the bad body-mass-index standing beside him. Thomas said, "Mr. Church, what if I could do all that, and have you finished with your entire training package after only this one night? Would that be worth it to you?"

Mr. Church nodded vigorously and the entire plant staff cheered. I smiled at the salesmanship.

Thomas gave a great politician smile before adding: "Here's the best part! You'll get all your training done tonight. It will all be part of the Lazarus Game! You play our game, you have a good time, and when the game ends you're fully trained and ready to go. How does *that* sound?"

Mr. Church joined his employees in giving Thomas a loud round of applause. Church said: "This is why I've been so excited to have our friends from Lazarus Corporation join us tonight for this special training meeting. I don't know about the rest of you, but I'm fired up to get started! I had a little speech prepared, but I think I'll skip it so we jump right in. What do you all think?"

I heard the loudest cheer yet come up from the employees. The plant manager, Mr. Church, laughed and shrugged.

"Okay, Mr. Thomas, you heard them! Let's get this game started!"

Thomas barked orders to a group of Lazarine hanging out at the edge of the crowd. At once the men jumped into action. I watched for a few minutes as the men rolled long carts of equipment into the room. Some of the guys from the moving trucks—including the drivers of our truck—joined the Lazarine with even more carts loaded with boxes and equipment. As the workers unloaded the carts Thomas yelled over the sudden commotion.

"Give us just a few minutes to get the game set up! Please, enjoy the refreshments while we finish. Once you've had your snacks, come back and pick up a headset. Take your seat on any of the comfortable chairs. Give us five minutes and we'll be ready to go."

I watched Lazarine and their helpers rapidly construct a series of game pods across the open factory floor. The pods resembled what I'd seen in the Lazarus Game Shop and inside Lazarus Corporation headquarters. Reclining chairs sat back to back; headsets were assembled and placed on each chair; cords ran beneath the chairs, connecting headsets to what I presumed to be computer servers on carts to the side of each circle of chairs. Within five minutes the center of the factory floor had been filled with dozens of identical pods.

Sidney leaned close to me, her hot body pushed up against me. She whispered in my ear.

"This is the big secret?" she asked, her voice dripping disappointment and a bit of mockery. "We hid inside coffins and came all this way to watch them do a training exercise?"

I shrugged. "Don't forget they brought a stack of coffins along as well. And there's a freaking mummy that's probably buck naked right now, dead parts and moldy old bones and everything. So I wouldn't *exactly* call this just a training exercise."

"Good point," she whispered back. "So what happens next?"

"We watch and see."

So we did. True to his word, Thomas had all the pods assembled and every single butt in a chair within five minutes. Even Mr. Church, the plant manager, was hooked up to a headset. Thomas fiddled around with a laptop while the workers settled into their chairs, headsets on heads, hands fidgeting nervously while the employees waited for the training to begin.

"There's the guy we saw by the mummy," Sidney said, nodding to my right.

I followed her gaze. The guy who had brought in the IV stand now approached Thomas. He carried a roll of cords over his shoulder. He backed his way toward Thomas, letting the cord trail behind him as he reversed his way across the floor.

"William," Thomas called, beckoning to a Lazarine. "Make the connection. Let's fire it up."

It was then that I noticed that a white cord extended from each pod toward where Thomas now stood. Thomas stood like a hub in the center of a wheel. White cords ran like spokes in the wheel from each of the pods. I noted that each player's headset had its own white cord. The headset cords connected to all the other headset cords, terminating and combining to form a single line that ran out of the pod. Thus all the people inside the hub were connected to a single cord, and that cord now extended across the floor to meet up with all the other pod cords. To my surprise, I realized that once the cords combined into a single point, every employee in the room would be networked together.

The IV-pushing Lazarine brought his cord across the floor and stuck it inside a small white box. He took the cords and connected them into the same white box. From that white box, a small cord, like a USB cord, connected to Thomas's laptop. *It's a whole lot of wires and connectors*, I thought.

No wonder Chaucer needs me. It's time to join the wireless age, my friends!

"I think I should go talk to Thomas," I said to Sidney. I was just about to stand up and end the sneaking around. "Chaucer hired me to help them, and I can see why. This is all so 1980s. I'm going to go over there and talk to Thomas about redesigning all this."

Sidney frowned. "You sure? I don't think he'll be happy to see you."

"I'm an employee of Chaucer same as him," I said. "I have a right to be here."

"Chaucer didn't want you here."

"He didn't think I was ready. That's what he said. But I'm ready for this! Why wouldn't I be?"

"Okay, but I still think—"

I turned to see what caused Sidney to stop talking.

Four Lazarine pushed a hospital gurney into the center of the room. Another man pushed a cart of medical equipment alongside the gurney, computer monitors and blinking lights and numbers and tubes and so on. The men pushed the gurney right up next to Thomas.

A naked body lay on the gurney. The body looked bad— shriveled, wrinkly, thin, and dry. Dead. No doubt that body was no longer alive. But, still, it was a body. A body with skin and muscle. Not bones. Not just a skeleton. This body had been wrapped up like a mummy.

Thomas smiled as he gazed down on the nasty dead body. He reached down and grabbed something connected to the dead man's head. Thomas held up a white cord, same as all the other cords from all the other headsets. Only this cord wasn't connected to a headset. It seemed to be connected directly to the dead man's skull!

"What's he doing, Carter?" Sidney asked, voice shaky. "What the crap is he doing?"

I waved her off, too mesmerized to speak. I could only watch.

Thomas took the cord that ran out of the man's skull and extended it to his laptop. He plugged the cord into the side of the computer, as simply and innocently as if he was plugging in a smartphone.

"Let's go," Thomas said. He punched a button on his laptop.

Chaos erupted from every part of the room.

Light bulbs exploded over head. Electrical outlets spewed sparks and smoke. A concussive explosion rippled over the room as mechanical panels blew off hinges. A conveyor belt kicked on and robotic arms started moving as though possessed by a satanic force. The arms rotated in crazy circles, chopping futilely at the air, crashing against each other as though sparring and fighting. Somewhere a fire alarm sounded and red strobe lights flickered and flared. Glass shattered and metal clattered and gears groaned and alarms wailed.

Chaos. The room had erupted into pure pandemonium. But that was not the worst of it.

"The workers!" Sidney screamed. She had jumped to her feet, all thought of hiding forgotten. She pointed as she jumped up and down in panic. "Look at them! Carter!"

I looked. I swore. I started running.

Men and women—factory workers, employees, colleagues, and friends, many of them fathers and mothers—convulsed and contorted as though struck with a traumatic electrical shock. Legs kicked and arms flailed. Faces twisted in pain. Blood flowed from nostrils and burst from ears and mouths. I watched a woman tossed five feet off her chair, thrown up into the air as though she were a rag doll. She went up and fell back down again, hitting the chair, arms and legs twisted unnaturally, bent and disfigured and broken. The headset remained on her head.

I ran to the pods, desperate to rip the headsets off the employees, the victims. I heard no cries from the employees, no screams, no moans, no . . . nothing! The bodies shook and trembled, bones shattered, necks turned about so violently that necks snapped. Yet still I heard no sound. They did not cry out, they did not whimper, they did not moan. Moreover, the headsets stayed on. Through all of it, the headsets stayed on.

"They're dying!" Sidney screamed as I ran, her voice propelling me forward. "Carter! You've got to do something!"

I skidded to a stop in front of the nearest pod. I reached for the headset of a woman trembling and twisting right in front of me. My hands extended, fingers grasping for the headset.

Arms slapped at me! The woman moved. Her arms shoved at mine, fingers groped for my wrists! I jumped back, terrified, revolted, horrified! The woman pushed me away, arms impossibly strong. Her eyes stared vacantly at me, zombie eyes, senseless, dead eyes. Yet somehow they saw me. Those eyes and those arms resisted me.

"Carter! Save her!" Sidney yelled as she reached my side. "Get it off her!"

"I can't!" I cried. "She won't let me!"

Sidney's eyes widened. I saw pure terror in those eyes.

"They're killing these people! Carter, don't you see it?"

I did see it. Some of the men and women had already stopped convulsing. Many lay motionless and inert on their reclining chairs, arms and legs already stiffening. Hearts had stopped beating. Brains had ceased functioning. Blood had stopped flowing and now coagulated and pooled. Dozens were dead, others were still dying. There was no denying it.

"Why?" Sidney croaked, her voice harsh with exertion and stress. "What's happening to them? Do you know what's happening to them?"

I nodded. I did know. It was the game.

The Lazarus Game was killing them.

Geoffrey Chaucer, my boss, my employer, was killing these people.

And I knew why. I knew why because just then I saw movement at my left side. I turned.

The man on the hospital gurney—the man who had just recently been dead—sat upright on the bed.

CHAPTER SEVENTEEN

'm not an overly black–and–white kind of a guy. I can handle the gray areas just fine. I like a surprise once in a while. I like a bit of unpredictability. But I also happen to believe in a few fundamental laws of science and mathematics: the earth really does go around the sun, one plus one always equals two, and once a person dies, they stay dead. Simple, reliable, absolute, right?

Wrong.

Apparently, sometimes the dead just don't stay dead.

The man stretched, pale white skin gleaming in the spectral light of showering sparks and glowing red flames. He gazed about the place, eyes blinking and arms moving as though he'd just awakened from a long nap.

Only he didn't wake from a nap. He'd been wrapped in linen. He came out of a gosh-darned coffin! I would swear on my grandmother's grave that this guy had been dead just a few minutes ago!

Two of the attending Lazarine reached around the back of the previously dead man's head and plucked out a long white cord. The cord had been plugged into the man's skull, like a lamp cord stuck in a socket. That cord had connected this man with the little white box. That white box connected to all of the headsets from all of the players in the room. In essence, this man had been hooked up to all the employees of the factory.

I knew why. It didn't take a genius to figure it out. People were dying, the employees of this factory were dying, their lives sucked away. And now this man lived. Simple math. Subtraction and addition. A balanced equation. A couple hundred lives on the one side of the equal side, a single once-dead life on the other. Simple, elegant, and horrific.

I heard Sidney moaning and whimpering behind me. I heard her mumbling, "This can't be true, this can't be true, this is all a bad dream, this can't be true."

I turned around and took Sidney's hand. She gazed at me unsteadily as though she were about to fall over. She looked more pale and sickly than the dead guy. Excuse me, than the previously dead guy.

"Carter," she managed. "What's going on? Did that guy really just . . . just . . ."

"Resurrect?"

That did it. Her eyes rolled back in her head. I moved forward, catching her as she fell to the ground. She fainted right there, in the middle of the factory floor, as electrical outlets hissed and popped and sparks flew and fires raged. She went out cold. I envied her.

I lowered her limp body to the floor. Turning, I saw Thomas standing before the newly undead guy. No one had noticed me or Sidney. Of course, there was a lot going on, with all the living people dying and the dead person now living. Thomas knelt before the guy on the gurney like a knight kneeling before a king. I crept closer so I could hear Thomas.

"It is a great honor and privilege to have you with us, Isaac."

The man on the table—who was looking better and better with each passing moment—sneered.

"I don't appreciate being so casually addressed. Surely you understand my rank and titles?"

The dude spoke with a strange, nasally, wimpy-sounding accent. British, I guessed.

Thomas bowed even lower.

"Yes, Sir Isaac Newton, of course. My apologies."

Wait a minute.

Before I could finish my thought, the guy on the gurney said, "I suppose that Sir Chaucer brought me here, is that right? Where is the old man? A remarkable chap, our Mr. Chaucer! I can't wait to see him again."

"He's nearby. He is looking forward to seeing you again."

"Geoffrey is such a dear friend. How kind of him to think of me. Now, where is Edmond? Did Chaucer bring him back, too?"

"Edmond Halley died nearly three hundred years ago. He is still dead. He did not agree to join us, Sir Newton, as you may recall."

"Ah, yes, I had forgotten. Poor Edmond. Forever in the grave. Well, what about Charles? Last time I came around Charles was still kicking. Is he dead too? I mean, is he still dead?"

"You mean Charles Darwin, I presume?"

"Of course! A lively young man. A bit arrogant and all, but overall a promising young scientist."

I coughed. No one noticed.

"Oh no, he's not dead."

I choked. Still they didn't notice.

"Oh, very good. Where is he?"

"Back in our offices."

My choking turned apoplectic.

"Well, good. Very good. And what is your name?"

"Thomas," he said. "Thomas Edison."

I started swearing really loudly. No one seemed to care or notice, and it made me feel better. Since I was losing my mind, I needed to vent a bit. Isaac Newton? Charles Darwin? Thomas Edison? *Seriously*?! I envied Sidney, peacefully and ignorantly asleep on the ground.

"I suppose you've done something important with your life?" Isaac Newton asked. "Are you part of the club too?"

"I've done a few things," Thomas—*Freaking*—Edison replied, in a historic understatement.

Newton shrugged. "So, why now? Why am I here?"

"It's time," Thomas said. "It's time to bring you all back."

"Wait, all of us? Is it possible? I mean, even for Geoffrey?"

Thomas smiled. "Mr. Chaucer is a remarkable chap, as you said. He's smarter than all of us, Sir Newton. Even you."

Isaac Newton considered that without speaking. Thomas said, "He will soon have the power to bring everyone back. Isn't it glorious? Isn't it miraculous?"

Newton nodded, a bit grudgingly, I thought. He said, "Well, I suppose that is true. It is a remarkable achievement. Do tell me more about young master Darwin. Did he ever amount to much? Any interesting scientific discoveries? I heard he had a thing for earthworms. I knew his grandfather, you know, back in the year—"

I never got to hear what year Newton knew Charles Darwin's grandfather. I never got to hear Newton talk about his laws of gravity or motion. I never got to hear Newton continue to belittle Thomas—*Freaking*—Edison. I didn't get to hear Sir Isaac Newton say anything else. I didn't get to hear it, because Isaac Newton wasn't talking anymore.

Isaac Newton lost his head. Literally.

A long wicked blade sliced clean through Sir Isaac Newton's head. One minute the old scientist was chatting away with Thomas Edison, reminiscing about Darwin's great-granddaddy, and the next minute an axe thingy chopped all the way through his skull. It was like a meat cleaver slicing through a ripe watermelon. Nothing to it, nice and easy. Axe thingy swung, blade connected to skin, tissue, and bone, and the top half of Newton's head went flying off. Slick as a whistle. Like an Indian scalping, only several inches lower.

As if to make sure he really stayed dead this time, the axe thingy reversed and swung back again, this time connecting just below the chin. The long powerful stroke took what was left of the head off at the neck. I counted that twice dead. Maybe thrice, if you counted the first time, all those years ago.

I vomited all over the floor. I tried to miss Sidney but didn't succeed. I couldn't exactly aim it.

I looked up from my puking to see Logan Pierce standing over the prone and bloody form of Isaac Newton. He held the axe thingy in his hand, brandishing it defiantly. Thomas Edison stumbled back, his mouth agape in obvious shock and horror. Pierce took a step toward Thomas, who took a step backward, tripped, and fell to his backside.

"Pierce!" Thomas shrieked. "How could . . . how could you . . . do you know what you've done?!"

Pierce nodded. He lifted the axe, getting it all positioned for the next killing blow.

"I killed him all the way dead," Pierce answered.

All the way dead. I shook my head. *The world has gone mad. Now there's different levels of dead!*

Thomas groaned. He said, "All the way dead! Pierce, do you know what you've done? Now he's never coming back! Isaac Newton! All his memories, his knowledge, his pure genius! Gone forever!"

"The way it should be," Pierce answered. "No more lives will be sacrificed in his behalf."

"No more lives? Are you insane? What are these little people? What are their lives compared to his? Hundreds of them, no, thousands of them don't equal his one life! You'd save a few pathetic creatures and lose one of the greatest geniuses in human history? Is that how deluded and naïve and idealistic you've become? Is it?"

"It is indeed."

He swung the axe with terrible force, swinging it down so fast I saw only a blur of motion and streak of reflected light. I gasped, knowing that Thomas Edison would be split right in half, like a piece of wood spliced into kindling. I tried to move, tried to reach my feet, but too slow, too late. The axe fell.

It missed Thomas by three feet. The blade never reached him. The axe thingy fell on top of Thomas's laptop, cutting right through it in a shower of sparks and sizzle of shorn electrical circuits. Two smoking pieces of severed computer tumbled from the makeshift desk to the ground.

Then things got really interesting.

Screams rent the air, a hundred voices set free to wail and screech and cry. It was as though a switch had been flipped, or a plug released. Every man and woman still living began screaming all at the same time. The screaming filled the air with a terrifying cacophony of hideous sound, like a thousand haunted houses had piped their ghoulish sound effects into this very room, all at once, magnified a hundredfold. The sound pounded at my ears, sent tendrils of pain through my forehead, made my eardrums reverberate until I feared they'd shatter.

The gamers awakened.

Men and women cast off the headsets, sitting up dumbly, as though coming out of a trance. Some sat blinking on the chairs, rubbing faces and foreheads, wiping at tear-filled eyes. Others fell in a tangle of limbs off the chairs, desperate to run away. Others moved not at all, bodies emaciated and empty, hollow shells. The dead remained still. The living screamed and writhed and began to flee the horrible nightmare.

But there were some who did not cast off their headsets. There were some who opened their eyes and gazed about, and once seeing and once knowing where they were they began to weep. Cries of disappointment added to the chaos. These men and women clutched at their headsets as though trying to force the dream back inside their waking minds. I watched them and realized that these people didn't want to be set free. They wanted to stay inside the game. They wanted to let the game kill them.

In the midst of all this chaos, Thomas managed to scramble to his feet. He stood a few feet from Logan Pierce, slowly backing away. Pierce ignored him as he scurried about the room, yanking headsets from those who still had them, taking vital signs of those who did not move, trying to help those who stood uneasily or fell with enervated muscles to the ground.

Seeing Pierce distracted, Thomas turned and began screaming orders to his men. Five black-clothed Lazarine stood numb and still at the edge of the room, as though unable to move or think without direction. Only when Thomas began shouting at them did they move to action. At once they had guns pulled from within the long folds of flowing black clothing. The guns came out, pointing at Pierce.

"LOGAN!" I screamed. "LOOK OUT!"

Pierce immediately hit the ground, ducking as bullets erupted overhead. He dove beneath a pod of chairs, gunfire shattering the metal seats as five guns unleashed a barrage of crackling bullets. Pierce rolled on the floor and came up running. I saw a blur of motion, a smudge of light, and then Pierce disappeared from view, vanishing like a wraith off the factory floor.

He's freaking fast!

I remembered the alley fight between Pierce and Chaucer. The two men had moved impossibly fast, unnaturally fast, so fast my eyes could not follow. Pierce displayed that extra-human speed again, disappearing in a blur from the open floor.

My yelling attracted Thomas's attention. He turned his gaze on me, eyes wide with surprise and anger. I understood both reactions. Surprise, because I shouldn't have been here in the first place. Fury, because I had just warned Pierce and saved his life.

Crap, what am I thinking? Thomas is going to kill me!

But Thomas didn't kill me. In fact, he didn't even stop to yell at me. His own sense of self-preservation must have kicked in. Thomas was leaving. He turned and ran. He fled toward the back of the room, the way I'd come in, the direction of the loading dock. He ran to the long rows of electrical panels and disappeared from my sight.

His men, however, stayed to fight. They ran after

Pierce, guns aloft, searching for a target. They ran to where Pierce had last been standing, the five men whirling this way and that, eyes darting about the factory for any sign of the big man.

Chaos, however, had upended the factory. People ran everywhere, scrambling to get away from the game and the smoke and the flame and the gunfire. I saw one of the Lazarine knocked to the ground by a mob of employees frantic to leave. Another Lazarine had his gun knocked from his grip by the pressing mass of fleeing bodies. Pierce remained nowhere to be found.

I ignored the Lazarine and Pierce. I ran back to Sidney. She had awakened and was struggling to her feet, eyes dazed, disoriented. I put my hand on her arm to steady her.

"What's happening?" Sidney asked as she gazed in wonder around the room. "Carter, what's going on?"

"Later!" I said as I took her hand in my own. "We've got to get out of here."

I started pulling Sidney toward the exit. I had taken only a few feet when one of the black-clothed Lazarine stepped in my way. The man held up his gun, pointing it at me.

"Where is Logan Pierce?" the man shouted at me.

"How should I know?" I shouted back.

"You're with him! You're helping him!"

"Are you an idiot?" I screamed. "I'm not with him!"

The man put his finger on the trigger.

"You helped him!"

Then the Lazarine lost his head. A blade went right through sinew, muscle, and bone. Pierce appeared behind the man as the head tumbled from the Lazarine's body. The blade remained shiny and clean, as though it had moved so quickly and so cleanly through the neck it had not absorbed or retained a single bit of muscle, fiber, or ligament.

Pierce beckoned to me.

"Come with me!"

I did the logical thing. I shook my head.

"I'm not with you! Didn't you hear what I just told that man?"

"That man's dead," Pierce reminded me. "You'll be next if you don't come with me."

"You gonna kill me too? Chop off my head?"

"Not me, you fool! Chaucer will kill you himself, now. You know too much! You've seen too much. Now come with me if you want to live!"

Sidney yanked on my arm, pulling the direction of Pierce. Was she an idiot too?

"I tried to save their lives!" Pierce shouted. "I tried to save them from the game!"

I started backing away. To my left I saw two of the Lazarine approaching. They would see Pierce any minute, and then the bullets would fly again. I had to get out of there.

"Sidney!" I cried. "We've got to go!"

Pierce stepped closer. The Lazarine had seen him now. They fought through the crowd of people still milling around the factory floor. They had no clear shot. But they carried their guns high, ready.

"Carter!" Pierce called as he moved toward me. "Your brother's inside the game!"

I froze. His words hit me like a sledge hammer. I felt the air knocked out of me. I couldn't even speak, couldn't make a sound.

"He's in there right now!" Pierce continued. "At the the-ater! Carter, they're going to kill him!"

I last saw my brother inside the theater. It was yesterday, when I went to see Chaucer at the store. Clinton had been standing in line. He'd been in the beta test line, the group of lucky kids who got to see behind the closed curtain, back where the really cool new games were being tested. Clinton had received a letter from the Lazarus Corporation. He went to the store that night to play the game.

Had he come home? I hadn't seen him this morning. I hadn't been looking, of course. I had been focused on get-ting out the door, excited to meet Darek and Sidney and take them with me to my office at Lazarus Headquarters. I hadn't stopped to look for Clinton. He could have come home last night. He could be there right now, curled up safe in his bed. Or he could be at the store. Still there. Still playing.

I knew the truth. Somehow, with some sixth sense, with some brotherly premonition, I knew the truth. Clinton had not come home. Pierce was correct. Clinton was still there playing the game.

"I can help you save him!" Pierce cried. "But you have to come with me now!"

The employees of this factory had played the game. Legs kicked and arms flailed as the headsets crackled to life. Blood flowed from noses and ears, screams were trapped inside throats, moans of agony had been stifled and unheard. I had played the game and felt none of that, but this was different. I knew it was different. This game had been different. This game had been lethal.

Maybe all of the games were lethal.

Kids getting sick. Virus spreading. Sickness worsens.

Kids start dying. Hospitals fill, parents weep, and the game plays on. The kids in my town shrivel up and die. The Lazarus Game plays on.

The Lazarus Game plays on . . . and my brother is playing it.

I squeezed Sidney's hand. I said, "Let's go with him."

The two Lazarine broke free of the mob. They raced toward Pierce, guns raised.

"Hey!" I shouted, waving my arms. "Thomas is looking for you! Thomas needs to see you!"

My words made no sense, my movement posed no threat, but my action startled the two men, causing them to pause, just for a moment, and look at me. It was all the time Pierce needed. I saw a blur in the corner of my eye, and then he was on top of the men, blade slashing and whirling. I didn't bother to study the outcome. I started moving toward the exit, Sidney in tow behind me.

Pierce reached my side as we ran toward the front of the building, leaving Thomas and the rest of the Lazarine behind us.

"You've got a lot of explaining to do," I said as I ran beside Pierce.

"I know," he said.

"You killed Isaac Newton," I said.

"I returned him to his natural state," he answered.

We pushed through the mob, seeing the front exit ahead of us. Night had fallen, but in the distance I could see the swirling red-and-blue strobe lights of police cars fast approaching.

"Is my brother already dead?"

"Not if we hurry. You can still save him."

We hit the outer doors. Pierce motioned us toward a

black Mercedes still idling, front and back doors open. The big man must have been expecting us to go back with him.

"What about Chaucer?" I asked. "You going to return him to his natural state too?"

Pierce grinned and nodded.

CHAPTER EIGHTEEN

Logan Pierce drove the Mercedes like a crazy man. I told him to drive faster.

I sat shotgun, across from Pierce, Sidney in the back. She appeared to be in a state of shock, eyes staring, mouth slightly open, a bit of spit on her chin. I thought it best to give her some space. Not so for Pierce.

"All right, pal, it's time to tell me what's going on here," I said. "You and I keep running into each other, and I still don't know whether you're the good guy or the bad guy. Are you trying to kill everyone in town or save them? You trying to kill me or help me? Who exactly are you?"

Pierce had the car at about ninety miles an hour. He could have used this as an excuse to stay silent, but he didn't. I found him remarkably talkative.

"You just asked me about six questions at once. You want to give me a place to start?"

A fair point, I thought. I shrugged.

"Okay, first, let's talk about the Lazarus Game. Let's talk about what just happened back there."

"What do you think was happening?" he returned. "Is this rhetorical, or do you really need me to spell it out to you? I thought you were a boy genius. Can't you figure it out?"

"I guess I'm looking for some validation for a theory I'm forming."

"And what is your theory?"

I sighed. My stomach had twisted into knots. My head ached. I felt queasy. I felt lousy. Ever since taking that stupid test I'd been pestered by these feelings. First, because I sacrificed my family for the game—it was all fantasy, mind you! Then because of my brother, that idiot. Now, this. Guilt at what my company did. Guilt that Thomas and his cronies killed those factory employees! Guilt that I was part of it at all!

Guilt! I went my whole life avoiding the emotion, and now here I was feeling all mopey and depressed all the time. Who needed it?

No one, I'm sure. But I couldn't avoid it.

"I think that the game Chaucer designed is killing people," I said. "I don't know how it's possible, but I think he's using the game to suck the life out of people. He sucked it out of those people back in the factory and channeled it into Isaac . . . uh . . . the dead guy. Freak, I can't believe you killed Isaac Newton."

"He had his time," Pierce said. "It's over. You think sacrificing a hundred people is worth bringing back one dead guy, no matter who he is?"

"Is that really what Chaucer is doing? I mean . . . I can't believe it's true. That he's really doing it."

"You saw it, didn't you? That's what happened back in the factory. All those people killed, the life drawn out of them, just to bring back one man. That's what's happening in your hometown too."

"The game store, right? That's what's really going on there? That's why kids are dying. Not because of some mystery virus?"

Pierce nodded. "There is no virus. It's the game, Carter. It's always the game. The gamers play it, they get addicted to it, and they die."

"But it's happening so slow at home, not like here, not like at the factory. Thomas no more than turned on the game and it started killing them. What's the difference?"

"Chaucer is in a hurry. He's about to launch a new version of the game. He needs to bring back his little posse of geniuses to help him make it work."

"That's why you killed Newton?"

"That's one reason. Anything to slow down or stop Chaucer."

"So why so fast here? Why so slow back home?"

"It's about efficiency and risk. What you just saw was actually the inefficient way of doing it. You saw how many had to participate in order generate enough power to bring back Newton? The slow way is much better, much surer, less costly and risky."

"The slow way. You mean what's happening back in Merewether?"

"Yes. Done right, the Lazarus Game is a one-for-one type of a deal. One player's life sacrificed for one life restored. Or extended. It's not usually about bringing back the dead, by the way. Usually it's about extending life."

"Extending? As in making old people younger? Like Thomas, right? When I first saw him he was pale and white as a ghost. Now he's as healthy as a teenager. Is that from the game?"

"Yes. He's been feeding well in your town. The game

gives continued life. It's the Fountain of Youth, Carter. It's the means of eternal life. Chaucer can rejuvenate dead tissue, resume dead brain function. And he can keep our cells from never dying, always dividing. Living forever."

"But Newton's been dead four hundred years! Can he make skeletons grow muscle and tissue as well?"

Pierce laughed, a strange, short bark.

"Newton's been around just fine for centuries. He takes naps on occasion, sometimes for a few years, but he's never truly been dead."

"But . . . that's . . . that's crazy. That means that . . ."

"That the Lazarus Game has been around a very long time, yes. Chaucer has been doing this for centuries. The technology has changed. It used to look like witchcraft and folk magic, the ability to draw the life from one person and give it to another. Now it's almost all automated. Now it can go large scale. Now it can go global."

I fell silent for a long time. I struggled to comprehend the meaning of Pierce's words. I struggled to believe it. How could such a thing be possible? How could it have gone on for centuries? Yet I had *seen* it!

"Has it always been like this? A life for a life?"

"Yes. The ability to extend life requires that another life be taken. But here's the kicker, and Chaucer has never found a way around it. For the process to work, the gamer—the victim—has to willingly give up his life."

"Willingly? You mean he has to let himself be killed? Why?"

"Because human willpower is more powerful than the beating of our heart, more fundamental that the DNA inside our cells, more complex than even our computer-like brains. When a person is murdered, when they are killed without their consent, the willpower is killed as well. It cannot be harnessed. When that willpower—when that agency—is given freely, then the full power of the human body can be taken and reused. This is the greatest trick of all. Not to harness and reuse the incredible power of our cells, but to harness and reuse it with the person's consent! With that consent goes their willpower, their agency for action, and all the power that comes with it. With that power, Chaucer can extend his own ancient life. He can bring Isaac Newton back from his long slumber. He can ensure the eternal life of the few elite humans on the earth."

It was all making sense to me. As sick and twisted and maniacal as it was, it was starting to make sense. I said, "This is the reason for the game, right? The reason he uses a video game. To trick people into giving up their lives!"

He nodded.

I added, "Because inside the game each player has a choice to continue or come back to the real world. I saw it myself. When I was inside the game. I wanted to stay. It was so real, I wanted to stay."

"It's not just that it is realistic, Carter. It's not just that it looks and feels and smells and tastes real. It's better than real. It's the ability for each player to live out their greatest fantasy, over and over, in the most realistic manner possible. For the players, that game—that fantasy—becomes their reality. They don't want to come back to the real world."

"But do they know it's killing them? Do they actually agree to it?"

"Of course. They are willing to sacrifice everything for a few days living out their fantasy. Besides, a few minutes in the real world are like hours inside the game; real-world hours can seem like decades. You can live a lifetime inside the game."

Like in that stupid book about the magic wardrobe, I thought. Time has no meaning.! A few minutes in the real world is a lifetime inside the game. An imagined lifetime of fantasy in exchange for your last few minutes of real-life. Your premature death would seem perfectly natural, perfectly normal. A few minutes of this nasty world in exchange for a lifetime of hallucinogenic utopia. Oh, crap. Double crap!

"That's nuts. That's totally screwed up! I can't believe anyone would sacrifice their lives for a fantasy. That just can't be true. No one would agree to it!"

Pierce turned to gaze at me. He looked surprised and disappointed at my words as though he just realized I was a complete moron.

"What?" I asked. "Am I wrong?"

"You're dead wrong. You see it all the time. You just don't recognize it for what it is. Chaucer didn't create the impulse to throw away your life for a fantasy, he's only harnessing it."

"You're wrong! I've never seen one person sacrifice everything for a fantasy."

"Never, huh? Do kids in your school do drugs?"

I shut my mouth and didn't respond. I hated getting tricked like that. He had a point. He was right, dead right, and I was wrong. Crap. But I didn't need him to turn this into an anti-drug lecture, so I said nothing.

I remained quiet for a long while. Sidney napped in the backseat, mercifully not hearing any of this crazy talk. After several minutes I dared ask another question.

"Who is Geoffrey Chaucer?"

Pierce slowed the car and came to a stop, idling in front of a street light. There wasn't a freaking car left in the entire county, and here he was waiting at a red light! I didn't mention that, though, because I didn't want to interrupt his answer. After the light finally blinked green and the car started moving again did he answer.

"He *is* Geoffrey Chaucer, for starters. The real deal. The author and poet. I think he likes that particular persona for some reason. It's a name he often assumes. You read much English lit in school?"

"Wait, wait just a minute. You mean he really is *the* Geoffrey Chaucer from the Middle Ages? The dude who wrote *Canterbury Tales*? I saw the book back in the office!"

"That's him," Pierce said. "But that's only one of his many names, one of his personas. He wrote that book—it was actually one of the early versions of the Lazarus Game. Back then he used stories like today he uses video games. Those stories are so powerful that they resonate even today, six hundred years later."

I nodded. It made sense. Stories were the power beneath the technology, behind the games, underpinning everything. Fantasy is nothing without story.

"But you said that's only one of his names," I said.

"Oh, yes, one of dozens. He was alive far before the medieval times, when *The Canterbury Tales* was written. He was already ancient by the fourteenth century."

"Then who was he before he was Geoffrey Chaucer?"

"Nobody you've ever heard of. He's older than memory. Older than history."

"But who is he?"

"He is Adam. Maybe not literally, but figuratively at least. He is the first, the original great man, the true father of genius. Today we toss around the term genius all the time, like it's a common thing. But Chaucer is the originator of the term. He's a fluke of human genetics, probably the smartest person who's ever walked the planet. Long ago, back before technology and science, he figured out the true meaning of the human body and its true potential. Don't ask me how he did it. I'm sure I'm not smart enough to understand. Point is, he learned how to extend his life, then how to do that for others. He started a secret society based on this most basic human desire to live forever. He has been the power behind thrones and dictators. He is undoubtedly the wealthiest person on the planet. Yet he cares nothing for riches or politics. He cares only for life. His own life. And extending his life forever."

Nothing is forever, I thought. Relationships don't last. People change their minds. Monuments fall, buildings crumble, time moves on. Nothing goes on forever. Not even the love of a father to a mother, and a mother to her child. Nothing endures.

Except a madman named Geoffrey Chaucer, it seemed.

Pierce paused for a moment, perhaps considering his next words. Then he said, "I told you he's been doing this a long time. That's true. But it's always been very small in scale. A few people, a handful of deaths over a long period of time. This is because of the difficulty of the method over the years."

"Before the Lazarus Game, you mean?"

"Yes. He's used various forms. He had to prepare each mind to be influenced. Then he had to tell stories, fantasies that he whispered into the victim's consciousness. He used board games before computers. Before that it was cards, tarot cards and the like. He's used hypnotism. He's used stories, like the *Canterbury Tales*, as I told you. He's always used stories and games to tap directly into each mind. But it's a long, slow process. Then here came computers and the Lazarus Game revolutionized everything."

"Now he can do it large scale, right? More victims? More common people to sacrifice? More of the elite to save?"

"People like you," Pierce said.

I swallowed hard. The feeling of guilt intensified.

"That's not why I signed up," I said.

"No, of course not. Not yet. But he can be very persuasive."

"He couldn't persuade me to do that!"

Pierce smiled. "Perhaps not. But you are working for him."

"It was a job! A chance to create amazing technology! I thought I was changing the world."

"You would be. Chaucer does do many great things. What you saw inside his headquarters—I know a bit of what goes on there—those things are not lies. He really is at the forefront of all those innovations and inventions. But it all comes at a terrible price, Carter. You'd have to ask yourself if all that advancement is worth the cost in human life."

I chewed on my lip, considering my next question. Finally I figured I had to know something else, something horrible, no matter how terrible the truth.

"Chaucer said he hired me to help take his game to the next level. Do you know what he's talking about?"

"It's the next platform for the game, the next evolution. Chaucer's been planning it for years. I've spent those years trying to stop him."

"You were involved too, weren't you? You were one of his Lazarine?"

"I was a fool. He recruited me, just like you. He taught me and mentored me. I did it knowingly. I am guilty, Carter. I am a monster, just like him."

"You're pretty fast," I said. "No normal human can move that fast. You're like a blur when you move. That can't be normal."

He nodded, face grim. "He engineered me that way. He changed my DNA. He told me I could live forever."

"Did you . . . have you . . .?"

"Been fed from the game? Taken a life to extend or enhance my own? Yes. I am a monster and murderer, just like him. This is why I must fight him. This is why I'll sacrifice my life to destroy his. Because I know the monster that I am, and I cannot live with that knowledge. Chaucer must be stopped before any more lives can be taken."

"How do we do that? How do we stop the game?"

He laughed, that same barking, terrible laugh.

"Stop the game? There's no way to stop the game without stopping Chaucer. You can't kill the game unless you kill him."

"Because he creates the games? Surely there are others now that could continue the game, keep on programming new ones after he's gone. Thomas, for example. Couldn't he engineer a new Lazarus Game after Chaucer is gone?"

Pierce shook his head.

"No, Carter, it doesn't work that way. There is truly only one game. Everything else is a shadow and a reflection, mirrored copies that are twisted and configured through technology to reach each player."

Pierce took his eyes off the road again to look at me. His eyes bore right into my soul, those eyes fierce and burning.

"You cannot kill the game without killing Chaucer," he repeated, "because the game is Chaucer."

Pierce paused and then said, "Geoffrey Chaucer *is* the Lazarus Game."

CHAPTER NINETEEN

There were two significant obstacles to invading the Lazarus Game Shop and rescuing my brother. For normal people this would have presented an insurmountable challenge. Given that I am who I am, it was no problem at all. Better to be lucky and a genius than good, I always say.

The first obstacle began presenting itself while we were still ten miles from Merewether. A large sign, one of those roadside construction signs that warned people to slow down or merge lanes or stop driving like lunatics or whatever, straddled the shoulder of the right side of the road. A large orange blinking message read: "Road Closed Ahead. Turn Back." Logan Pierce cursed when he saw the sign. I told him to ignore it and keep driving.

Five miles later we encountered an identical sign. Again Pierce swore and again I directed him forward. Three miles from there, we found yet another sign.

"They've got the town closed down," Pierce said. "We'll have to ditch the car and go in on foot."

"Keep going," I said. "Don't worry about it."

About a minute later the night sky lit up like the freaking Aurora Borealis, all red and blue and white—police lights. Additionally, a big strobe light tracked lazily across the night sky, meaning either our high school team just won homecoming or there was some danger ahead. Given the sorry state of our football team, I knew it couldn't be that.

We reached the police barricade two minutes later. Our local police force had been augmented by a couple of Highway Patrol cruisers. A total of five Crown Vic police cars sprawled across the narrow highway. A tight knot of uniformed cops stood in the middle of the road, sipping coffee from long black thermoses while they chatted and kept unsuspecting visitors away.

Pierce cursed once more and slowed the car.

"They're not going to let us in," Sidney said, who had finally been roused from slumber. "They won't let anyone in or out. Not with this virus still loose."

"It's not a virus," I said. "It's the Lazarus Game."

"What?"

I sighed. She'd missed only the most important revelation in history—slept right through it. I really didn't have the time or patience to explain it to her.

Fortunately she wasn't as big an idiot as I thought she was. She said, "It's the same as back at the factory, right? Oh my gosh! The game was killing those workers. I saw it happening. That's what's happening in town too, right? That's why Jordan and Kenyon died, isn't it? They didn't wither away from a virus. It was the game that killed them!"

I nodded, immensely relieved I didn't have to waste effort explaining it to her. I said, "Yes, that's exactly right. Problem is, Clinton's inside the store right now, playing the game. For all I know, he could already be dead."

"That's awful!" she cried. "Carter, what are you going to do?"

I felt my stomach lurch, but I gritted my teeth and steeled my nerves.

"I'm going to rescue him."

I didn't have any other good options. I mean, my brother is an embarrassment to the family, really to several generations of the Chance family. He dropped out of football when he could have had a scholarship. He stopped playing when maybe he could have even made the NFL and done something meaningful with him life. He would barely qualify to go to the local state college on academics. He had no meaningful ambitions or interests. Like I said, an embarrassment.

And he drove me crazy. He wouldn't stop talking about Mom, which was totally unacceptable. I mean, it was because of Clinton that Mom left in the first place. Which was another matter. If not for my stupid brother, my mom might still be with my dad. We'd be one big happy family. But Clinton screwed that all up. Like I said, he drives me crazy!

But, as much as it pained me to admit it, he was still my brother. That meant something, even to a huge, callous, arrogant jerk like me. It meant that I had to save him.

Then there was Chaucer. I was really angry about my job. I could have really made a difference in this pathetic world! It all seemed too good to be true. I guess it was. I have no problem working for egomaniacs who want to monopolize industries and make billions of dollars and drive the competition into the ground. I did, however, have a problem working for really huge egomaniacs who wanted to kill thousands of innocent people. Yes, even I have a few basic principles.

The cops stopped us just short of the barricade. Pierce rolled down the window. One of our local guys, Fitz Sheridan, leaned his thick head through the window. He started explaining about the killer virus and the quarantine zone and blah, blah, blah. I stopped him.

"We gotta get in there, Fitz," I said. "You need to let us through."

"Carter? Carter Chance, is that you?"

He stuck his flashlight in my face. Yep, it was me, the idiot.

"Your dad's going crazy looking for you!"

"That's why you gotta let me in."

The cop hesitated, chewed on his lip, obviously considering. I sighed.

"Look, we're not going to make these people any sicker! The virus is in there! We're not going to get anyone else infected if we go in! You just need to keep people from going out!"

"It's for your own safety," Fitz Sheridan said.

"My dad's going to want to see me, Fitz. You know he'll tell you to let me through. Can we quit wasting time here? I'm in a bit of a hurry."

The guy gave a halfhearted attempt at considering a reason to keep me out, shrugged, and finally waved us through. I smiled and thanked him.

Pierce stepped on the gas, racing us toward the game store. There was no need to worry about traffic cops pulling us over. Every cop in town was at the barricades.

The second obstacle required Pierce letting me out a block away from our destination. I could get us past the police barricades, but I couldn't get me and Sidney AND Pierce past the Lazarine who would be guarding the game store. There was no way Pierce could get into the store without slicing and dicing his way through. I could get in, though, no problem.

I stepped from the car to the curb. To my surprise Sidney opened the back door and followed me out. Before I could say anything, she said: "Shut up, Carter. I'm coming with you."

"To do what?" I asked.

"Help you save Clinton."

"Just what are you going to do, exactly?"

She smirked at me. "If there's a situation requiring common sense and basic human goodness, then you'll need me. You don't have any of that."

I nodded. No arguing that. I was happy to have her along. Pierce was another story.

"They'll kill you if you stick your face around the store," I said to him. "Chaucer has everyone geared up looking for you."

"What about you? Thomas knows you're not on his side."

I shrugged. "Maybe word hasn't gotten out yet."

"Be careful," Pierce said. "Carter, don't listen to anything Chaucer tries to tell you. And don't underestimate him! He'll sound so reasonable and logical you'll forget all the reasons you have to kill him. Don't believe anything he says."

"I'm not going in there to kill Chaucer," I said. "I'm going to save my brother."

Pierce grinned and nodded. "Good! That's exactly right! I'll be along in a few minutes. I'll kill Chaucer. You just keep him distracted."

"How do I do that?"

"You'll figure it out."

He revved the car and pulled away from the curb. Sidney and I jogged to the store.

The building looked deserted. Granted, it was past midnight. It had been a long ride from the factory to Merewether. Maybe everyone had gone home to bed. Or maybe everyone was dead. I honestly wouldn't have been surprised either way.

The neon lights were off. Weak light filtered around shaded windows. I could see three hulking bodies loitering by the front door, but otherwise no one else at all. If there were still gamers inside the store, I could see no evidence from the outside. Perhaps the only evidence that remained would be stacks of occupied coffins.

I shuddered at the morbid thought. I ran faster, Sidney right on my heels.

Once again my credentials gained us entrance into the store. Three black-clothed Lazarine attempted to block our way through the front door. I flashed my sideways figure eight diamond necklace at them. They immediately apologized and let us through.

The interior of the store was dark, quiet. We jogged through the showroom, all empty now. No three-dimensional digital figures danced on the ceilings, no horses pranced across the walls, no game displays stalked me across the floor. I couldn't see a shred of evidence the store had even existed. Even the walls had been stripped clean.

"Has the store closed down?" Sidney whispered as we hurried through the room. "It looks like they were never even here! We were just here yesterday!"

"They're getting ready to leave," I said. "I guess they've sucked the town dry."

"What about Clinton?" she asked.

"There's still someone here or those guards wouldn't be hanging around."

I pushed on through the swinging double doors into the main theater hall. Here I found a regular hive of activity. I found normal living-and-breathing men busily packing equipment and wires and electrical devices into boxes. I found the back door propped open and a steady stream of the workers moving boxes from the hall to the dock. I found Lazarine walking around barking orders to the normal "only-got-one-life-to-live" men.

I found the hall being swept clean of any evidence of the Lazarus Game Shop. I found empty seats and abandoned headsets on the few remaining circular-configured pods. I found no coffins, no dead bodies, no emaciated victims. I found none of what I had once seen inside this hall.

I also did not find my brother. I did, however, find three interesting things.

First, I found the long heavy drape still closed across the stage—the area where the "beta" version of the game had been played. Someone could still be back there.

Second, I found Thomas standing on top of the stage—the old inventor had somehow beaten me back to the store.

Third, I found that Thomas had a very large, very black, very scary-looking handgun in his hand. He pointed it right at me.

"I thought you would come," Thomas said, sounding quite satisfied. "Chaucer believed you would abandon your brother—he still thinks you've been converted to the true cause. But for all your potential, you are nothing but a simpleton at heart. Sentimental, emotional, and common."

"I've come back for my brother. I couldn't care less what Chaucer thinks. I'll let Pierce deal with him."

Thomas's eyes flashed at mention of Pierce's name. "Where is Logan Pierce? Is he here with you? Don't tell me he was stupid enough to come here with you."

"He's gone. Looking for Chaucer, I guess. Wants to chop him up just like he did Isaac Newton."

This appeared to agitate Thomas. The gun started shaking. I took a deep breath and swallowed hard. It was probably not a good idea to irritate the guy holding the gun.

"So where is Chaucer?" I asked. "Is he here? Maybe I'd like to talk to him after all. I'm having second thoughts about my employment."

"He's not here right now," Thomas said. "But he'll be back."

"That's good, real good. Pierce will be excited to see him."

"Pierce will be dead. You too, if you don't watch yourself. Geoffrey is willing to give you another chance. I'm not."

"I don't want another chance. I'm just here for my brother."

Thomas nodded. "Feel free to come see him. He's back behind the curtain. You can join him. We'll have a little party while waiting for Geoffrey to return. Come on, don't be shy."

He motioned me and Sidney forward, waving the gun like a finger. I figured he didn't know a thing about proper gun safety. I walked to the stage. Sidney followed me, the poor girl. Out of the frying pan and into the fire.

I trotted up the stairs to the stage. No sense in making Thomas wait around to kill me. He didn't kill me, though. He pulled the curtain back. He nodded with his head, inviting me through.

"You'll find your brother in the back. He's been our guest a couple days now. He has been most cooperative. I am amazed at everything we've been able to get out of him. He has been . . . how shall I say it . . . an excellent *resource* for us."

I paused at the edge of the stage, hesitating before walking past the curtain. Sidney stood right beside me, not talking, her expression filled with worry, fear. She'd been a real warrior following me around, never complaining, and I knew she'd follow me through this curtain no matter how nasty things could get on the other side. I *really don't deserve her friendship*, I thought. Seriously, I didn't. I'm nothing but a huge jerk, always rude to people, treating them like crap. Yes, usually they deserve it, but not Sidney.

She couldn't follow me. I had to keep her out of whatever happened with Clinton. The problem would be trying to talk her out of it. I knew she'd take a lot of convincing to stay behind.

"Hey, Sid, I think you should stay here," I said. "I don't know what we're going find on the other side of that curtain and I just think—"

"Okay!" she interrupted. "I'll stay!"

I grinned. "You okay with that?"

"I've got your back," she said, patting me on the arm.

"Okay. Stay right here. I'll be right back."

She nodded and patted my arm again. I left her there, right at the foot of the stage. Thomas looked on from a few feet away. I didn't fear Thomas hurting her. Sidney posed no threat to him. She would be nothing more than a bug to him, insignificant, unimportant.

I entered a dark room, an old stage once used for community theater and local talent shows and the selling of war bonds or whatever. There were no props or sets or dusty old costumes or anything like that. There was no evidence the area had ever been used for an innocent purpose. The room now reeked of rot and decay and death. I squinted my eyes against the gloom. I stepped further onto the stage.

The pulsating glow of hospital monitors lured me into what seemed to be the center of the stage. Soft repetitive beeps confirmed that someone was still alive. Through the milky sheen of fake light I could see a dozen or so empty chairs, recliners like I observed at the office building—at the game store—at the factory. Headsets rested on empty chairs, leftovers from prior games, the game players now gone . . . or dead. Only four chairs had occupants.

Dylan Thomas lay on one of the chairs. I knew Dylan. I had a math class with him once. Of all the idiots I encountered in high school, Dylan was one of the least moronic. He actually had a reasonable grasp of trigonometry. He had been decent to me too. He was a big-time athlete, like Clinton, but he never treated me like a loser for being so smart. I liked Dylan.

Dylan's chair had been arranged back-to-back with one of the other occupants of the room. Dylan wore a headset: he played the game. A cord snaked out of Dylan's headset to connect right into the skull of a bloodsucking monster behind him. The two were tethered together, the teenager and the Lazarine. It was feeding time. My friend was the prey.

I stepped close, ready to rip the headset off Dylan's skull. Dylan did not move. I placed my hand on his chest. It felt hollow, empty, fragile. He looked like an empty shell. His chest did not move. I felt no breathing. I fumbled about his neck, testing for a pulse. I felt nothing.

The creature on the other end of the tether moved. I had barely noticed him, my attention centered on Dylan. The man stirred and looked up at me. He rubbed at his arms, probing the bones and muscles. He seemed a bit dazed, his movements shaky, uncertain. He was coming awake, I realized. He was coming back from the dead.

The dude was huge. I don't know how the chair could hold him. He must have been three hundred pounds, and I'm not talking three hundred pounds of jelly. It was all muscle. He wore no shirt, revealing chiseled, bulging muscles, which was pretty impressive given the guy had likely been dead a while. This guy was so ripped even death couldn't make him flabby.

He looked like a Chinese sumo wrestler, only without the blubber rolls. He was clearly of Asian descent: black hair, black goatee. Weird tattoos marked his body in inky, arcane symbols.

The guy rubbed a naked knife blade across his six-pack belly as he stared at me. A thin line of blood followed the knife's edge. Maybe it helped him wake up, maybe he needed to sharpen the blade. His rock-hard abs would do it. I gulped and backed away from the man, away from my poor friend Dylan. The big Asian moved and stretched; Dylan did not. I gritted my teeth and kept moving.

I passed another twosome, a recovering Lazarine and his teenager victim. I didn't know the kid. He looked younger than me, maybe twelve or thirteen, probably from the junior high. The kid looked frail and thin, like Dylan, only he seemed alive. I could see his chest moving. His companion Lazarine sat upright on his chair behind the teenager. Like with Dylan and the Asian guy, a tube came out of the kid's headset to connect directly into the skull of the receiver.

The "receiver" sat on the chair as nonchalantly and

casually as a guy sitting in a dentist waiting room. He had his legs crossed and a book propped on his lap. I couldn't believe it. The guy sat there reading a book while sucking out the life from another human being! I could just make out the title of the book. Something in another language. Maybe German. I stared at this smallish man—middle aged, maybe around forty or fifty, small little mustache, brownish hair—and felt a growing horror. I'd seen pictures of this monster in grade school. Every history book has pictures of this butcher. He had been one of the most despicable tyrants in history. He had started a world war, killed millions.

Now he sat reading a book, brought back from the dead.

He bounced his leg lightly as he read, no cares in the world. He glanced up as I approached, dark eyes on me. He gave me a cursory glance, apparently found nothing interesting or threatening in me, and went back to his book.

I should have strangled him. I really should have. There is not one moral person on this planet that could have blamed me for killing him. But I didn't. I couldn't. I didn't have time. I had to find Clinton.

I found a third pod in the corner of the room, another two people sitting back to back, wires connecting them: cord from the headset of the player running right into the skull of the receiver. The Lazarine twitched and shook, hands trembling. His eyes were closed, his breathing labored. I watched him for a moment, sickened and yet fascinated at what I saw. It could have been a trick of the light, yet it seemed that even while I watched I could detect a change of coloration in the man's skin. In the few brief moments his pale skin imbued with a healthy pink color. Life appeared to be pouring into the man—life was pouring out of the game player.

I found my brother on the other side. I gasped when I saw him. Clinton Chance, one-time middle linebacker for Merewether's football team, recruited by USC and Nebraska and Ohio State to play college ball, All-State in football, basketball, and track, big, hulking, powerful All-American boy, now lay emaciated and gaunt and at least fifty pounds lighter. His once plump, meaty face had withered into a sagging mask, protruding cheekbones like ancient half-excavated dinosaur bones sticking out of the ground. I saw no movement, no sign of life. His skin had turned pasty, chalky white. His arms hung limp and lifeless to the ground.

I put my hands on his face. Cold. Clammy.

My fingers needled his neck, frantic for a pulse.

Nothing. Still. Lifeless.

Then, faintly, the slightest tap against my index finger.

Something. Motion. Life.

"Clinton!" I cried, voice ragged. "Clinton!"

No response. No movement. But another light heartbeat nudged against my finger.

I shook him hard, hands on his shoulders. His bones seemed to creak, complain. His skin felt like parchment beneath my fingers. My hands came off his shoulders wet, sticky. Blood seeped through his shirt where my hands had been, skin bruised and oozing from my touch.

I gagged, stomach pitching. I staggered back. I vomited on the floor, heaving and rocking back and forth as I spit and coughed. I knelt on the floor, dry heaving again and again as the image of my brother's bleeding shoulders blazed in my consciousness. After the retching stopped, I gazed at my hands, stained red with blood, and puked again.

I huddled on the floor on hands and knees, staring at the ground. Anger grew in me, a boiling volcano of rage. I beat the cracked wood boards with my fists, furious at my brother.

Clinton! You idiot! How could you do this to me?

I pounded the floor until my hands throbbed. Tears mixed with vomit on the floor.

My brother's going to die, I thought. *I can't stop it. He's leaving me. Leaving me! Just like Mom.*

Nothing lasts forever. Relationships don't last. Nothing lasts. Nothing endures.

Except for Geoffrey Chaucer and his monsters.

I scrambled to my feet.

No! I could still save Clinton! I could stop Chaucer!

I returned to Clinton's side, leaning over him. He wore a headset, a Lazarus Game headset that poured the infectious game inside my brother's mind. I wrapped my fingers around the headset, ready to rip it off his skull.

A guttural roar rent the silence, causing me to jump back in surprise. Spinning, I saw the Asian on his feet, cord on the floor, ripped from his skull. He pointed at me and shouted. He brandished the long blade in the air. I took a step backward, heart pounding. He screamed again and waved the knife at me.

"You don't want to mess with him!" called a thin, raspy voice.

Thomas Edison appeared out of the dark gloom, his face shining in the dark, his seemingly disembodied head hovering in the air near the big Asian's shoulder. He continued moving forward until he stood at the side of the Asian Lazarine. The Asian glanced at him and then turned back to me, knife slashing the air, threatening me.

"I said, you don't want to mess with him," Thomas repeated. "He is Chaucer's personal bodyguard. You may have heard of him? He once went by the name Attila."

"I don't want to mess with him," I said, my voice surprisingly clear and strong. "I just want to save my brother."

"You sure he wants to be saved? He had plenty of chances to stop playing. It was his choice to proceed. Just like all the other players. It's always their choice. We don't force them."

"You tricked him! You lied to him!"

Thomas smiled. "No. We did not. It's his choice. He doesn't want to be in the real world."

"I'm bringing him back," I said. My fingers touched the headset.

The Asian screamed at me. I couldn't help myself. I took a step back, hands free from the headset. Clinching my teeth, steeling my resolve, I regained those lost steps, moving back to the table. The Asian shouted something. I ignored him.

"He said don't touch the headset!" Thomas said.

"I'm going to save him."

Thomas laughed. "You'll be dead first."

I reached for the headset. The Asian Lazarine started moving. He took one step, two steps. The knife came up.

He pulled the knife back to throw it. I winced and ripped at the headset. It came free. I tore it off Clinton's head. I saw a blur of motion from the corner of my eye.

The knife!

The headset rattled to the floor. I winced and closed my eyes, too slow to duck, not enough time to evade. He had me.

I heard a grunt and a startled, choking cry. I opened my eyes and turned to look at Attila.

The big man stumbled. His eyes widened in shock, in stunned disbelief. His mouth moved, mandibles closing and opening, opening and closing, but without sound. His jaw opened again. Blood flowed out of his mouth like water from a faucet.

What?

He took one more step, eyes blinking, and fell to the floor. He hit the ground in a tremendous concussion. Something glittered in the pale mechanical light. Half of a ninja throwing star protruded from the back of the big Asian's skull.

Thomas shrieked in fury. He emitted a roar of blood-curdling anger. I have to say, in the midst of all the tension, that this sort of surprised me. The Thomas Edison I knew from dusty old schoolbooks portrayed a kindly old man going around happily inventing all sorts of useful stuff, not a madman who would shriek and scream and try to kill people. Guess that just goes to show how much we really know about our history, right?

He whipped his gun from inside the folds of his black cloak. The gun started to come up. It didn't make it far.

Logan Pierce emerged from the shadows. The axe thingy flashed and both of Thomas's hands fell to the stage, severed at the wrists. Thomas screamed and stumbled. Pierce stepped toward him.

"Logan!" Thomas cried, blood spurting from oozing stumps on the end of his forearms. "Logan, don't do this!"

The axe thingy came up.

"I am Thomas Edison!" the man roared. "You can't just kill me!"

"Yes, Thomas, I certainly can."

"But I'm a genius! The world needs me!"

"Genius is a bit overrated these days. We'll get by just fine without you."

The axe thingy swept up and Thomas's head flew from his neck. The body tipped, wavered, and fell to the wooden floor. Logan Pierce stepped over it on his way to greet me.

I yelled at Pierce, trying to stop him. I pointed at the German who still sat on his chair, book still on his knee. The German gazed at me quizzically.

"Logan! Kill that man! Don't let him go!"

The German dictator started to stand. He never made it to his feet. His head rolled across the floor like a bowling ball. Logan Pierce hadn't even slowed down as he swept the blade through the man's neck. Der Führer would not live to torment the world a second time.

A final Lazarine remained, the one connected to my brother. Pierce didn't even slow down. He swept the blade through the chest of the Lazarine, chopping the man in half. Pierce kicked both halves of the man off the chair, bloody stumps tumbling to the floor. My brother was free from the Lazarine. But he did not move.

Four Lazarine dead. My brother alive but unconscious. I heaved a sigh of relief. My knees buckled. I darn near fell to the floor.

I leaned against my brother's chair, my strength almost spent. Pierce reached me before I could faint. He put a hand on my arm to steady me.

"You . . . you . . . killed Thomas Edison!" I said between sucking mouthfuls of air. "The man who invented the incandescent light bulb!"

He shrugged.

"Yeah, well, it's all LED lights now anyways. Who was the little guy?"

"Adolf Hitler."

"You're kidding!" Pierce exclaimed. He laughed. "Really?"

"Yep. You've earned your brownie points for the day."

"Wow. That *does* make me feel better. What about you? You okay?"

"I'm fine. A bit grossed out, but fine. Thanks, by the way. I was going to be Chinese stir fry."

Pierce smiled. "No problem. We won't have any other interruptions, either."

I raised my eyebrows. "All the other Lazarine? The ones out in the hall? You didn't . . ."

He shrugged again. "They won't be bothering us. Ever. Come, your brother needs you. There's still time, but you have to hurry."

I gazed at my brother in surprise. I don't know what I had been expecting. That he would be sitting up? Eyes open? Ready to go play a pickup game of football? I had removed the headset, but nothing seemed to be different. The Lazarine he'd been feeding was dead, but nothing seemed to change for Clinton. His eyes remained closed, breathing shallow.

"When's he going to wake up?" I asked.

"He isn't."

"Isn't? What do you mean, isn't?"

"Not like that. Not by just taking off the headset. He's been playing too long. You can't wake him up like that now."

Fear and dread returned to me in a nauseous wave.

"What do you mean? What are you saying?"

Pierce gripped my shoulder with his massive hand. His eyes looked worried. He said, "He's too far into the game now, Carter. The headset doesn't matter now. The game is inside him. Geoffrey Chaucer has invaded your brother's mind. There's only one way to get him out now."

He took a deep breath.

"You've got to go in after him."

"Go in?"

"Inside the game. Carter, you have to play the game to save him."

He picked up the headset. He handed it to me.

I didn't hesitate. I took the chair beside my brother. I put on the headset.

I entered the Lazarus Game.

CHAPTER TWENTY

A loudspeaker crackled and squawked as if the announcer had a microphone jammed down his throat. The voice was mechanical and magnified, booming out over the frenzied crowd. I stood in a pack of jumping, jigging, gyrating teenagers and twenty-somethings. The announcer berated the crowd.

"Deee—fense!"

Clap. Clap.

"Deee-FENSE!"

Clap. Clap.

A football game. No big surprise here. Of course Clinton's fantasy would be a football game. That was his dream. That had always been his dream.

The guy to my left reeked of beer and warm urine. He stood with his back to the field, yelling up into the crowd, something about "gib uz a hommmrunnnn!" The guy was so slammed he didn't even know what game was playing. The lady to my right stared at me uneasily, probably wondering where I'd come from. I smiled at her encouragingly. She scooted several inches away from me.

All at once the crowd started booing the refs. Some

life-altering, cataclysmic, end-of-the-world bad call, I guess, maybe resulting in a penalty or something. I knew this from the profanity-laced tirade raining down from the fans around me. I ignored the crowd and looked for Clinton.

He'd be on the football field, of course. Starting quarterback. Not in real life. He'd played middle linebacker—receiver and tight end once or twice. In his fantasy? Definitely quarterback.

I studied the players standing in a loose huddle while the refs figured out where to place the ball. Pretty much rocket science the way the zebras debated and pointed. Finally they must have figured it out, because the ball got placed and the two teams lined up.

The center hiked the ball and the quarterback took three steps back. He surveyed the field, checked off his first receiver, then his second, then threw to the tight end coming across the middle. Poor throw, right at his knees. The quarterback twisted when he threw it, showing off the name sprawled across his back.

Anderson.

I knew before seeing the name this was not my brother. My brother wouldn't miss an easy pass in his own football fantasy. And Clinton would never play for the New York Giants, the team now on offense. Clinton was a Dallas Cowboys fanatic.

Dallas played defense, meaning Clinton would be off the field. I studied the Cowboys standing about on the opposite sideline, shuffling around, sitting, spitting, drinking Gatorade, studying Xs and Os with coaches, riding stationary bikes, stretching, scratching, and so on. I couldn't find Clinton. I waited for the offense to take the field.

I didn't have to wait long. Anderson threw an

interception, tipped ball, batted by the safety right to the cornerback. The ball advanced fifteen yards before a Giant could take out the legs of the Cowboys corner. After a brief on-field celebration—and much enthusiastic pandemonium in the stands—the Dallas defense retreated and the offense trotted on the field.

The offense went into huddle, stood around for a few seconds, and broke the circle after some hand-clapping and butt-slapping. They lined up and hunched over, quarterback over center. I frowned. The ball hiked, quarterback falling back. No. All wrong. Not Clinton. Some guy I'd never heard of. Not Roger Staubach. Not Troy Aikman. Not even Tony Romo. Definitely not my brother. The guy went back to throw and missed an open receiver by five yards. Clearly not my brother.

Where was he? I scanned both sidelines, searching, my eyes darting over faces and reading names on jerseys. No sign of him. Where could he be? This was his fantasy, right? Then why wasn't he out on the field? I couldn't believe Clinton's fantasy was being a bench warmer or water boy.

A woman screamed, somewhere behind me in the stand. I ignored it. Probably beer spilled down her shirt. Substitutes ran in and players came out. I kept my eyes on the field, certain I'd find Clinton eventually. Three guys in, three guys out. No Clinton.

Another scream, a different woman, different pitch and tone, just as frantic. Then I heard yelling and gasps and cries. Chaos erupted in the stands behind me. I heard someone yell the word *gun*. I turned.

Gunshots fired. Once. Twice. Three times. More screaming and more scrambling from the crowd. People climbed over each other in a panic, desperate to get out.

Two masked gunmen stood in the midst of the crowd. One of the gunmen fired his gun, a short blunt rifle, a submachine gun. The other guy held a small black box in his hand, small wires, red trigger. Bomb! A terrorist attack!

I started moving up the stands just as hundreds of people scrambled down. I was picked up by the pressing mob and carried back down the stand like a paper boat caught on an opposing tide. I fought my way free of the grasping hands, weaving and snaking my way around the fleeing fans. I made three rows in about five seconds.

The gun fired again, and I heard more screaming. A man fell in a sprawling heap a few feet away from me, bullet hole through his forehead. I heard someone shouting. I looked up. The trigger man pulled back the flap of his jacket, revealing a girdle of explosives. Suicide bomber. He put his finger on the trigger.

I would not make it in time. I could not move fast enough.

A huge shape came out of the crowd, hurtling sideways across the row of seats. A crazy fan dove at the terrorist, trying to tackle him to the ground. The fan drove his shoulder into the right arm of the terrorist. The trigger box went flying through the air, clattering harmlessly on the cement ground two rows away. The terrorist stumbled at the impact, staggered backward, and fell.

The fan rolled on top of the terrorist, big hammer-like fists pummeling the bad man's face and head. Three heavy blows rained down in rapid succession, bam, bam, snap. I heard bones breaking.

The terrorist's partner turned his machine gun at the fan. Too slow. The big man leaped up and slapped the gun away before the terrorist could squeeze the trigger. It only took

STEPHEN J. VALENTINE

one blow to snap the terrorist's head back. I heard another crack and the terrorist fell to the ground, neck broken.

The remaining crowd started cheering. The fan stood huffing and puffing, sweat all over him, hands still shaking from adrenaline. The crowd's cheering turned into a rolling roar, pure adulation and love for this man, this savior. The fan wiped sweat from his brow, seemed to notice the crowd for the first time, and gave a timid wave.

My brother. Clinton.

I laughed. I never would have guessed it. This was my brother's secret fantasy? A one man counter-terrorist unit? Jason Bourne, James Bond, and Jack Bauer rolled into one? Who knew?

I started toward him, jumping up a row. I froze before I made the next step.

Four rows above stood my brother. Two unconscious terrorists lay beside him. The row to the left of Clinton had emptied completely, a few spilled buckets of popcorn and a half-eaten hot dog the only thing remaining on the row. To the right, however, came another figure, sliding sideways down the narrow aisle. I sucked a deep breath at the sight of the boy.

It was me.

My identical twin reached my brother and started hugging him. The two exchanged hearty backslaps. They stood together laughing and talking, pointing, gesturing, nodding, grinning, chattering excitedly. My twin looked like me in every conceivable detail. Well, almost. The real me was certainly slimmer and taller than this imposter, and I hoped better looking. Other than that, he looked just like me.

Another Carter Chance? How could this be?

The crowd continued to cheer as Clinton and Imposter-Me congratulated each other on the heroic deed. Someone in the crowd started to yell, "Clinton, Clinton!" and soon the rest of the crowd took up the chant. My imposter stood next to Clinton and beamed like a proud papa.

What was going on?

I smelled the sweet mixture of beer and urine again as I stood gazing on my brother and myself. The big drunk stood beside me, cheering my brother. He held a freshly refilled cup of Budweiser or whatever. My brother waved to the crowd, and the drunkard lifted his hands to celebrate. Beer plastered me.

I acted on reflex, raising my arm, closing my eyes. Beer splattered my face. My eyes stung through closed eyelids. I dabbed the liquid with my shirt sleeve. I carefully opened my eyes.

I stood inside a dimly lit room. Candles flickered, the wax melted down to blunt stubs. The smell of smoke hung in the air. Dirty dishes cluttered a table beside me, stacks of pizza crust in the center of the table. Chairs had been pushed back and dishes forgotten as though the inhabitants had suddenly fled. There were no people in the room.

I knew the place. It was all too familiar. My house. My kitchen. But wrong. Power had been cut. Candles. Panic and fear, hasty departure. What had happened here?

Low talking came from somewhere beyond my location, hushed voices. My heart leapt at the sound. Someone still in the house! I took a step forward, trying to tune my hearing. I could just hear a woman's voice. She sounded worried, stressed. I moved faster.

"You're going to kill me, aren't you?" the woman asked. I knew that voice. My mother! "You're going to destroy me."

"That's right," answered a male voice. "But first I'm going to pick you apart piece by piece. You'll beg me to stop before I'm through. You'll try to surrender, but I won't let you. I'm going to wipe you off the face of the earth."

I broke into a run.

I burst down the hall, feet loud on the floor. I skidded to a stop at the corner, just outside our family room. Candlelight cast disjointed, frightening shadows on the opposite wall. I could see three figures leaning over a table. I could hear my mother groaning softly. Did they have her on that table? Were they torturing her?

I peeked around the corner, terrified at what I would find, prepared for just about anything.

Nope. I wasn't prepared for what I saw. I nearly burst out laughing.

I saw Clinton, my mother, and another cloned imposter of myself sitting around a card table in our family room. The three of us bent low over the table. My brother was shaking his closed fist, up and down, rapidly, rhythmically. He flipped his wrist, tossing a pair of dice to the table. Clinton cheered while my mother groaned.

"That's two sixes!" he cried, triumph in his voice. "Alberta is mine! I've swept your armies off North America. Do you surrender yet, or must I clean you all the way off the map?"

"Surrender, Mom!" called my phony self. He (me) sat hunched over the table, face in my hands as though bored to death. "Please, put us out of our misery!"

"Then we'll play again!" Clinton said. "So I can whip your sorry butts one more time."

"No, no more Risk," said Imposter-Me. "You're killing

us at Risk. Why not a nice game of Monopoly? That only takes three or four hours. Anything but another game of Risk."

"Just because you can't beat me, you want to quit?" Clinton asked. My Imposter-Me grunted but didn't say anything.

I rolled my eyes. Now I knew for sure I was inside a fantasy. I never lost at Risk. Particularly not to Clinton. He's never beat me at any game, not Risk, not Stratego, not Tiddly-Winks.

My mother laughed. "I surrender! I surrender! And if you won't make me play another game, I'll make you guys brownies. You can beat each other up in chess."

As if, I thought. No way Clinton—even Fantasy Clinton—is beating me in chess.

"No electricity, remember?" Clinton said. "Power's out. Good thing we had that leftover pizza. Guess we have no choice but to play again."

My mother made a big show out of mock-sighing. She said: "Well, okay, if we have to. We could wait for your father to get home. He should be here any minute. You know how he loves to play."

I snorted so hard I about swallowed my sinuses. My dad? Play Risk? Are you kidding me? He never played *anything* with *anyone*! He sure didn't play with me and Clinton! Not one time in all my long years of living had my dad put his fat butt on a chair and played a game with us. The only game I could even recall was the old famous "you get to go out and pick the stick I'm going to whip you with for getting your muddy shoes on my carpet." That was his idea of a game, the big moron.

And then there's my mom. What exactly was *she* doing

here? What was she doing in the house, playing games, eating pizza, acting like nothing had happened? She LEFT us! She walked out and left us with Dad, abandoned, forgotten.

But here she was, back at the house like nothing happened. What kind of crappy fantasy is this?

I heard the game being restarted. Little plastic army pieces being cleared and counted. Cards shuffled. Armies reassembled. So much for Monopoly. So much for me lurking in this hallway too. There was no way I'd stand around for the next three hours while they played a board game.

Wait a minute. Something was still wrong. I backed up and padded down the hallway, going into the kitchen. There had to be something more to this fantasy. There had to be something dramatic about to happen. Terrorists would burst through the windows. A gang of gun-wielding criminals would break down the door and kidnap my mom. Something crazy would happen, requiring my brother to save our meager lives. He would be the hero again, just like he'd been at the football game. He would save the day. He would save us all.

Because that was his fantasy, right? To be the big hero? That's what I saw at the game. That had to be his fantasy!

Nothing happened. I crept around the kitchen for the next hour, just waiting for a meteorite to blow through the ceiling or an earthquake to crack open the floor or monsters to crawl out the chimney. Something life-threatening and dangerous and terrible would happen, I just knew it. When it did, Clinton would save us. It made perfect sense.

Only, nothing happened. The only remotely bad thing that happened was that Clinton continued to wipe my armies from the board. I lost Ukraine and Ural in the first round. Before I knew it he controlled all of Europe, getting his little army bonus for controlling not one but TWO continents! I listened to the game with mounting disgust. How could I lose to my brother?

An hour passed. Then two. I sat at the table and chewed on discarded pizza crusts. I devised strategies for attacking Clinton's armies in a daring naval battle. I found new candles and relit them. I calculated the odds of my remaining five armies defeating his vastly superior force. How many rolls of fives and sixes would I need to ensure victory? I did the math. I figured the statistics based on his available rolls versus mine. Not good. There was no chance I could beat him.

I nearly fell asleep. Then I got angry.

What kind of fantasy is this? What sort of lame boring Lazarus Game is Clinton playing? I expected to come in here and have to fight to get Clinton back. I didn't expect to come in here and die of boredom.

I closed my eyes. I really could use a nap. Maybe if I just dozed off for a bit something exciting would happen. Maybe the terrorists were just late. Freeway closure or bad traffic or something like that. I just needed to rest my eyes before the really exciting stuff happened.

"Great catch, Carter!"

My eyes opened. An icy breeze tussled my hair. I shivered against a sudden cold. The grass felt stiff and crunchy at my feet. I reached for my coat to pull it closer. I wore no coat. I stood outside in the freezing cold with no coat. Where am I?

"Hit me while I run!" cried my brother's voice. "Yeah! That's it! Great pass!"

I stood shivering at the side of our old rusty metal shed.

I huddled on the east side of the shed, over against our neighbor's fence. I could hear voices on the other side of the shed.

"Ten-hut! Ten-hut! HIKE!"

That was my voice. Or, rather, my impostor's voice. I heard myself shout something, then I said: "Dude, you dropped it! I hit you right on the numbers! Freaking Payton Manning right here! Who's the man, Clinton? Who is DA MAN?"

"Ball's as hard as cement out here," Clinton returned, laughing. "'Bout broke my fingers. You sure you don't want to go in?"

"Naw," my clone said. "Just a bit longer. We need to stay out here until I can properly school you on catching the ball!"

I peeked around the corner of the shed. Clinton and Carter-Clone ran about our backyard. The back porch light poured weak yellow light into the yard. Stars gleamed overhead. My clone passed the ball to Clinton. He caught it, made a big show out of dodging and darting around imaginary defenders, then spiked the ball to the ground.

"Touchdown!" he proclaimed.

My clone clapped his hands.

Another fantasy, I realized. Another ridiculous fantasy. Me and Clinton outside playing catch. I laughed at the thought of it. Me and Clinton outside playing catch? Seriously?

I shook my head. I scratched my chin. I furrowed my brow. I thought and thought. What was going on here? What kind of fantasy is this? Why would Clinton let himself die out in the real world to stay inside this stupid fantasy?

Saving the football crowd from a terrorist? That I could understand. That was cool. Board games? Playing catch? That I couldn't get.

I thought harder, really getting my genius brain working. I realized that even the football game didn't make sense. Why wasn't Clinton out there playing? Why wasn't he the quarterback of the Cowboys? Even the Giants, for that matter, perish the thought. Why up in the stands? Why a hero? Why not a Superbowl-winning quarterback?

What's the missing link here? What is the common element between the fantasies? What am I missing?

I had been with him at the game. He knocked out those terrorists, but I had been with him. Did he want to show off to me? The Risk game! He'd beaten me twice! That never happened in the real world. Was this some sort of competition against me? Trying to show me up?

The game of catch continued. I watched myself catching the football, all unnaturally acrobatic and athletic. Now that made no sense. Clinton wasn't showing me up here. Inside this fantasy, I was a good athlete. I was just as good as Clinton. I was able to stand out here in the darkness and play catch just like one of his buddies. Just like one of his friends.

Me and Clinton. Out playing catch.

Me and Clinton. Playing a board game.

Me and Clinton. At a Cowboys game.

Oh, great. That's it. That's the fantasy.

I swore. I really let out a nasty. I got it. I saw it, and I didn't like it. In fact, it made me feel like total crap.

You've got to be kidding me. That's the fantasy!

That's when the pain hit me. Pain. Guilt. Regret.

Me and Clinton, at a football game.

Me and Clinton and Mom, hanging out at home, having a good old time.

Me and Clinton, out playing ball, trash-talking and joking, best buds.

Except that had never happened!

Buddies? No. Best friends? No.

My throat constricted. My head started aching. Tears started.

I slumped against the side of the shed. My head suddenly weighed a thousand pounds. My chest felt pierced and bleeding, like one of those old jousting javelins had been stuck through my heart. My hands came to my face. I felt wetness.

Why did he want this? Of all the stupid things? Why this?

Why did he have to want this?! Clinton!

I cried. I stood there in the stinking freezing darkness and cried like a baby. Tears like ice on my face. My chest heaved and buckled. My throat constricted, my vision swam. I sobbed. I sobbed like I hadn't sobbed since Mom walked out. I sobbed until I cried every tear that had ever existed in the world. Then I cried some more.

Clinton! Why this? Why are you doing this to me? Why do you have to make me feel so totally rotten! So totally guilty?

I was guilty. I was guilty as charged. Throw me in prison, lock the door, throw away the key. The fantasy should be the truth. My world was upside down. Clinton turned it upside down.

I came inside this fantasy wanting to confirm that Clinton was the shallow, narrow, common-man loser that I *needed* him to be. I came inside fearing nothing, because

I knew that Clinton wanted only to be a big football star, the game-winning jock, the guy all the girls and popular guys want to be around. Clinton the big stud was no threat to me. Clinton the popular winner meant he could continue on in his own life without needing anything at all from me. I could continue to be the huge jerk that I always pretended to be, and he could go on perfectly happy without me.

It would have been so easy this way, because then I felt no guilt at all. Clinton didn't need me. Clinton didn't care about me. He had his fame. He had his success. He had all the good fortune that superior athletic genetics bestowed on him.

Clinton! Why do you want this? Why do you have to make me feel so guilty?

I am guilty. Terribly, truthfully, totally guilty. I had made a practice out of treating Clinton like crap. I did it out of my own stupid insecurity. My own stupid sense of guilt when Mom left us. My own need to push him down to build myself up. And it didn't matter to me that I did it. I could justify it all. I could treat him like dirt because Clinton wouldn't care. He wouldn't feel it. He was just a big dumb athlete. He felt nothing at all. Nothing for Mom. Nothing for me.

The tears came harder until I thought I'd drown. My heart lurched and twisted and rent inside my chest.

Clinton! Why do you have to care?!

He did care. He really did care. There was no doubt now, no way around it, no way for my supposedly genius mind to justify it. He cared.

He loved me.

The proof was indisputable. He could have had anything

inside this game, anything at all. It was his fantasy, his imaginary paradise. And what did he want? What did he dream of?

You've got to be kidding me. That big idiot. He just wanted to spend time with me.

With me! With *me*? I'm the biggest jerk in the world, and he wants to spend time with me?

He really is an idiot.

I stepped out from beside the shed. I walked across the frozen ground to confront him.

Clinton saw me coming. His eyes widened. He looked at me—the real me—and then at my cloned imposter. His eyes darted back and forth, back and forth. The fake Carter threw the ball at him. It hit Clinton in the chest. He never saw it coming. He couldn't take his eyes off the two of me.

"Clinton!" I shouted. "It's me! Carter!"

He opened his mouth. His lips moved but nothing came out. He pointed at me, then at the other me, then back to me again.

"It's really me," I said. "That other guy is fake."

"Huh?" he stammered. He may have a big heart, but that didn't mean he magically had a big vocabulary.

"It's really me, Clinton. I'm inside the game with you. You remember the game? The Lazarus Game? You're play-ing the game right now. None of this is real. That Carter over there, he isn't real, either."

Clinton's eyes narrowed. He shook his head.

"You're lying. You're lying! That's my brother! Not you! The other one!"

I laughed. It sounded strange coming out of my swollen, strangled throat.

"Are you an idiot? Think about it! When have I ever been

able to catch a pass? Look at that guy! He's an imposter! He can catch the football!"

Clinton gazed back at the fake me. He seemed to consider it. My imposter just stood there, not saying anything.

"Try it!" I said. "Test it out!"

Clinton picked up the ball. He threw it at my clone. Imposter-Me caught the ball with no problem.

"See! You big moron! Do you see it? That's not me!"

Clinton gazed at me, confusion and pain on his face. He kept shaking his head.

I went on. "Clinton, you need to come out of the game. You've got to decide to quit playing! You've got to stop right now!"

"He doesn't want to stop," the imposter said. My clone-self tossed the ball back to Clinton. Clinton caught it without even looking.

Clinton threw the ball back to my fake self. When he caught it his face changed. The voice changed. My clone's body convulsed and twitched and shimmered and became someone else.

Geoffrey Chaucer caught the pass. Geoffrey Chaucer took over my clone's body. He smiled at Clinton and threw it back.

"Clinton wants to stay here, don't you, Clinton?" Chaucer asked. "Because this is where you are happy. This is where you belong."

Clinton looked at me. He looked at Chaucer. The football fell forgotten at his feet. Clinton frowned. I could see confusion in his eyes, uncertainty, pain.

"You don't belong in here," I said. "This is all a lie. Clinton! Look at me! This isn't really where you are. You aren't in our backyard. You weren't really inside our kitchen playing

Risk with me and Mom. You weren't really at a Cowboys game. You weren't really doing any of those things. This is a game!"

"Where am I, Carter?" Clinton asked. "Where am I, really?"

"In the Lazarus Game Shop. Don't you remember? You went there yesterday. You went to test out a game. You are still inside that game. Right now you're strapped to a chair with a tube coming out of your body. Chaucer and his monsters are sucking the life out of you! They're killing you! This game is killing you!"

Clinton's face screwed up, eyebrows up, mouth twisted. He looked dazed, confused.

"I feel fine, Carter. Perfectly fine. I like it here."

"It's fake! It's not real!"

He shrugged. "I'm happy here."

"Of course you're happy!" Chaucer said. He started walking toward Clinton. I ran across the lawn, standing in front of Clinton, putting my body between my brother and Chaucer. The big man stopped walking. He smiled.

"Clinton, you're happy here because finally all of your dreams are coming true. This is the world you've always wanted, my friend, right here. Why would you want to go anywhere else?"

"Is it fake?" Clinton asked. He looked at Chaucer when he said it.

Chaucer shrugged.

"Does it matter? You said you wanted this life. I asked you, didn't I? I asked you if you wanted to sacrifice your real life in order to stay inside this world. You said yes, didn't you? Every time I asked, you said yes. Isn't that correct?"

Clinton nodded. I felt my heart sinking. I felt the

pressure inside my head mounting, a piercing pain all through my forehead.

Clinton had said yes. He had told Chaucer he wanted to sacrifice the real world for this. Oh, Clinton! Had I really made your life that terrible?

Chaucer continued, "Didn't I deliver exactly what you wanted? You wanted to spend time with your little brother. You wanted to spend time with your mom. You wanted the family life you deserved but never had. And didn't I get that for you? Isn't that what you have here?"

"Yes," Clinton said, his voice a whisper. "I have that here."

"Then why would you go back?" Chaucer asked. "Why would you want to leave this?"

"I don't," Clinton said. "I don't want to leave."

"You do!" I cried, my voice wild, strained. "Clinton, you do!"

"Why?" he asked.

"Why?" Chaucer echoed. "Why would he want to leave?"

"It's not real here!" I said. "It's all fake!"

"It's better than real," Clinton returned. "I don't want real. I want this."

"You're dying!" I shouted. "They're killing you!"

Clinton looked at Chaucer. The big man smiled.

"A small price for true happiness, wouldn't you say?"

I bowed my head. The pressure was overwhelming me. The pain raged unabated inside my head. I was losing my brother. I would not be able to get him back.

"But it's not real!" I tried again, futilely, desperately. "Don't you want it to be real? This is only fantasy. Come back to the real world, Clinton! Come back!"

Clinton turned away from Chaucer. He turned until he faced only me.

"Why? I ask you again. Why would I want to?"

Tears came again. Emotion. Anger. Frustration. Fear. Worry. Pain.

I sank to my knees. I bowed my head. I had nothing left. Nothing to say. No argument left inside me. I had only one thing. One last thing buried deep down inside.

I took a deep breath. I swallowed hard. "I want you to come back. I want you to come back! I don't want you to die! I don't want to go through the real world without you, Clinton. You're my brother!"

Clinton blinked. I could see liquid in his eyes, reflected in the dim porch light.

"You want me to come back?"

I knelt on the ground in front of him, like a beggar, like a sinner, like a brother pleading for his brother's life.

"I want you to come back."

"Why?"

The big jerk! He was going to force me to say it! I gritted my teeth.

"Because, you great, big, moronic freak of nature, I love you!"

Chaucer started roaring. I heard him shouting something, anger in his voice. He burst forward, sprinting toward Clinton, his arms raised in front of him, his hands reaching, stretching, cupped into a noose, ready to clasp around my brother's neck and squeeze him to death.

Clinton laughed. He let Chaucer come at him. He swatted the big man aside like a fly. Like a nothing. Chaucer's body disintegrated when it hit the ground. Not even vapor or dust remained. He was gone.

Clinton grabbed me by both arms and lifted me off the

ground. He crushed my chest in a rather embarrassing hug. He laughed again.

"Now you tell me? After all this, now you get around to saying it?"

I shrugged, as much as I could, anyway, given I was being crushed to death.

"I shouldn't have to say it, you jerk. What boy wants to say anything that mushy, anyway? We're brothers, aren't we?"

He grinned. He wiped his eyes, and he grinned.

"Yeah, Carter, that's right. We're brothers."

And with that, I woke up.

CHAPTER
TWENTY-ONE

My eyelids flittered open. I sucked a deep breath. I blinked several times, eyes stinging and blurred. My vision focused and sharpened. I blinked again and swore.

I stared up into the face of Geoffrey Chaucer.

"Welcome back, Carter," said Chaucer. He smiled at me as he gazed down upon me, a kindly father, a wise old friend. *Father Adam*, I thought. Ancient of years, patriarch of generations, eternal and immortal.

Poet. Author. Scientist. Inventor. Genius.

Monster.

Murderous leech, sucking the life of the innocent. Parasite of humanity.

I struggled upright, heart pounding. The headset tangled and pulled at me, a leash, a harness. I tore it from my forehead and tossed it to the floor. Chaucer made no move to stop me.

I swung my feet off the chair, shoes touching the floor. I stood and turned to face Chaucer, arms raised, hands balled into fists.

I froze. My arms hung suspended in the air, marionette arms, wooden and lifeless, pulled aloft by strings. Chaucer kept smiling. The person at his side did not.

Sidney stood next to Chaucer. Her eyes were wide, fear pooling in the liquid depths. She stood perfectly still, ramrod straight. Her lips had turned pale blue, as though she could not get enough oxygen. She did not call to me. She did not come to me. She only stared, terror brimming for her eyes.

Then I realized that she wasn't staring at me. She gazed on something to the side of me, something low, on the floor. I followed her line of sight, twisting around. I found a dark mass on the floor beside the chair, a long, bulky shape.

Logan Pierce.

I knelt at his side, fingers on his throat, searching for a pulse. His heart beat strong. He did not move, but he lived. Chaucer had immobilized him, not killed him.

"He's not dead," Chaucer said, voice calm and soothing. "Not yet. Logan Pierce cannot die so easily. And he has other purposes to fill this night."

"What did you do to him?"

He shrugged. "Not much. Not yet. You will do the rest of the work, Carter . . . when you take him inside the game with you."

I did not respond. Why would I take Pierce inside the Lazarus Game? I had no plans to ever return again. I wanted nothing more to do with the Lazarus Game. I almost lost Clinton to the game.

Memory returned, and with it a rush of fear. Where was Clinton? Had Chaucer attacked him?

I raced around Chaucer and Sidney, pushing past them. My brother reclined on the chair. He looked better than the last time I saw him. Color had already returned. His eyes were closed as though sleeping. My hands went to his face, his neck, his chest. I felt movement, breathing. His face felt warm. I took a breath and lay my head against his chest.

"It will take him a while to come all the way back," Chaucer said, his voice hovering above me. "He was inside the game for a long time. He's out now, thanks to you. It will take him some time to return all the way to the real world."

I lifted my head from Clinton's chest. I looked up at Chaucer. The big man, bearded, black-clothed, massive in the near darkness, stood motionless. Sidney teetered at his side, leaning up against Chaucer as though she were unable to stand on her own.

"Sidney?" I asked. "You okay?"

Sidney shook her head. A tear trickled slowly down her cheek.

"Carter, I'm scared . . . ," Sidney whispered, but Chaucer laughed as she whimpered.

"She's fine, Carter," Chaucer said. "A bit shaken up is all! She's fine; your brother is fine. Even Pierce is fine. Everything is well. Everything is exactly right."

"Exactly right? You think so? Nothing is right, Chaucer!"

He kept on smiling, as though enjoying a private joke. Or as if immensely pleased with himself. As if some grand plan, some evil plot, was unfolding exactly the way he wanted.

"Oh, there's a few setbacks, don't get me wrong. Losing Isaac Newton, Thomas Edison, and Attila the Hun all in one night, now that is a bit unfortunate. Men like that don't come along all the time, you know. Actually, men like that come along about once every couple hundred years! Pierce did do me a favor on the little German man, though. Most disagreeable fellow. Darwin really wanted him along, but I had my reservations. Thanks to Pierce I don't have to deal with him. But, really, none of that matters, anyway. Not Newton. Not Edison. I have you now, and that's what truly matters."

I stood up, facing him. Fear and loathing and weakness were replaced by anger, by righteous indignation at what this man had done.

"Have me? You really think so? Are you insane? I know what you've been doing! I know the truth about the Lazarus Game! I know what you've been doing to the players!"

Chaucer nodded. The demeanor of satisfaction seemed to be growing. His eyes twinkled merrily.

"Yes! So you do! That is excellent. It was only a matter of time, Carter. You had to know sooner or later. And sooner is much better than later, particularly since we are so close to launching the next phase of the game."

"The next phase?"

"Of course! That's why I hired you! Nothing has changed. Now you know the truth, which, frankly, saves me a whole lot of time. So everything is just right, as I said."

"You don't care that I know?" I asked, stunned at his words. "That I know the truth? About you? About the game?"

"Why would I? How could you ever be my equal partner without full understanding? It was always part of the plan for you to learn everything. It just so happens you got there on your own, and that's no problem. One way or the other we'd get to this point."

He paused a moment, considering. Then he said, "It's actually better this way. You've demonstrated your ability to manipulate the game. You beat your brother's game. You beat your own game, your very own personalized fantasy. That's two for two, Carter. That's never happened before. No one has ever had this level of mastery. So, as I said, your training is progressing quite nicely."

I shook my head, amazed and disgusted.

"You can't really think I'll still work for you? After all this?"

"Yes, Carter, I do believe that. I know you. I know what you really want out of this life. Besides, what have I really done? What is this terrible thing that so appalls you?"

"You really are an idiot! You've murdered thousands! You've sucked the life from innocent victims to extend your own miserable existence. You are a monster. There's no way I would join you."

"Innocent victims? Honestly, Carter, you should know better. I have killed no one. I have offered a choice."

"A choice? Seriously? You think that these players—my own brother!—knew what was going to happen to them? You tricked them! You didn't offer a choice."

"But I do, my friend. I truly do. Each player is offered a choice as they progress through the game. They are asked if they wish to proceed with the fantasy or return to the real world. They choose between their meager, pathetic lives or the richness of a fantasy more realistic and more tangible and more meaningful than anything they've ever experienced inside the so-called *real world*. They could return at any point, but they choose not to."

"Because you tricked them! You trick them with this fantasy!"

"No, Carter. To them the fantasy is real. You have seen it yourself. Could you see the difference? Could you feel the difference? Of course not. It is better than real, because it is the life that these people have always wanted. It is the life they want to experience but never will."

"So you give them what they want, then you kill them. You are a murderer, plain and simple."

"A murderer? I am a savior! I give these people an entire lifetime of happiness! In the hours or days that they are inside the game they are living out hundreds of years or more of experiences. They have a full rich life, Carter! There is no sacrifice on their part, none at all. They want this!"

"Death? Being sucked dry by you and your monsters?"

"Not death—life! Carter, don't be so naïve, so ignorant. How many wretched people would give anything for just a few hours of true happiness? How many people go through their lives never knowing peace, never knowing joy, never knowing what it is like to have dreams fulfilled? I'm talking about the vast percentage of every person on the earth, Carter! Do you see what I'm saying? Every person on this planet seeks after their own happiness, their own self-interest. It is the most basic of human motivations. Is it wrong for me to give it to them?"

I said nothing. I looked at Sidney. She stared wide-eyed at me but did not speak. I turned my focus back to Chaucer.

His words pounded in my head, an insidious poison corrupting me. His logic was perverse and evil, and yet, I had to admit, as sick and twisted as it was, also correct. There must be millions of people who would indeed trade their real existence for a fake one, a fake one that seemed entirely real to them. The world is filled with misery and disappointment, I knew. Even in the United States, the richest country in the history of the world, there is boundless despair.

How many people achieve even of fraction of their dreams? How many people live each day in happiness?

The list of problems is endless. Poverty. Disease. Crime. Abuse. Neglect. Even the seemingly happy people are riddled with problems. Stressful jobs. Debt. A never-ending "to-do list" and no time to ever be at peace. Broken hearts and broken homes. Divorce. Relationships that do not endure.

I knew this myself. I felt that pain. Nothing lasts. Nothing endures.

The Lazarus Game could change that. Inside the game, people could find happiness. What did it matter if it was real or fake? I knew exactly what Chaucer meant, for what is "real" anyway? Our consciousness is nothing but sensory input. Why not change that input from the tangible world to a digital one? The brain would not know the difference.

I tried to shake off the insidious logic.

"You have no right to kill them," I said. "Why not just give them the fantasy? You could do that, you know. You don't have to kill them!"

"It is a necessary thing," Chaucer said, calm and collected, a teacher reasoning with a student. "It is necessary so that the lives of my followers can be extended. If I do not live, if my Lazarine do not live, then the game cannot continue. The fantasy truly does end when I am gone. If I am not here, then the terrible real world intrudes once again."

"What you're saying is that it's up to you to decide who lives and who dies! You use these people to extend your own life! You and your cronies feed on these people in order to keep on living, right? You think it is okay to kill other people so that you can go on living?"

He emitted a short, barking laugh.

"Of course I do! It is entirely logical! Carter, my boy, get over your sentimentality! You've seen it yourself! Most people on this earth are satisfied only to be entertained! They have no ambition, no desire to do something important. Trust me, if you were to give these people all the money they needed to survive, without any need to hold a job, what would they do with their time? They would glut themselves on entertainment. That's it. Nonstop sports and action and games and movies. Thrill seeking. Amusement parks and skydiving. Never-ending amusement. Nothing productive. Nothing that advances the human race!"

I said nothing. I knew he was right. He had just described every person in my town.

"You've seen what we are doing!" He was excited now, energized, his eyes lit up by the fire of his belief. "You've seen the scientific breakthroughs. That's all real, Carter. All of it. We are on the verge of curing disease, solving poverty, eliminating crime. We are discovering sustainable energy, sources of food for our ever-growing world. We are advancing the arts and education. We are preserving our world's culture and history. We are as Prometheus, taking fire from the gods and giving it to mankind! I am doing more good for society than any person in the history of our planet. And you think I'm evil? You call me a monster, but I am doing more *good* than any person who has ever lived! I advance our human race. I bring happiness to those without it. Am I not a saint? Am I not a hero? Am I not a god?"

I closed my eyes. His logic beat against my brain. I felt guilty. I felt dirty. I felt ashamed that even some small part of his reasoning seemed right.

"You are just like me, Carter," Chaucer said. "You have the same genius. You were born to do more. You were born to make a difference. You know it is true. I am giving you this opportunity. Would you throw away your chance to change the world, to live forever, for a few meaningless lives?"

"Why me? You had Edison, Newton. You have a whole stable of geniuses. Why me?"

"I've waited generations for someone like you. You see, I am all by myself. I am alone, without peer, without equal. I control the game. I alone can control it. But to extend the game beyond a few hundred or thousand each year, I need an equal. I need redundancy, Carter. I need another server, another instance of the game. You can be that equal. You can host the game inside your mind, just like me. Your brain is more powerful than all the combined computers in the world. I can teach you how to harness that power to launch and control the Lazarus Game. With your help, we can extend the game to millions of players. Just think of what we could do with all that power!"

The next version of the game. That's what Pierce said. That's what Chaucer himself had said. I would help him launch the next version of the game. Now I knew what that meant. I would not simply *create* a new version of the game, I would *become* the next version of the game.

I looked at Sidney. She looked small and timid next to Chaucer. Would she make the cut? Would she be one of the lucky few worthy enough to live or would she be sacrificed to feed the best and brightest of society, people like me. I gazed on my brother, asleep on the chair. What about him? He was a good man, a kind man. But would he be part of the next evolution in human advancement? Would he be part of new scientific discoveries, new advances in art or economics or government? Or would he be content to fall in love, have a family, hold a job, and go through his life without ever truly making a difference?

My brother would not make the cut, I thought. *He would not be worthy.*

My father wouldn't either. We would not need police in the new world.

I thought of Chambers. I thought of Darek. Would either of them? Darek, perhaps. Chambers? No. For all his charm with the ladies, it would not be enough.

I turned my eyes back to Sidney. So beautiful. So filled with goodness. So filled with potential. Was there anything she couldn't do if she really put her mind to it? Who was I to judge human potential? Who was Chaucer?

Could I play god? Could I decide who was worthy to live and who not? What would that mean anyway? What was worth? Was a new mathematical formula worth more than a mother raising her child?

I thought of my mother. I thought of how much I missed her. What would I give to be a family again? Wasn't that worth more than all of Chaucer's so-called advancements? Maybe not to him, but it was to me. Could I let him decide that his desires were more important than mine?

I rubbed at my eyes. I took a deep breath. I felt the guilt flowing out of me. I felt peace in my heart, right down into my soul, if I had such a thing. I knew deep down inside that I could never be like Chaucer.

I was not a monster.

"Sorry, Chaucer," I said, "but I don't buy it. You have no right to decide who lives and who dies. You have no right to judge which life is worthy and what contribution is sufficient. That is up to each of us. Each living person has that right, and only that person. It's not up to you."

"It is, Carter," Chaucer said. "I have made it my right."

I smiled, cold, hard. "Then I'll make it my mission in life to stop you."

Chaucer said nothing. Silence filled the space between us. He regarded me for several long moments. His eyes seemed to harden. His jaw tightened.

"This is your final answer?" he asked. "You have made up your mind?"

I nodded. He paused. I could see the gears of his mind turning.

Finally, after a long delay, he seemed to come to some decision. I could see anger in his eyes. Disappointment. Resolve.

"No chance of reconsidering?" he added. "You are convinced that you do not need me?"

"I know I don't need you."

He shrugged.

"Perhaps this will change your mind."

He pushed Sidney away from him, and for the first time I could see Chaucer's right hand. I saw at once why Sidney had stood so quiet and still. Chaucer held a handgun, muzzle pointed at Sidney. He had held it against her the entire time. Sidney had had a gun stuck in her rib cage while I conversed with the devil.

"Sidney!" I cried. I started moving.

Too late.

Chaucer pulled the trigger. I saw his finger moving, squeezing, pulling the metal trigger toward him. I could not move fast enough.

The gun roared. Smoke and flame came from the barrel. Sidney fell.

Geoffrey Chaucer shot her in the chest.

I dove to the ground, reaching her within seconds of her

body striking the floor. The bullet had opened a hole in her chest. Blood already pooled through her shirt, a coursing river of redness. Her eyes blinked open and closed once, twice. She gasped and convulsed.

Then her body stiffened. Her eyes stared open. She did not move.

"SIDNEY!" I screamed. "SIDNEY!"

"She's dead," Chaucer said, his voice soft. "Her heart has stopped."

I cradled her in my arms, my chest sticky and wet with her blood. I rocked her back and forth.

"You killed her! You murdered her! SIDNEY!"

"You can still save her, Carter," Chaucer said. "You can bring her back."

I looked up. Through my tears I could see Chaucer smiling down on me.

"You can save her inside the game, Carter. Pierce is still living. You can use his life to save hers. You can bring her back."

I continued to rock her back and forth, like a baby in my arms. I sobbed. I buried my face in her hair, against her cheek. Then, after lifting my head up again, I asked, "How?"

"Come back with me to the office. Create your own game. You can use it to save her."

He stood there staring at me. He stood there waiting for me to answer. I held Sidney in my arms, her body already growing cold. I knew I had no choice.

"I'll do it," I said. "Let's go."

CHAPTER
TWENTY-TWO

Five people flew in Chaucer's helicopter to the Lazarus Corporation skyscraper. Three of the five lay unmoving: two unconscious, one dead. My brother remained asleep, still recovering. Logan Pierce had been carried aboard, also unconscious, brought along as bait and fuel. Sidney Locke's body had been loaded to the chopper. Sidney remained—for now—dead.

I sat behind the copilot's chair. Chaucer sat beside me. He talked all the way from Merewether to Portland. He told me all the secrets of the Lazarus Game, how he created it, how he maintained it, how he used it to suck the life from the players, how he used that captured life force to resurrect the dead, extend life, and make himself and his followers immortal. He taught me how I could create my own Lazarus Game, a parallel game to exist beside his own, with me at the top of the pyramid of my own game just like the head of a multi-level marketing scheme. He told me all this while we flew from my hometown to his office. He told me this while I sat and stared out the chopper window in dull horror.

A pack of black-robed, white-skinned Lazarine met us

on the rooftop helipad. They unloaded the three prostrate bodies. I stumbled along behind Chaucer. I wondered about the pigmentation problems of the Lazarine as I walked. Had they not been getting enough fresh young victims? Did they "pale up" when going too long between feedings? Did their bodies know they really should be dead, and were trying to return them to that natural state? Thomas had alternated between albino and ruddy several times since I'd first met him. *Must be hard work on a body*, I mused, *to live forever*.

Chaucer brought us to one of the myriad game pods situated all over the building. Each floor contained some sort of laboratory and game pod. I got the point now. The pods were basically the lunchroom for the scientists working on that floor. The Lazarine had been developing all sorts of scientific and social breakthroughs, for certain, no doubt about that, but they needed lots of sustenance to keep them going. They needed a little afternoon snack now and again.

I vomited all over the floor when the Lazarine laid Sidney in one pod chair and arranged Logan Pierce right behind her. I mostly dry heaved. I couldn't remember the last time I had eaten anything. I spewed out a bit of liquid puke and heaved and panted and sweated. By the time I could pull myself upright, the Lazarine had a cord stuck into the back of Sidney's head.

Geoffrey Chaucer himself placed the headset over the forehead of his old friend. He got it all snug and situated. I vaguely wondered if Chaucer would give Pierce a good night kiss on the head, like a father tucking in his son. Chaucer looked immensely pleased with himself, as if all his diabolical dreams were at last coming true. I guess they were.

"This is all so twentieth century," Chaucer said as he finished fiddling with Pierce's headset. "All these cords and direct connections and proximity restrictions. Soon all that will be a thing of the past."

He sat me down on a chair right between Sidney and Pierce, as though I were about to teach a Sunday school lesson or read them a story. It was a high-backed office chair, leather, on rollers. Very comfortable. Chaucer spared no expense. Only the best for the immortals and their victims.

I gagged again, bile strong in my throat. My hands were shaking. My face was wet and sticky; salt tinged my lips. I couldn't recall when I started crying. I couldn't imagine when I would stop.

Chaucer put a headset over my forehead as well. One of his cronies connected a thin wire from my headset to Logan Pierce's headset. Another goon ran a wire from my headset to Sidney and plugged it in to a dual socket that now protruded out of the back of my girlfriend's skull. Sidney was now doubly wired. One cord went from her to Pierce and one cord went from her to me. The three of us were networked together.

"This is all very crude," Chaucer explained, his voice apologetic, as though he were embarrassed about the entire event. "These wires and headsets and so forth. Because this is your first time creating the game you will have to be wired-in. In the future, when you are a bit stronger and better trained, you can create and control remotely, like I do. Soon, in our next version, you and I will not need these cords at all, not even between the giver and recipient. In fact, they won't even need to be in the same room."

I watched as a Lazarine took all three cords—one each from me, Sidney, and Pierce—and pushed the ends into a six-foot tall computer terminal. A series of computer servers lit up green as the cords connected into the device. I felt a jolt of electricity. My feet kicked up from the floor.

"With your help, Carter," Chaucer said, "we will create a Lazarus Game that will run completely over the Internet. It will connect our friends to potential donors who may reside anywhere in the world. Just think of it! One of my Lazarine brethren needing a donation can be here, in Portland, and his donor—the game player—can be living in Argentina or Australia or Antarctica! No matter where they live, as long as they can play via the Internet, we can tap into them. Isn't that marvelous?! It's a new era for all of us! A new era for the Lazarus Game!"

Chaucer walked to the computer terminal. He typed in quick staccato on the keyboard. I gazed about the room as Chaucer bent toward the screen, studying it intently. The other Lazarine had left the room, closing the door behind. The only two conscious people were me and Chaucer. Sidney and Logan Pierce reclined on their chairs. My brother had been laid on the floor at the edge of the room. He seemed to be sleeping peacefully. I envied him. No matter what nightmare he could possibly find inside his deepest, darkest consciousness, nothing could compare to the horror I faced wide awake. I wondered if I should have left Clinton inside the game. He would have at least been happy.

Chaucer returned to my side. He pulled a chair alongside me, all collegial and friendly. He coached me through my next steps, teaching me how to enter the game and shape it. He told me how I could use the game to steal the life force from Pierce and give it to Sidney. I was tutored and taught by the very Master of Evil. I became his young apprentice.

"All you need to do is to create Logan's fantasy," he summarized. "You are connected to his consciousness. You can see his thoughts, read his mind. You will know what he wants as clearly and surely as you know your own thoughts. Once you tap into his deepest desires the rest is easy. Construct a fantasy so compelling that he will do anything to have it, a fantasy so essential and desirable that he would sacrifice his own life to realize it."

The perfect fantasy, I thought, *would be driving a stake right through your rotten heart.* But killing Chaucer was my fantasy, I knew, and perhaps not Logan Pierce's. Maybe he dreamed of unicorns and rainbows. Whatever it was, I had to find it. I had to use it. I had to kill Pierce with his own fantasy. Or Sidney would remain dead.

"Close your eyes, now, Carter," Chaucer said. "And here you go."

CHAPTER
TWENTY-THREE

had to kill Logan Pierce. I had to extract his life force and give it to Sidney. I had to kill him to save her. I had no other choice.

So I constructed the perfect fantasy for Pierce. It was all too easy.

Men are incredibly predictable when it comes to fantasies. It all comes down to power, money, or women. Maniacs like Chaucer crave power. Losers like my friend Darek Branderson want money. Logan Pierce? It was a woman.

Plugged in to Pierce's conscious it didn't take me long to learn his deepest, darkest secrets. I had hoped his fantasy would be killing Chaucer. It was, but that was surface motivation, a plan and an ambition, but not a fantasy. I found that the only passion Pierce had was for a woman.

I wish I had never known.

Chaucer told me how to construct the fantasy scenario. It was ridiculously, laughably easy, at least for me, as I was accustomed to thinking in multiple dimensions. I built a Lazarus Game for Logan Pierce completely inside my imagination, using Pierce's innermost desires as the foundation and blueprint. Once constructed, I transferred this virtual reality scenario through the medium of the headset, planting the game directly into his consciousness. It was a perfect, beautiful, terrible fantasy.

I wish I had never done it.

I hated myself as I built it. I outright loathed myself when I transferred the deception into his mind. It was a terrible, deceitful, betraying fantasy.

Why this fantasy? Why did Logan Pierce have to have this particular fantasy?

I could have handled a gruesome death wish, Pierce torturing and dismembering Chaucer in all sorts of vile and twisted ways. I could have endured a power-hungry delusion of ruling the world, a dictator over millions of oppressed followers, a conqueror of nations and people. I would have been okay with any number of the usual male vices. But this fantasy? Did it have to be this rotten fantasy?

I sat in orchestra box seats a row behind Pierce. I looked pretty good in the black tuxedo. Pierce looked better. He was clean-shaved, hair slicked back, big bulk neatly packaged beneath white dress shirt and black tux suit. Hobo Warrior really cleaned up well.

I felt rotten. Terrible. Guilty as sin. Guilty as the devil.

Pierce leaned forward in his seat, gaze riveted on the stage. He didn't notice me sitting behind him. His eyes were fixed on the woman dancing on the stage. Not that I could blame him. She was dazzling, breathtaking. She leapt and pirouetted and did all sorts of impressive ballerina moves as she glided about the stage. She wore a tutu, skin tight leggings, ballerina shoes. She was stunning, absolutely beautiful.

This was Allison Hale Pierce, Logan's wife.

Pierce watched the entire ballet, reveling in the way a man did when gazing at the woman he loves. It ended and then Pierce was backstage, congratulating the company. He took the woman in his arms, holding her close, kissing her. I couldn't bear watching.

We went out to dinner. It was a different day. I sat at a table behind them, a voyeur, an intruder on their intimate evening. Logan fumbled with something under the table. The woman bent close, laughing, teasing him. His hand came up, a ring clenched between two fingers. The woman gasped. She laughed and cried. She pushed back from the table and grabbed Pierce and pulled him up and planted a kiss on his lips. She told him "yes" over and over. They hugged and she cried. I buried my face in my hands.

I came with them to a soccer game. The day was crisp and cool, a clear autumn day. A mob of kids in red and blue uniforms packed the center of the field. They stood around a soccer ball, kicking at it, every single kid in a neat little circle. Then a scrawny blond-haired kid broke from the pack, streaking away from the scrum, dribbling the ball with his feet at the breakneck speed of three miles per hour. He kicked the ball past the outstretched hands of the goalie and the crowd went wild.

Logan Pierce and his wife jumped up and down as though just winning the lottery, as though their five-year old had just won the World Cup. They raced onto the field and scooped the kid up in their arms. They hugged him while he struggled to get free, obviously embarrassed at the public display of affection. The kid blushed and squirmed, but Logan and Allison only held him closer, laughing triumphantly. I stood on the sideline, next to the coach and the referee, feeling like a murderer.

Happy times, I thought, standing there in the warm fall sunshine, wanting to kill myself. Memories of a simple time, a young family, a bright future ahead of them. Memories of a life Pierce could have had. A wife. A child. A family. No Lazarine. No Chaucer. No Lazarus Game.

But these memories had never happened. This life had never been. Pierce had no wife. He had no child. I knew this. I had read his mind, scanned his memories. The woman in his fantasies had died more than two hundred years ago. She had died of tuberculosis at only sixteen. She had loved to dance. She loved to dance with him. They had been childhood sweethearts, Logan and Allison. They grew up in Boston, in the years after the Revolutionary War. He was brilliant, a genius, another Benjamin Franklin. He was going to marry her, go to Harvard, and be a lawyer or diplomat or politician, and they would have children and grandchildren and grow old together. It never happened. She died. He lived on, brokenhearted, full of bitterness and despair.

Chaucer had found him. Chaucer had a nose for talent, for genius, and he found Pierce before Logan could drink himself to death. He showed Pierce how death could be cheated, how life could be extended. It was too late for Allison, Chaucer said, but it was not too late for Pierce. He could defeat death. So Pierce joined with Chaucer, and for two hundred years helped him steal life from the innocent. For two hundred years he fought his own conscience, justifying the deaths, rationalizing the sacrifices. Chaucer did much good over the years. He and the Lazarine were behind nearly all the major breakthroughs of the past couple centuries, from electricity to penicillin to the computer. All that good, all at the expense of innocent lives. Pierce justified and rationalized and went along with it.

Then came the advent of the Internet. Pierce could see what would happen, how Chaucer would use the Internet to kill millions with the push of a button. In the past the evil had been contained, quarantined, slow and difficult. Now there would be no stopping it. Chaucer could feed forever, no shortage of supply, and he could expand his society until only the truly elite would live and everyone else would die. It was too much. Pierce knew he had to stop Chaucer. He turned on his friend and ally and dedicated his life to destroying the Lazarine, to doing what he should have done two hundred years before.

I knew this. I knew all of it. I saw inside Pierce, right down into his consciousness. I felt the guilt and agony and anger. And the loss. The nagging ache for Allison. The love that never died.

He would sacrifice anything for her. He would sacrifice anything to be with her, even if only for a day, only for a few moments. Would he care if it were true or not? Would he care if it were all a lie? Would he not sacrifice his life to spend his last few hours on earth with her?

Of course he would. I knew it. That's why I built this particular fantasy.

I was sitting at a dance recital. I looked around me, seeing the faces of parents and grandparents, restless siblings, teenagers poking at phones and listening to headphones. Pierce sat in front of me, the row just ahead. I could not see Allison. A boy sat beside Logan Pierce, about ten years old. I recognized him. The kid from the soccer game. Older now, taller, bigger, but the same kid. He sat beside his father looking bored out of his mind.

I looked at the stage. I found Allison there, but not as a dancer. She was guiding a group of young fidgety girls onto the stage. They wore little tutus, some of them hanging down nearly to knees, others pulled up high around scrawny chests. Allison herded the girls to the stage, whispering encouragement, giving smiles and waves. A teacher, I saw. Allison was a dance teacher.

A girl at the front of the stage caught my eye. She had long dark hair, green eyes, a beautiful girl. She looked just like Allison. She looked just like her mother. There could be no doubt about it. Pierce had his smartphone aimed at the girl, taking video. He looked like the proudest papa in the auditorium.

The girl spied her father video recording her. She flapped her hand and smiled excitedly. Pierce waved back, big grin on his face. Even the ten-year-old boy waved, though with a degree of reserve, in the way all brothers act toward younger sisters. *I love you*, he seemed to be saying, *and I'm proud of you, but don't make me say it out loud.*

The music started. The girls started dancing, twirling around. Some turned one direction, some another, and all order and choreography broke down. The audience tittered with laughter, everyone smiling and chuckling. Everyone, that is, but me. I wanted to throw up. I couldn't take it anymore.

I leaned forward and tapped Pierce on the shoulder. He twisted about in his chair. His brow furrowed when he saw me. He frowned.

"Carter?" he asked. "Carter Chance? What are you doing here?"

"I'm terminating your game, that's what I'm doing."

"You're what?"

"Ending the game."

"Game? What game? What . . . ?" Pierce's mouth froze open. His eyes widened.

"Is this the Lazarus Game?" he asked, shock draining the color from his face. "Is this all part of the Game?"

I dropped my head. I stared at the floor, unable to look into Pierce's accusing eyes.

"Yes," I said. "It's all fake. None of this is real. You're back inside the office right now. Hooked up to a headset. Hooked up to Sidney."

"It's all fake?" he asked again. "Allison? Anna? My son? All fake?"

I nodded, still not looking at him. His voice was frantic, strained, anguished.

"You brought Allison back? You brought her back to do this to me? To trick me? To kill me?"

I nodded, unable to speak. I just went on nodding.

"Why did you do this to me, Carter? Why this? Why Allison? How could you do this?"

"Sidney's dead," I said. "I was just trying to save her. I'm sorry. I'll send you back."

"No."

My head snapped up. Pierce stared at me, eyes steely with determination.

"No? What do you mean, no?"

"I'm not going back," Pierce said. "I'm staying here. Inside the game."

"It's fake! You know this! You're the one trying to stop Chaucer from doing this!"

"I don't care! Allison is here. You've brought her back to me. Carter, I can't leave her again."

"It's not really her! Logan, you know it's not really her! I can't let you stay here. I can't let you stay here and die. Not for Sidney. Not for me. You're going back."

"I won't! You can't make me!"

I shook my head, smiling grimly, sadly. "I built the game, Pierce. I can send you back."

And I did. I blinked, and a moment later he disappeared. He vanished into thin air. The boy was gone, the other parents, the girls up on the stage. Allison Hale Pierce and her daughter and all the rest, vanished as if they had never existed, because, in essence, they never had. Not like this. The game ended, and the fantasy died with it.

Only I still sat on the hard metal chair. I did not go back. Pierce had gone, the game had stopped, yet I still sat there. I stayed inside the game. Why? What the crap was going on?

"Not bad, for your first attempt," said a voice behind me. "A little spare in the details. The parents all looked the same, did you notice that? All the guys looked like all the other guys, and vice versa on the women. You didn't give much attention to making the supporting cast look believable, Carter. But that's to be expected on a first try. Overall, an admirable effort."

Geoffrey Chaucer sat behind me. I stood up. He followed me. He extended his hand like he wanted to shake mine. I didn't take it.

"What are you doing here?" I asked. "I didn't put you in this game."

He nodded. "I know. Interesting, isn't it? You built a custom fantasy for Logan Pierce. You didn't expect to find me in here."

"So why are you? What are you doing here?"

"I'm guessing you have to thank you brother for this, or maybe that friend you brought along and left here last night. Someone knocked me over the head."

I laughed. "Really?"

"Yes, really. Someone must have knocked me out and stuck the headset on my head. You don't think I'd come inside on purpose, do you? Inside *your* game? I was put inside here on purpose."

I kept laughing. Darek! Darek is at the office building! Darek must have done it!

"So now what?" Chaucer asked. "We going to waste time standing around or are you going to bring us back to the real world?"

I stopped laughing. The real world, he said. The real world. There was nothing good happening back in the real world. My brother barely alive, narrowly escaping his own Lazarus Game. Logan Pierce injured, nearly dead. And Sidney. My dear friend Sidney. Dead. Not nearly. But really. She was dead. And now I could not save her. I sent Pierce back, and that meant that I had sentenced Sidney to death without hope. There was no way now to bring her back.

"I'm disappointed in you, Carter," Chaucer said. "You sent Pierce back."

I rolled my eyes. "Oh, yeah, well, sorry to disappoint you. Yes, it's true. I'm guilty. Guilty of actually having a conscience. Guilty of having to do the right thing!"

"You could have saved your girlfriend," Chaucer said. "But you sent Pierce back. You are still weak, naïve. You still think that one life is as good as another. You are still bound by petty morals. But it is a common problem, this delusion of righteousness. I can overcome it with time."

"No, I don't think you can. For a genius you're also pretty stupid, you know that? How can you think I'll still work with you? You tried to kill my brother! You killed Sidney! I don't know how . . . but I swear I'll stop you. I won't let you hurt anyone else. I'll kill you if I can."

It was his turn to laugh.

"You can't kill me, Carter! Don't you know that by now? I have lived hundreds upon hundreds of years. I have out-lived entire nations! Empires have come and gone, great cathedrals built and crumbled, generations of people born and died, and yet I remain. I will always remain. I am immortal, Carter. You cannot kill me. Didn't Pierce teach you this? So, come, let us quit wasting our time. Send us back."

I shrugged. I was in no hurry to make things easy on Chaucer.

"You do it," I said. "Bring yourself back. It's your freaking Lazarus Game."

He shook his head.

"I can't go back. It's not my *freaking* Lazarus Game. It's yours. So let's get this over with. Let's go back, and perhaps we can still find a way to save Sidney. Perhaps I can help you find a way. Come, Carter. I'm growing impatient."

A shiver of excitement went through me, coursing down my arms and legs, a jolt of electricity. I was Newton when the apple fell on his head. I was Archimedes running naked through the halls screaming "Eureka! Eureka!" I had my Edison light bulb moment, my Einstein "just discovered the theory of relativity" epiphany.

In short, I figured out how to defeat Chaucer.

Logan Pierce had given me the clue, when we were driving to Merewether, on our way to rescue Clinton. He told me exactly what I needed to know.

Chaucer is the Lazarus Game.

The game played inside Chaucer's head. His imagination fueled it. His life force was connected to it. He had lived for hundreds of years because of this connection to the game he created. It sustained and nourished him, extending his life. His body could no longer die, not like normal men. But he could be killed. He could be killed inside the game!

I had to force myself to remain calm. I nearly laughed hysterically, giddy with excitement. I knew I could do it! Chaucer himself had all but admitted it. He couldn't escape. He was my prisoner here. I could do with him whatever I wanted!

He was trapped inside my game.

I can't go back, he had said. *It's not my freaking Lazarus Game. It's yours.*

It's my game. I create the fantasies here. I can do whatever I want.

Now, how to kill Geoffrey Chaucer?

CHAPTER TWENTY-FOUR

A gangbanger shot Geoffrey Chaucer in the head. Chaucer was in East L.A., selling drugs. The deal went bad. A rival gang member blew a four-inch hole through Chaucer's forehead, a mist of red and a splatter of blood on the brick wall.

A vampire hunter hammered a wooden stake right through Chaucer's chest. Chaucer had been hunted through the dense forest, hounds nipping at his heels. Villagers with rakes and pitchforks caught him, dragging him over the ground, tearing at him with their nails. They dragged Chaucer to the center of town and tied him to a stake. The local priest doused him with holy water, then the Inquisitor pounded a stake through Chaucer's heart.

A crew of pirates forced Chaucer to the end of a gang plank. They wrapped a fifty-pound iron chain around his naked shoulders. Chaucer had captained a rival ship, a competitor to the pirates who roamed the Caribbean waters. His ship had been boarded, crew shot or stabbed to death. Chaucer himself had been found drunken and blubbering, too scared to fight back like a man. So the pirates treated him like the coward he was. They placed the mantle of iron around his neck and shoved him into the deep waters. He sank like an extremely heavy rock. The crocodiles didn't get a chance to catch him.

A drone missile blew him to smithereens. An Eastern European terrorist group had captured Chaucer, mistaking him for an American senator traveling in the region. They were going to put Chaucer on television and execute him in front of the whole world. Before that could happen, a US military drone launched a missile through the roof of the building. Chaucer was blown to a million little bits.

Except that Chaucer didn't die. I mean, he definitely blew up. And got poisoned to death. And he got shot. And stabbed. And drowned. He died over and over again. But, just like the hero in a bad boxing movie, he got right up again and kept on fighting. Chaucer wouldn't let a little thing like death slow him down.

Each time he came back from the dead, he had a little smirk on his face. He laughed and slapped his knee and rolled his eyes at me. Then I launched him into a different scenario, a different fantasy. I dreamed up some new way to kill him, and I played it all out. Chaucer was killed a dozen times, two dozen, a hundred! But he always came right back.

"Getting tired of this yet?" he asked after my last attempt to kill him. I made him allergic to peanuts and then dropped him inside a huge vat of Skippy peanut butter. His body swelled up about three times the normal size, turned fire-engine red, sprayed pus from gaping pustules the size Yellowstone Park geysers, and then died. Or not.

I cursed him. I swore and yelled and ranted like a two-year-old.

"I really thought you were smarter than this, Carter,"

he said. We sat inside the dance hall auditorium. It was our "limbo" zone, apparently, the area where we always returned after my latest attempt to kill him. "I am actually starting to question my faith in you."

I said nothing. I was starting to lose faith in myself as well. Nothing I did fazed him. I had him trapped inside my own game, my version of the Lazarus Game, where I could create any fantasy I wanted, and I could not hurt him.

Why? What was I doing wrong?

I sent him into another scenario—a creaky old house filled with black widow spiders and poisonous snakes—to give me time to think.

It wasn't working. I obviously couldn't kill him like this. It was my game, but nothing I did affected him. I couldn't use my fantasy to kill him.

Then I saw it. I was trying to use *my* fantasy on *him*! I couldn't use my fantasy. I'd have to use *his* fantasy! The only way to kill Chaucer was to keep him inside the game, trap his mind in a digital fantasy until his physical body withered and died. Just like he did with my classmates, just like he tried to do with my brother. I had to use his fantasy against him.

I had to convince Chaucer to stay forever inside the game. He had to willingly give his life in order to stay. It all came down to will. Chaucer himself had said it. The human will is stronger than our bones, stronger than our muscles and sinews, more inherent and foundational and essential than our DNA. Chaucer could not steal the life force from the game players. They had to give it willingly. The game only worked if the player agreed to stay inside the fantasy.

This is what I had to do to Chaucer. I had to convince him to willingly exchange his real life for a fantasy I constructed inside the game. I had to tap inside his dreams and desires and find the one fantasy that would keep him here forever. I had to find the one thing he would sacrifice everything to possess. I had to convince him to relinquish his will—his agency—to me.

I reached inside his consciousness. I peeked inside his mind. I saw horrors there beyond comprehension, thousands of lives lost, homes ruined, families shattered by pain and loss. I found beauty and wonder and accomplishment there as well, breakthroughs and miracles of science and human advancement. Literary genius. Poetry, imagination, wonder. I probed beneath all of that, seeking for his fantasy, looking for his innermost desire. It didn't take long to find it. The desire for immortality—not just to live forever, but to be remembered forever— everywhere inside his mind.

I yanked Chaucer out of the haunted house and put him inside the Colosseum in Rome. Roman legions marched past him. He stood reviewing the parade of soldiers and horses, slaves and concubines, elephants and lions. Thousands of people cheered and chanted his name.

"Caesar! Caesar! Caesar!"

He rode inside a chariot, his arm raised to the crowd. The bowed and paid him tribute. Rose petals showered down from above. They hailed him the conquering hero, the greatest Caesar in history.

Chaucer drove the chariot out the front gate of the Coliseum and right into the dance hall. I jumped back as the horses trampled the metal folding chairs. Chaucer— bedecked in gold armor and horse-mane helmet, leaped from the chariot. He pulled a sword and held it to my throat.

"I know what you're doing, Carter!" Chaucer cried. He looked pretty impressive in the Roman armor. I fell back from him. "It won't work! You can't trick me to stay here!"

"You're the hero!" I cried. "Don't you want to be the hero?"

"I am the hero, Carter! I am already the hero!"

The scene changed. He stood on the steps of the Capitol Building in Washington, DC. The heads of state of every nation gathered on the steps below him. One by one these leaders bowed before Chaucer, swearing their fealty to him. Chaucer had conquered the entire world. The armies and navies of the United States had invaded each unfriendly country, defeated each opposing military.

"On this day I say we are no longer a collection of individual countries and nations," Chaucer proclaimed. "On this day we no longer have distinct cultures and people. We have today only a single language, a single culture. On this day we no longer have the United States of America; we have the United States of Earth!"

The presidents and kings and ministers of the various countries applauded their new dictator, the new ruler of the world. Chaucer had done what no one before him had accomplished. He had truly conquered the whole earth. He was king and God over all of it.

He raised his hands, motioning for the heads-of-state to quiet down. Once the cheering stopped he said: "You have come here to name me your ruler, your emperor. You think that I want this thing above anything else. You think I would sacrifice everything to be ruler over the whole earth. But you are wrong. This is not my fantasy. Do you hear me, Carter Chance? You can end the game now, because you're wrong! This is not my fantasy! You can't trick me to stay here!"

I was back in the dance hall, sitting on the cold hard metal chair. I was alone. I don't know where Chaucer was. I didn't care. He was probably roaming the halls of my broken game, finding amusement in my failure. I buried my head in my hands.

He had seen right through it. I presented him with the whole world. Chaucer, king of everything, and he rejected it. He would not trade his life for that fantasy. He wouldn't even trade a pack of chewing gum. I had been wrong. I had failed.

My genius had failed me. All this intelligence, and for what?

I laughed. I laughed long and hard and bitter. Genius! What genius? Oh, yeah, I had a perfect memory. I could recall anything I've ever read. Yes, the most advanced mathematical formulas were easy to me, natural as breathing. I could create some computer code, I could invent new technologies, and I could think clearly and creatively. But it wasn't enough. All of that, and I couldn't defeat Chaucer.

You have to kill him in the game. That's what Pierce said. Inside the game!

But I couldn't do it. Chaucer was beyond me. I couldn't defeat him here.

I sat on the chair a long time, thinking. I thought about Chaucer. I thought about the deepest desires I found inside his mind. I thought about Sidney back in the real world, her heart no longer beating. I thought of my brother, still recovering, nearly dead. I thought of an office building full of Lazarine, any of which would soon find us and take the headset off Chaucer and bring him back to the real world. I was out of time. Chaucer had won.

Chaucer would live forever. That much was certain. He

would live for all time. Wasn't that what really drove him? The desire to live forever? Was that his true passion? Was that his deepest fantasy?

And then I saw it. All at once, I saw it.

I could beat Chaucer. I could make him sacrifice everything. I could make him give up his own life. But not like this. Not when he knew it was a game.

I had to take him back to the real world.

CHAPTER
TWENTY-FIVE

blinked. My eyes opened and my vision cleared. I sat upright. I reached up and yanked off the headset. I gazed about the room, white walls, circle of chairs, medical equipment. I smiled. I was back inside the Lazarus Corporation laboratory.

"He's waking up!" called a familiar voice. "Hey, he's waking up!"

Darek Branderson rushed to my side. He slapped me on the back as I struggled to get off the chair. "You made it back!"

"Of course I made it back!" I swatted my friend away, but I grinned at him.

"Did you forgot about me? I knew you would. You abandoned me here, Carter. You left me here all by myself. You ran off to that factory or whatever and left me here. Good thing, too, or Chaucer would have had you."

"Chaucer!" I cried. "Where is he?"

"Over there," Darek said, pointing. "He's still out cold."

I followed Darek's gesture. I saw Chaucer sitting on one of the game pod chairs a few feet away. The headset still rested on his forehead. Chaucer's eyes were closed, face pale. He was still inside the game.

"You did that to him?" I asked. "You sneak up on him or what?"

Darek laughed. "Yeah. Smacked him over the head, strapped the headset on him. I sent him inside the game for you. A little present. You like it?"

"Very much so. What about Pierce?"

"Still asleep," he said. "Out cold. Just like Clinton."

I nodded. I glanced at Sidney. She remained on a chair situated behind Pierce. She still had the cord stuck into the back of her head. She did not move. She would never move again.

"Let's wake up Chaucer," I said.

"You sure? You really want to bring him back?"

"The world needs him, Darek. Without Chaucer the world would fall into chaos. Billions will die of disease and malnutrition. Crime will rage out of control. Our economy will collapse. The world must have Geoffrey Chaucer."

I got up and walked slowly and gingerly to Chaucer's chair. I felt stiff and sore, like I'd been asleep for many hours. Maybe I had.

I put my hand on Chaucer's headset. His eyes opened before I removed the headset. He smiled.

"So, Carter, you have come to your senses at last?"

"My senses? What do you mean?"

"I heard you. I heard you just then, talking. The world needs me? Is that right? Do you see this at last? Do you finally see how indispensable I am?"

I shrugged. I reached down and took him by the arm and helped him to his feet. I pulled the headset off him and tossed it to the chair.

"Carter?" he asked again. "Do you truly see it? Are you ready to acknowledge that I am the only truly indispensable man?"

I nodded my head. I shrugged my shoulders. I smiled at him, a bit wry, a bit rueful. I said, "Okay, sure, I'll give you that. You win. You really are worth more than all the rest of us combined. You are the only person that really matters."

I took my hand off him and walked away. I went to Sidney's side. I touched her cheek, cold, motionless. I bent near my brother. His breathing had improved as had his color. I put my hand on his shoulder and shook him. He groaned and stirred. I figured he'd be awake soon.

"Carter!" Chaucer called after me. "What are you doing?"

"I'm leaving. Just as soon as my brother's ready. How about you, Darek? You ready to go?"

My friend nodded. "You bet your hairy old butt I am. Let's get out of here."

Clinton kept groaning and moving. His eyes flickered open and shut. He was coming out of it quickly now. It wouldn't be much longer.

"What do you mean, you are leaving?" Chaucer asked. "What does this mean?"

"I'm walking out of here, that's what it means. Me, Darek, and Clinton. We're going back home."

"Back . . . back home? But . . . after what you said? You're staying, aren't you? To help me! To make a difference here! To live forever!"

I snorted. "I don't want to stay here, Chaucer. I want to be out in the real world, out where people will actually know who I am. I may only do small things out there in my lifetime, but at least I'll be remembered for it."

Chaucer—who had been moving toward me—froze. He frowned at my words. He looked puzzled, anxious.

"What do you mean? Remembered? Remembered for what?"

"For whatever! You don't get it, do you? You're doing all these great things in here, Chaucer, because you want to be remembered. You don't just want to live forever. You want to be memorialized and loved. You want people a thousand years from now to know what you did. But no one even knows that you exist. No one knows what you're doing in here. You're invisible. You are nothing."

"I am a god! You know this! You've seen what I have done! What I can do!"

I shrugged. "No one else has. You want to live forever? Go for it. I don't care. No one else does, either. Because no one knows that you are even alive."

I paused. I gazed at him. I shook my head, trying for my best look of pity. "You're not a god, Chaucer. You're not even a common man. Heck, you're not even a loser, like Darek here! You're worse than that. You're nothing."

Chaucer said nothing. He blinked rapidly as though the processor inside his brain was spinning and churning, trying to decipher my meaning. I wondered if blue smoke would come streaming out his ears and nostrils. That would be something to see.

"So you're leaving? Just like that? What about Sidney?"

"She's gone," I said. "You killed her. Nothing can change that. That's the way of nature. The way of the world. You murdered her, but there's not one thing I can do to change that now. So, yes, I'm leaving. I'm going back to where I can be known and admired. Back to where I can live forever in the memories of my friends and family."

I walked to the door of the laboratory. Darek came right behind me, Clinton—up now, at last—followed at Darek's heels. I heard Chaucer calling behind me, begging me, pleading for me to stay.

I paused at the door, my hand on the handle. I turned back, glancing just over my shoulder.

"You could come with me," I said.

"What?"

"You could come with me! You could leave this place. Leave your shiny offices, leave your corporation, leave the Lazarus Game! You could walk away from all of it. You could come into the real world and let everyone know who you are. You could collaborate with real scientists and real teachers and real government leaders. You could be known by millions, Chaucer! You could be remembered! You would live forever as the greatest genius of all time! Why not come with me? Why not do this?"

Chaucer hesitated. His eyes went to the door, to my hand on the handle, and back, to the pod of chairs, to Pierce's prostrate body, to Sidney's corpse. He looked at me again, his eyes filled with conflict, uncertainty.

"The world will remember me," he said. "I will live forever. I will never die. I will—"

"Be forgotten," I finished. "You are already forgotten. No one knows you. No one will ever know you. Your body may live, but your soul is already gone. Come with me, Geoffrey! Come back to Merewether. Help me rebuild what you've destroyed! Come out into the light and be known!"

"NO!" he screamed. "I cannot go! I WILL NOT GO! I AM the Lazarus Game! I am immortal!"

"You are nothing," I said. I turned the handle.

"Carter!" Chaucer cried. "Don't throw this all away!"

"Chaucer!" I called back. "You *should* throw it all away! Sacrifice the Game! Sacrifice all of it and come back to the world!"

"I will not! I will stay here! I will stay with the Lazarus Game forever!"

"Even if it means killing thousands of innocents?"

"Yes."

"Even if it means sacrificing your own soul?"

"Yes!"

"Your own life?"

"YES!"

I gazed back at him one last time.

"You're sure about that? You would sacrifice your life to stay here, inside your precious Lazarus Corporation, inside your precious game?"

"You know I will stay. I could never leave all I've built here. I would sacrifice the whole world for this. I would sacrifice my life, my very soul."

I nodded, just once. I couldn't help it, then. A single tear came from my eye, dripping down my cheek. No matter all the evil he had done, all the tragedy and heartache, I still pitied him.

"Good-bye, Chaucer," I said. "Enjoy your fantasy."

I opened the door. I stepped through. I closed the door behind me. I sealed Geoffrey Chaucer inside the Lazarus Game.

The game ended.

And then I really did wake up.

CHAPTER
TWENTY-SIX

opened my eyes—for real this time. I knew at once something was wrong. Call it a sixth sense, or maybe I heard something while waking up, or maybe I'm just naturally paranoid, but I knew my life was in danger. I opened my eyes and rolled off the chair.

I hit the ground hard. I landed on my hands and knees, jolting myself fully awake. The game headset tangled about my neck, half-strangling me. I heard a swish as something sliced through the air. Then I heard a *thwock* and a thump. A metal blade hacked into the chair where I had just been sitting. The blade severed the dangling headset, sending splintered plastic parts flying off the chair. That would have been my head had I been a second slower.

I saw a blur of black and a flash of silver above me. I rolled. Metal clanged on hard linoleum flooring, a blade again narrowly missing my head. I kept rolling like a kid somersaulting down a hill. The blade followed me like the tines on a tractor, cutting and chopping, slicing and dicing, biting into the floor, tearing out chunks of linoleum.

Someone was trying really hard to kill me.

I heard someone yelling, someone behind me, out of sight. My shoulder hit a hall. I stopped rolling. I looked up.

Geoffrey Chaucer leered down at me, face pale, eyes bloodshot. He held an axe thingy above his head. A Lazarus Game headset cradled his skull, the cord dangling loose like a wayward ponytail. He looked old—ancient and thin, ravaged by years. His hulking frame had shrunken. His black beard had thinned and grayed. Dark spots and black bruises colored the skin of his hands and arms.

I was shocked by Chaucer's appearance. But I was even more dismayed by the implication of his unfortunate not-deadness. If Chaucer was alive—old, haggard, but alive—then Sidney was still dead. I thought I could exchange his life for Sidney's. Guess I was wrong.

Chaucer held the blade above him like a wacked-out lumberjack. I cringed and waited for him to chop me in half. I had nowhere to run . . . or roll.

"You destroyed the game!" Chaucer rasped, voice all nasty and Yoda-ish. "You destroyed my game!"

I heaved a sigh of relief.

"Whew!" I exclaimed, feeling much better about things. "I thought it was a total failure."

"It *is* a total failure!" Chaucer screamed, voice hysterical. The guy was losing it. He had a freaking axe pointed right at me, and he was losing it. Not good.

"You destroyed the Lazarus Game! You cannot even imagine what you've done. You've ruined everything! All these lives . . . all these lifetimes . . . the greatest collection of intelligence, of talent . . . lost. The greatest hope for the world . . . gone. GONE, YOU STUPID BOY!"

I shrugged. "You're still alive. You look terrible, but still alive."

"It's gone," he kept repeating. "The Lazarus Game is gone. You traded my life for a girl. For a STUPID, MEANINGLESS GIRL! I am the savior of this world! I am God! You have killed your god!"

I felt a thrill of hope. Maybe it had worked after all. Chaucer looked pretty darn bad. He wasn't quite dead, not yet, but *something* had happened. I had drained the immortality out of him—that was for sure. If life came out of him, then where did it go?

Sidney! Was Sidney alive?

"Where's Sidney?" I cried, to no one in particular, my excitement and hope overtaking me. "Where is Sidney?"

Chaucer said nothing; he just stood there, holding that blade high above him, staring down at me. He looked really pissed, and he looked like he really hated me. He was also looking older and nastier and stinkier by the minute. He looked like Thomas before Pierce chopped his head in half. He was looking more like the rest of his Lazarine. He looked almost dead.

Something must have occurred to Chaucer, for all at once his eyes lit up, as though he'd just had an epiphany, a little miniature revelation. His arms were shaking. Given that I was on the ground beneath him, and those trembling arms held a razor sharp blade above me, I didn't much care for Chaucer's sudden lack of arm strength.

"My game is gone. I cannot bring it back. But your game . . . your game can continue! You can continue the Lazarus Game! Carter, you can save me!"

I started laughing. I really didn't mean to, because pasty white or not, Chaucer could still probably chop off all the important parts of my body. But his words were just so preposterous I couldn't help myself.

"Save you! *Save you?* You really are nuts! Why would I want to save—?"

The laboratory door shuddered. Heavy pounding came from the other side, from the outer hallway. Someone was trying to come in. Chaucer's goons, I guessed.

I peered around Chaucer, straining to see beyond his quivering, swaying frame. I could see my friend, Darek Branderson, propped against the door. Darek! He really was alive! Maybe I didn't just dream up his part in the fantasy. Maybe I knew, somehow, subconsciously, that he was here in the room with me. Darek, my old loser friend, the kid not worth a bucket of warm spit, was helping me!

Darek was trying to keep the door closed. The door rocked from repeated blows. Darek stumbled back. The door inched open. I saw five arms stick through like cockroaches slithering through a cracked wall. A tangle of arms propped against the doorframe. The door came open.

A knot of black-clothed Lazarine spilled into the room. One went down, momentum carrying him too far forward. Three more came behind him, swarming around their comrade, coming after Darek.

The guys looked bad. I don't mean *bad* as in tough or cool; I mean, they looked awful. Their skin looked mottled and spotted. It sagged. It looked thin as parchment, stretched taut over bones. They moved with a certain zombie-like determination, but they appeared waifish, wasted.

Darek must not have thought they looked too harmless, for he ran away from the doorway. Chaucer turned to look at his cronies, forgetting about me for the moment. I took the opportunity to get up and I ran toward Darek.

I heard Chaucer turning, I heard a thrumming noise. I felt my shirt tearing, fabric ripping. I felt a red-hot flash of pain across my back. The axe thingy blade sliced through my skin.

I howled and fell to the ground. I heard Chaucer behind me, cursing, panting. I rolled and came up on one knee. Chaucer stepped toward me, blade up, ready.

Darek—in an act of insane and completely unjustified bravery—shoved me out of the way and jumped in front of Chaucer. The big man didn't hesitate. He swung the blade toward Darek's head.

The blade never made it. Chaucer pitched sideway before he could complete the motion. A massive figure slammed into Chaucer's side. Chaucer's head snapped back, neck whiplashed from impact. Chaucer's arms flailed and the axe went flying. Chaucer hit the ground, the dark shape on top of him.

Clinton Chance sat atop Chaucer. Clinton raised his right hand, fingers balled into a fist. Chaucer raised his head. Clinton smashed Chaucer's nose with his fist. I heard bones crunching and saw blood splattering the wall and floor.

My brother! How long had he been awake? Probably the whole time. Just hanging out, playing it cool, waiting for the perfect chance to kick Chaucer's butt. You go, bro!

"Clinton!" I cried. "Get him! Beat the crap out of him!"

The four Lazarine turned toward me. Darek stayed in front of me, my own personal bodyguard. But it wouldn't do much good. Two of the four men held handguns.

Then Logan Pierce made it to the party. I'd been waiting for him the entire time. The whole reason I was rolling around the floor and making small-talk with Chaucer was to give Pierce time to wake up.

Pierce came off the pod chair in a fluid, running motion.

He shot across the floor, reaching down to snatch Chaucer's axe thingy off the floor as he ran. He flung the blade up into the air as he barreled toward the four Lazarine. He took five steps, six, seven, and was on top of them.

One of the Lazarine saw him coming. He whirled and raised the pistol.

Pierce swept the blade toward the Lazarine. Metal struck metal and sparks spat across the room. The Lazarine yelped and fell back, gun knocked from jarred fingers. The blade continued its arc of motion, flying past the man. Pierce spun around, reversing the angle and trajectory, sending the blade back. Metal caught cheek bone. The blade cut right through the man's face.

The head exploded. I reeled back at the sight of it. It was not an explosion of bone and blood, of cartilage and sinew. It was an explosion of dust, as though the bones had simply disintegrated. Knees buckled and the Lazarine's body hit the ground. His body erupted, shards of bone like shattered glass showering the ground.

His companions saw it. Their eyes widened in shocked disbelief. The three remaining Lazarine looked terrible, worse with every passing minute. There had been two Lazarine with handguns; one was now disabled. The second guy tried to lift his gun. It wasn't happening. The guy couldn't get the gun into the air. It was if the gun weighed five hundred pounds. I watched the Lazarine try to raise the gun, saw the strain on his face, the confusion and frustration. Then Pierce drove the head of the axe through the man's forehead. Fine particles of bone-dust remained where the man once stood. An empty set of clothes hit the ground.

One of the remaining Lazarine tried to flee. He made it a couple feet before collapsing. No one touched him. Pierce didn't even move. The guy took three steps and clutched at his chest. He convulsed and gurgled. His body went rigid. He managed a weak gasping scream and fell to the floor. I figured he had a heart attack. I'll never know. His heart— and all the rest of his body—disintegrated on impact with the floor.

The final Lazarine did nothing at all. He didn't run. He didn't fight. He just sat down on the floor. I watched in sickened horror as his skin rotted right before my eyes. It was like he aged twenty years in a dozen seconds. His hair went gray, then white, then fell out. His hands shriveled and turned knotted and black. His eyes rolled back in his head.

Pierce kicked him over, more out of pity, I think, than malice. The old Lazarine died before his body hit the ground. Like his comrades, nothing but clothes and jewelry remained of the man. Not even bones, only a trace of dust on the floor.

I heard struggling and swearing behind me. My brother! I spun around, frantic that I'd been distracted, fearful of what I'd find.

I found Geoffrey Chaucer pinning my brother to the ground. He'd swapped roles with Clinton. Clinton is a big, strapping, tough teenager, yet Chaucer got the better of him.

It didn't seem possible. Chaucer looked bad, wrinkly and aging. But he had aged slower than his followers. He still had strength enough to hold my brother down, strength enough to kill him.

Chaucer had a knife in his hand. I don't know where he found it. Maybe inside the folds of his robe, maybe in his shoe. Who knows. He held the knife to Clinton's throat.

I didn't stop to barter with Chaucer. I'm sure he wanted to give me demands, bargain for Clinton's life. He would have asked me to restart the Lazarus Game. He would have promised to preserve Clinton. He may have made promises to change his habits, to do no more evil, to use his great genius to help people, to eradicate disease and poverty and greenhouse gases and after-burrito gases or whatever. I'm sure he would have made a convincing argument. But I didn't stop to listen.

What I did next surprised even me. Now, I've never played football. Okay, I tried one time. I showed up to the first day of Little League and promptly got knocked on my butt by a scrawny eight-year-old thirty pounds lighter and three inches shorter. I couldn't tackle, I couldn't block, and I couldn't catch the ball. I was a lousy football player. I'd never played since.

That day, however, at the Lazarus Corporation, I made a flying tackle so hard and so crushing and so perfect in form and technique it would have made Mean Joe Greene proud. I ran at full speed and dove through the air, driving my shoulder right into the face of Geoffrey Chaucer.

The big man sailed back. I sailed forward. Chaucer landed on the floor beneath me. I kept on going. The first thing that hit the hard floor was my fat face. Then my shoulder. Then my belly. My head bounced on the linoleum like a basketball. My teeth chattered in my head.

I heard a croaking noise behind me. My vision swam, my head pounded. Through the double vision I just caught a glimpse of Chaucer on the floor. His head had split open. Blood oozed slowly through the crack in his skull, black ichor seeping out. Somehow the old man still lived, however. I heard him whispering.

"I'm going to live forever. The people will remember me. I'm going to live . . ."

I heard Logan Pierce say something. I heard the swish of metal slicing through air and the sickening slosh of blade through bone and skin.

I heard nothing more from Chaucer. I guess he didn't live forever.

My vision spun and my stomach churned. I closed my eyes.

Darkness took me.

CHAPTER
TWENTY-SEVEN

I awoke to a kiss.

Soft lips pressed against mine. Somehow—through the murk of half-consciousness—I thought of Sleeping Beauty. Hadn't she been awakened by a kiss? That meant that I was Sleeping Beauty and a handsome prince was waking me up. The only options in the room were my brother, Darek, and Logan Pierce. I didn't want any of those slimy lips on mine.

I forced my eyes open. My arms flailed, desperate to push the kisser away. This person, whoever it was, only kissed harder.

I fought, I struggled, I tried to escape—but I was weak. Wasted. Like I hadn't moved a muscle in days. I couldn't get the mystery kisser off me. Besides, after a time I didn't really want to. The person smelled nice. Maybe Logan or Darek had started using aftershave.

My eyes focused on a mass of dark curly hair. Darek didn't have long dark hair. Nor did my brother. The only person with hair like that was Sidney Locke. But, of course, it couldn't be Sidney Locke, because Sidney Locke was . . .

Alive!

I pushed the body off me as I struggled upright. I heard laughter, giggling. Then I heard, "He's awake! Our hero is finally awake!"

Sidney Locke stood beside me. She didn't look dead in the least bit. In fact, she looked pretty darn hot. I mean, for a girl who had recently been dead, she looked drop-dead gorgeous, if you'll excuse the pun. I told her as much. She rewarded me with a kiss.

"Weren't you just dead?" I asked. My throat was raw and dry. It hurt to talk.

"That's what they tell me," she said. "But I'm feeling fine now. Thanks to you."

Thanks to me. Yes, that's right! Thanks to me!

I gazed about the room. I saw Logan Pierce sitting on the pod chair that had once held my girlfriend's dead body. He was sipping a carton of orange juice. He gave me a little wave. He kicked his feet while drinking the juice.

I saw Clinton Chance, my brother. He sat on one of the game pod chairs too. Across from him sat Darek Branderson, my sometimes best friend, depending on the day. Sometimes him, sometimes Chambers. Of course, Chambers had missed all this fun, the huge jerk. He was probably home staring at himself in the mirror. What a gift to society he was.

I cleared my throat. Clinton ignored me. He and Darek were having a good old time chewing the fat. Pierce sipped his juice as if he had no care in the world. I'd never seen the big man actually look this happy.

I had a splitting headache. My shoulder hurt too, as if I'd just run full speed into a brick wall. The pain brought with it memory. Chaucer. Where was Chaucer?

I searched the room for Geoffrey Chaucer. I didn't see him. I asked Sidney about it.

"That old corpse? Pierce here dragged him out a while ago. He was stinking up the place."

"He's dead, then?"

Logan stopped kicking his legs. He looked at me and smiled. "You mean, he's dead, finally? Yes, he's dead. Not just dead. Disintegrated."

"What happened?" I asked. "To the Lazarine? To Chaucer?"

"*You* happened to them," Pierce said. "You destroyed the Lazarus Game. Once the game ended, it was only a matter of time for Chaucer and his boys. The timer started ticking the moment you beat the game."

"Did I really beat the game? I tried to trick Chaucer into sacrificing his life for his fantasy. Did it really work?"

Pierce laughed, low and soft. He nodded.

"Oh, yes, it worked. The moment Chaucer agreed to sacrifice his life in exchange for his fantasy, the Lazarus Game was over. Geoffrey Chaucer *is* the Lazarus Game. It is inside his very soul. When he agreed to die for the game, his immortality ended. He became mortal. That's when the timer really started."

"Timer?"

"Old Father Time," Pierce explained. "Chaucer and his boys should have died long ago. His body knew it. His molecular biology sentenced him to death hundreds of years ago. Only by feeding on the innocent had he extended his life. Only the power he gained through his continual connection to the Game kept him alive. He and all his followers. Once that connection ended, the power ended too. Chaucer's body, and all of the rest of his Lazarine, reverted back to its natural state."

"The natural state should have been death, right?" I asked.

"Yes. That's why those men were falling apart in front of you. That's why Chaucer was a dead man the moment he agreed to your devilish contract. His body—kept alive for so long—just needed a few minutes to adjust to the new reality."

"But you killed him," I said, remembering the sickening sound of axe hitting flesh.

"I put him out of his misery, really," Pierce said. "He would have died anyway. Like I said, Old Father Time had caught up to him. Thanks to you."

I shook my head, amazed it was over. I asked, "How did it happen? I mean, one minute I'm inside the game with you, the next Chaucer is in there with me. What happened?"

Pierce gave me the story.

"Darek snuck in here after you went inside the game. I guess he's been hiding out the past twenty-four hours or so. Remember that you left him here? He heard the commotion when Chaucer came back. You weren't hard to find. He waited until Chaucer wasn't watching and came in and beat him over the head. It all sounds fairly cowardly to me."

"Cowardly?" Darek asked. He rolled his eyes. He and Clinton had stopped talking and were staring at us. "What you mean is that through my daring bravery I saved each and every one of your sorry hides. Without me, you'd all be toast."

Pierce shrugged. "I hate to admit it, but yes. I was in no shape to do anything. Chaucer got the jump on me back at the store. I was out cold. Here I was, the warrior who had trained and prepared for the chance to kill Geoffrey

Chaucer, and I was sleeping right through the action. I'm pretty embarrassed about it."

"You should be," Darek interrupted, "but let's get back to me, shall we? I saw Chaucer and his goons drag you in here. He forced you into the game, made you put on that headset while he connected it to Pierce here. And that got me thinking. I remembered all our friends back at the game store, the headsets on them. The way everyone thought it was a virus killing people, but that was never it. This whole thing was connected to the game, right? So after I clunked Chaucer over the head, I dragged his wrinkly butt over to one of the chairs and stuck a headset on his skull. Wasn't that a genius thing to do? And I was right, right? So who's the genius now, eh? Come on, give it to me. Who's the genius now?"

I laughed. "You are, Darek. You are the world's first idiot genius."

"Thank you! I like that!"

I laughed. I looked at Sidney. She was smiling at me. She looked awesome, as always. Maybe even better than usual. She looked young and vibrant. She looked alive. I took her hand and gave it a squeeze.

"Tell me what you did . . . what you . . . what you did to Chaucer," Pierce said. He started coughing as he talked. His voice sounded raspy, hoarse. He tried to clear his voice and started coughing again. When he finally could control himself, he added: "It must have been some powerful fantasy you gave him."

"He was obsessed with the Lazarus Game. He was obsessed with his own immortality. I gave him the chance to leave the Lazarus Game behind him. I offered him a simple choice: his life, or the game. I gave him the chance to come back to the real world, but he couldn't do it. He had spent hundreds of years perfecting his game, and when it came down to it, he couldn't let go. He sacrificed his life rather than leave the Game behind him."

"So you used his obsession for the Lazarus Game to trap him inside his own Lazarus Game?"

I grinned. "Exactly."

Pierce laughed. He coughed and spluttered. He wheezed like an old smoker with bad lungs. After a long spell of choking, he said: "Maybe you are a genius after all. You saved us, Carter. You did it. You saved Sidney."

I looked up at Sidney again. I still had her hand in mine. It felt soft, warm. I said, "You really came back. We sucked the life out of Geoffrey Chaucer and gave it to you, and you came back."

She smiled. "Yes, I really did."

"And you're okay with that?" I asked. "You have no moral problems with it?"

She shook her head. "Not really. Should I? From what I hear, this guy should have been dead long ago."

Dead long ago. That's what Pierce said. The body reverting to its natural state. Chaucer and all his followers would die. All of his followers.

Pierce sat down. He leaned back in the game pod chair. I gasped as I studied him. His long dark hair was now peppered with gray. His face looked haggard, drawn. I saw bubbles of red liquid on his lips. When he coughed, he choked up blood.

"Pierce!" I cried. "Logan! What's happening to you?"

Logan smiled. He closed his eyes. He took a deep breath but started coughing again. When he could talk again he said: "I'm dying, Carter. Just like Chaucer."

"But . . . but you can't die! You're the good guy!"

He laughed, a choking, gagging bark.

"Good or bad, it doesn't matter. We are all destined to die someday. I should have had my final day two hundred years ago. I should have died back with Allison. No, don't feel bad for me. I've already worn out my welcome."

"You knew it, didn't you?" I asked, astounded as I realized the truth, as I finally understood the impact of my actions. "You knew that when Chaucer died, you would die to! You knew that all along!"

"Of course. My whole reason to live was based on stopping Chaucer. Stopping him before he could do more damage. Stopping him before he truly became immortal."

"And you knew you'd die the moment you succeeded," I said. I shook my head. "And you did it anyway."

Pierce seemed to sink lower in his chair. He was shrinking right before my eyes. His hair had turned almost perfectly white. His voice was weak and shaky when he spoke.

"You know you're going to die someday too, Carter. Yet does that stop you from living? No. It makes you live better. That knowledge motivates you to make better choices. To do something good with your time here."

He paused to rest, to take a breath. He said, softly, so hushed that I had to lean forward to hear him, "That's the true deception of the Lazarus Game. Because death was temporarily cheated, Chaucer thought he could do anything he wanted. He lived on borrowed time, never worrying about the consequence. We mortals are much luckier than that. Faced with our own mortality, we can make the best choices for how we spend the time given us. We can make a real, meaningful difference. Better than living forever, we can be remembered forever. Isn't that right, Carter? Isn't that what you want?"

I nodded. I grinned. I laughed. I knew he was right.

"I can make a difference," I said to him. "You're right. I can create something to endure."

"Not just things," Pierce said. "People too. Relationships. Relationships that endure. I would give anything for just one more day with Allison. Remember that."

Relationships can endure. They don't have to end. Even in divorce, I thought, they don't have to end. I thought of my mom. I thought of my dad. Sure, they had issues. They weren't together. But that didn't mean I had to stop loving them. Or my big idiot brother, for that matter.

Then there was Sidney. She still stood there, holding my hand. Would our relationship endure? It was puppy love, really, a crush, a teenage sort of love. Could it be more? I had lots of time to figure that out. But, maybe.

"Logan," I said. "I just want to thank you for . . . Logan? Logan!"

But Logan Pierce had gone perfectly still. Life had faded out of him. After more than two hundred years, he had finally gone to find his childhood sweetheart. He and Allison were back together again.

Clinton and Darek came over to join me and Sidney. We stood around in a circle, looking at each other, not speaking. I think we all realized it was a time of endings, but also beginnings. Everyone was looking so darn serious, I felt I was back in Sunday school.

Clinton grabbed me by the arm and pulled me into a crushing bear hug. I was a bit embarrassed by it, with Sidney and Darek looking on and all. But Clinton's bigger and stronger than I and I couldn't stop him from hugging me. I guess I'm just irresistible.

"Thank you, little brother," he said as my rib cage creaked and groaned. "Thanks for saving me."

I squeezed him back. "Thank you, big brother."

"For what?"

"Saving me too."

Darek swore and spit on the floor. "Can't you save this for home? Freak, guys! I feel like throwing up! Way too mushy!"

Sidney laughed. "No kidding! Way too much brotherly love here. Can we go, now?"

I nodded. "Yeah, sure. Let's get going. I think we need to get out and have some fun, you know? Take a break from all this serious crap."

"Sounds good to me," said Darek. "Whatcha have in mind?"

"You know Williams Speedway? About twenty miles from town? Unlimited speed on the raceway."

Darek nodded. "I know the place. You can drive as fast as you want. But the only car we've got between us is Chamber's Volvo, and there's no way his mom will let him take it."

"I'm not talking about a Volvo," I said.

"What? Your dad's Crown Vic? A bit beat up, isn't it?"

I grinned. "I'm thinking about a little race. Me in the Lamborghini Veneo, you in the Bugatti Veyron. Maybe we let Clinton take the Testa Rossa."

Darek rolled his eyes. "Oh, yeah, that sounds great! Dream on, Carter! Just where in the crap are we going to get cars like . . . oh. Oh, that's right! Yeah!"

I raced Darek to the door.

EPILOGUE

'd like to say that everything in my life got neatly resolved after I defeated Chaucer and brought down his empire and destroyed the Lazarus Game. Life isn't like that, though, you know? We never really get to a point where everything is wrapped up with a bow on it. Life just moves on to the next thing. There are more beginnings and next steps than endings in life.

One thing that did end, though, was the Lazarus Game. Logan Pierce had been right all along. Geoffrey Chaucer *was* the Lazarus Game. The whole platform stemmed from his incredible—albeit twisted—brain. He had controlled the whole thing. There had probably been hundreds of kids playing the game in homes or stores. Every single one of them connected directly with Chaucer. Somehow his supercomputer brain had controlled all of it. Once he died, the game died with him. Good riddance, I say.

Sidney's dad came out of the coma about a week later. He's doing pretty good for a guy who had a near-death experience. Sidney is doing quite well herself for a girl who had an actual death experience. Of course I tell her I need to give her extra-special attention, just to be sure she doesn't have a relapse. I've offered several times to play doctor, but she's playing a bit hard to get.

My mom is starting to visit us once a week. That's one of those things that will take a while to sort out. I can do advanced computations for breakfast, but figuring out relationships is still beyond me. It's good to see her, though. This whole thing will take a while to work through, but I think we'll get there.

Clinton and I are getting along great. I mean, he's still a bit of a moron, and I'm still a genius, so nothing's changed there. But I put up with all of his deficiencies and he puts up with all my superiorities, so I think we're doing okay. What do you expect? He's my big brother, after all.

The town is slowly getting back to normal after the terrible tragedies caused by the Lazarus Game. In all, thirteen people died from the Game. Thirteen families were torn apart by Geoffrey Chaucer and his evil scheme to live forever. It will take a long time for all those wounds to completely heal. I think that none of us are taking each other for granted any more. That's got to be a good first step.

My little gang is back together: me, Chambers, Darek, Clinton, and Sidney. We're back to fighting crime, keeping the streets of Merewether safe. I've put my PlayStation Artificial Intelligence device to good use since quitting my job with the Lazarus Corporation.

About two months after Chaucer's death, I tracked a crime syndicate to a warehouse at the edge of town. In the past few weeks we had had a series of very strange thefts: black leather jackets, gold necklaces, cheap polyester pants, gaudy gold watches. Like I said, a strange profile for a criminal. I had my guesses about who was behind it, but I let my predictive analytics do their algorithmic magic. The program led me right to the warehouse.

Since I still didn't have my driver's license, Chambers drove my Lamborghini Z 2025 Prototype to the back of the warehouse. We could have flown it right over the building, but I thought it might be a bit too conspicuous. There was a security guard prowling the area. Fortunately for us, the guard was a female and thus we had no problems getting past her. Chambers worked his strange charms on her and she let us by without question. As a bonus, Chambers got himself a date for Friday night. Some guys are blessed with brains, some guys with chick magnetism. The lucky dog.

Darek used his electromechanical talents to hot-wire the warehouse alarm system. He turned off the cameras and made the back door swing open. It was pretty nicely done. He has a bright future as a door-to-door home alarm system representative.

Clinton got me past the last barrier. We entered the back door of the warehouse, but needed access into the management offices, and this door was locked shut. It was an old door, solid metal dead bolt lock, thick wood frame, no way around it. So Clinton went through it. He kicked the door in. Some people are blessed with brains, others with brawn. *The lucky dog!*

That left me to confront the criminal mastermind. I found him in the plant manager's office. He was watching reruns of *The Sopranos*. He never heard me coming. I put him under citizen's arrest. He didn't comply willingly.

The Russian mobster jumped up and pulled out his gun. He aimed it at me. He started groaning and whining the moment he saw me.

"You! Not again you! You leave alone!"

I bit my lip to stop from laughing. I needed to act tough on crime.

"You're under arrest! Don't make me Taser your Russian buns."

"You no cop! You no put arrest on buns! No Taser on buns either!"

"I am the fashion police, and I'm here to arrest you for hoarding all the terrible gangster fashion in this town. You are under arrest for violating the Fashion Treaty of Paris. Come quietly or I'll have my brother head-butt you to death."

"You threaten me no. You shut face."

"Dude, really. Remember your definite articles! Please just try to get a sentence right, or I'll sic the grammar police on you as well."

He waved the gun at me, his finger on the trigger.

"I kick you buns, you no kick my buns. Now, you, get out . . . the. The out. Now!"

"Just my buns?"

"Not just the buns! All buns! You and buns. Out!"

He wasn't being reasonable, and he was butchering the King's English, so I had no choice but to let Clinton head-butt the guy—and his buns—into submission. I had used my genius brain to track down the Russian and bring him to justice, and my brother used his brain as a battering ram. It was a great team effort.

Hey, at least Clinton got to use his head for something.

ACKNOWLEDGMENTS

First and foremost, I want to thank my original support group: Steve Anderson, Todd Jensen, and Emily Schultz. You read my books, grinned bravely, and kept on supporting me. Thank you so much for the feedback, encouragement, and friendship over the years. I have to credit my sister, Kristine, for being the earliest reader of my crazy stories. Thank you for being my scribe when I was too young to even read, let alone write.

My poor children are my beta test team. Thanks to Amanda, Kimberly, Spencer, Anna, and Ethan for surviving one draft after another. Also thanks to Merrijane Rice for polishing up the manuscript before submission. You made me look like a far better writer than I am!

I could not have made this dream a reality without the incredible staff at Cedar Fort. Special thanks to Melissa Caldwell and Emma Parker for excellence in editing! Kristen Reeves captured the essence of the story in the stunning artwork. Kudos to Kelly Martinez and Meagan Piiparinen for the awesome marketing plan. Thanks to all who helped make this book read great and look stunning!

Finally, and most important, is the debt of gratitude owed to my dear wife, Linda. She never accepted my lame excuses to stop writing. She always gently prodded and pushed. She made it easy for me to write. Thank you, Linda, for making this possible! This one is for you!

DISCUSSION QUESTIONS

1. Why do so many people today sacrifice reality for fantasy? Why does a person take illegal drugs to escape reality? Is an addiction to video games similar to an addiction to drugs? Is any addiction to fantasy at the expense of reality morally wrong?

2. If you could ensure that your children achieve their greatest potential, would this be worth curtailing their freedom? If you could ensure their safety in a dangerous world, would you restrict their agency?

3. What would you sacrifice in order to achieve your greatest desires? If you could live your dream life—and if that dream life seemed perfectly real—what would you sacrifice to achieve it? Would it matter that your reality was actually fake? Or is perception of reality all that matters?

4. What is the acceptable price of human progress? Revolutions in government, technology, industry, and so forth often take a severe human toll. Is this not acceptable in the grand scheme of

things as long as progress is achieved at the end? (The American Revolution is an example, as is the Industrial Revolution, even the recent Information Revolution, with many jobs displaced through out-sourcing, job elimination, and so on.) If the Lazarus Corporation could truly cure disease and eradicate poverty, wouldn't this be worth the sacrifice of a few hundred lives for the benefit of billions on the earth?

5. Are all human lives equal? Is a prison inmate on death row worth the same as Nobel Prize winner? If you could extend the life of the Nobel Prize winner at the expense of a murderer, would you do it?

ABOUT THE AUTHOR

Stephen J. Valentine received his bachelor's and master's degrees from Utah State University. He is senior program manager for FamilySearch International, responsible for the online publication of billions of historical records. Stephen loves history, hiking, cooking, reading, and traveling, especially to Disneyland. Stephen resides in Utah with his beautiful wife, talented children, brilliant Schnauzer, and massive J. R. R. Tolkien collection.